Praise for bestselling author

MAGGIE SHAYNE

"Maggie Shayne is better than chocolate.
She satisfies every wicked craving."
—National bestselling author Suzanne Forster

"Shayne's gift has made her one of the
preeminent voices in paranormal romance today!"
—*Romantic Times*

"…the magnificent Ms. Shayne demonstrates why
she is among the top writers of any genre!"
—*Affaire de Coeur*

"Shayne's talents know no bounds!"
—*Rendezvous*

"Shayne's haunting tale is intricately woven….
A moving mix of high suspense and romance,
this haunting thriller will propel readers
to bolt their doors at night."
—*Publishers Weekly* on THE GINGERBREAD MAN

Books by Maggie Shayne

MAGGIE SHAYNE,

a *USA TODAY* bestselling author whom *Romantic Times* calls "brilliantly inventive," has written more than twenty-five novels for Silhouette.

Maggie has won numerous awards, including two *Romantic Times* magazine Career Achievement Awards. A five-time finalist for the Romance Writers of America's prestigious RITA® Award, Maggie also writes mainstream contemporary fantasy and romantic suspense, and has contributed story lines to network daytime soap operas.

She lives in rural Otselic, New York, with her husband, Rick, with whom she shares five beautiful daughters, two English bulldogs and two grandchildren.

MAGGIE SHAYNE

TWO BY TWILIGHT

Silhouette Books

Published by Silhouette Books
America's Publisher of Contemporary Romance

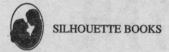 SILHOUETTE BOOKS

TWO BY TWILIGHT

Copyright © 2003 by Harlequin Books S.A.

ISBN 0-373-21809-5

The publisher acknowledges the copyright holder of the individual works as follows:

RUN FROM TWILIGHT
Copyright © 2003 by Margaret Benson

TWILIGHT VOWS
Copyright ©1998 by Margaret Benson

Visit Silhouette at www.eHarlequin.com

Printed in U.S.A.

CONTENTS

Dear Reader,

With the reissue of the other books in the WINGS IN THE NIGHT series, I've been hearing almost daily from readers asking how to find the one story that still hadn't been reissued, "Twilight Vows." That story was a half-length novel, originally published within the Intimate Moments line, along with another story of the same length by Marilyn Tracy. It was obvious to me that we needed to reissue "Twilight Vows," but how? It was too short to go in a book all by itself, and all the other books in the series, except for the very newest, had already been reissued. The solution that came to me was the obvious one: write another story of similar length and release the two together. That's what I've done here in *Two by Twilight*.

This book is an odd little combination of one reissued story and one brand-new story, both part of the ongoing saga we call WINGS IN THE NIGHT. "Twilight Vows" was originally published in October 1998. It's the story of Donovan O'Roark and Rachel Sullivan, set in a castle in Ireland. The new one is titled "Run from Twilight," and it introduces former gangland cop Michael Gray and bartender Mary McLean.

Happy reading!

Maggie Shayne

RUN FROM TWILIGHT

Prologue

There were only a handful of cops in the area. Just the few who'd been close enough to hear the gunshots. Officer Michael Gray stood in an alley between two buildings, his gun drawn but basically useless, as rival gangs fired at each other from opposite sides of the street. Tommy guns spat fire in the darkness. Windows shattered, and people ran for their lives. A car sped past, only to stop short as its windows exploded and the driver slumped over the wheel.

That was when he saw the boy. He must have been seven or eight years old, and scared half to death by the noise. He came out of nowhere and ran right into the street—right into the crisscrossing storm of bullets.

Michael reacted on sheer instinct. He ran out of the alley, shoving his gun into his holster as he went,

knowing he would need both hands. He dove on the
kid, pinning him to the pavement, covering him with
his own body. Sheer adrenaline drove him, and he
didn't even feel the pain until he was lying still, holding the kid underneath him. And then it hurt. It hurt
like hell, from a dozen places on his body. But not
for very long.

When Michael woke he was in a hospital bed, in
some kind of a daze. He didn't feel anything. He
couldn't seem to speak, but he could see and hear
what was going on around him. He heard a doctor
saying there was nothing that could be done. He saw
a nurse shake her head and dab at her eyes, but then
she slid a sideways glance in his direction and gave
him a wink. As if she knew something he didn't. What
the hell? He was lying here, dying, and the nurse was
winking at him? What kind of a hospital was this?

That thought fled, though, when he saw his wife,
Sally, sitting in a chair in the corner of the room, pale
as a ghost, shaking. Then the doctor took her arm,
pulled her to her feet and led her from the room.

As soon as they were gone, the flirtatious nurse hurried to close the door behind them. Then she closed
the window curtains tight and came to his bed.
"About time," she said. "It's damn near morning. I
thought they'd never leave. Listen, they'll be back
soon. We don't have much time."

She was cute, with short dark hair and huge eyes.
He tried to move his lips, to give voice to the questions swirling in his mind, but he couldn't get them
out.

"Don't try to talk," she said. "Just listen, okay?
I'm not a nurse. My name's Cuyler Jade. I saw what

happened in the street, the way you saved that kid, and I followed the car that brought you in. Then I sneaked in, borrowed this uniform from some nurse's locker.'' She turned in a little circle, arms out. ''Nice fit for a quick grab, isn't it?''

He blinked slowly, wondering if this was all some kind of hallucination.

''We have to make this quick,'' she said. ''You're a hell of a guy. A hero. You don't deserve to die, but you're going to. Probably a few minutes from now. You've got more holes in you than Swiss cheese, and I'm not whistlin' Dixie.''

Was this information supposed to comfort him somehow?

''I can see to it you don't die, Michael Gray. I can see to it you live. You won't be like you were before, but you'll be alive. You'll be strong. Healthy. But different. Very different. Do you understand?''

He blinked, thinking the woman was insane, and shook his head slightly, side to side.

''Hell, of course you don't understand. And I don't have time for the full rundown. Just suffice it to say I went out the same way you did. Cross fire, lots of bullets. And look at me. I'm okay. You can be the same. So lemme ask you this. Do you want to live?''

He managed to nod. Barely.

''Okay, then. It's gonna feel odd at first. You need to just lie still, just like you are now, no matter what you feel. Within a few minutes, the sun will be up, and you'll sleep more soundly than you've ever slept in your life. You'll sleep all day. I'll be there when you wake up. Understand?''

Again he nodded.

Then the woman pulled the curtains closed around his bed, bent over him and sank her teeth into his neck.

It happened just the way she'd said it would. He felt power zinging through him—as if he'd been struck by lightning. Every nerve ending tingled, and right on the heels of that sensation came another: excruciating pain. Every bullet hole in his body burned like fire. He hurt a thousand times more than when he'd first been shot. His entire being screamed in agony, and blood rushed from the wounds, soaking the bed.

The woman, whatever, whoever, she had been, was gone. The doors burst open; doctors and nurses rushed into the room. Beyond them he saw Sally, biting her knuckles and weeping, and beyond her, the first rays of the morning sun peered through a distant window. Then the pain faded, and everything went black.

Vaguely he felt a hand on his wrist, and heard a doctor's voice saying, "I'm sorry, Mrs. Gray. He's gone."

But he wasn't gone. Not really. When he woke again, hours later, in the hospital morgue, he felt more alive than he ever had. Like magic, the bullet holes had vanished. And the woman, Cuyler Jade, explained to him what he was now. What he had become, and what that meant, as she led him out the back doors of the hospital and into the night that was to be his home from then on.

He really cared very little for all the things she told him. All he cared about was getting back to Sally. Taking away her pain. Showing her that he was still alive, that it was okay after all.

Cuyler told him that was a very bad idea, but he

didn't listen. He didn't believe her when she said Sally wouldn't understand, that she wouldn't accept him now. He *couldn't* believe it. It was something he had to learn for himself.

And he did, hours later, when he finally convinced the woman to leave him alone, let him do what he had to do. He went home. Where else would he go, besides home?

Sally was lying in their bed, but she wasn't sleeping. She was wide-awake, weeping. She hadn't even locked the house that night, so he was able to walk inside, just as if he were coming home from a hard day's work. It felt good to come home. And while his mind was still reeling from nearly dying and from the day's revelations, from all the impossible things Cuyler Jade had told him and the myriad new sensations racing through his body, he couldn't digest any of it, or even begin to explore what it all might mean. Not until he talked to Sally.

God, he missed her.

He slipped into the bedroom. She sat up in bed, with a little shriek of alarm, and he said, "It's okay, honey. It's me. I'm here. I'm all right." He found the light switch, turned it on so she could see for herself.

Her eyes widened as they skimmed down his body, and it was only then that he stopped to think about what he must look like, still dressed in the bullet-riddled uniform that was stiff with dried blood. "Look, it's okay. I didn't really die. I'm all right."

She slid up in the bed, pressing her back to the headboard. He thought she would have backed right through the wall if she could. "You're dead," she said. "I sat with you for hours. I held your hand while it went cold as ice. You're dead."

"No. No, there was this nurse—not a nurse, really. She said I could live. And she did something and— I'm not the same anymore, she says. But I'm still me. I'm still Michael, still your husband."

"You get away. Get away!"

He shook his head slowly. "Honey, it's okay. Look, the bullet holes are all gone." He lifted his shirt to show her.

"Get out!"

"But—"

"My Michael died. I don't know what you are—a walking corpse. A ghost."

"A vampire," he said, and then wished he could take it back when he saw the sheer horror on her face. "It's not like in the books, honey. It's not. It's nothing like that."

"My husband is dead," she said. But her voice and eyes looked more dead than anything he could ever imagine being. "Now I want you to leave." In a burst of motion she rolled to the side and yanked something from the nightstand. His gun. His revolver. She pointed it at him. "Go. Get out—now—and don't ever come back!"

He held up his hands, palms toward her. Cuyler had told him bullets would hurt like hell—pain, she said, was magnified in his kind, just like every other sense. But bullets wouldn't kill him—unless he bled to death from the wounds. Still, he didn't have any urge to try it out.

"Honey, don't. Look, I'll go, okay? I'll go, if that's what you want. But you have to believe me, I'm all right. And it really is me. It's me."

She shook her head hard and thumbed back the hammer.

"I'm going." He backed toward the door, his mind racing with ways to prove to her that he was who he said he was. And then it hit him that he knew things no one else would know about her. So he kept backing up, slowly, but talking all the while, needing her to believe him and to accept him in a way he'd never needed anything, ever. "Your maiden name is Litchfield. You wore a white satin nightgown with tiny pink roses at the shoulders on our wedding night. You collect seashells. You hate green vegetables, except for peas, but only baby peas, and…

Tears fell from her eyes. "If you're not dead, Michael, then you're damned. And I can't live with that, either."

"No, no, honey, you have it all wrong. Just listen to me and I can—"

She turned the gun quickly, pressed the barrel to her head and pulled the trigger. Just like that. She was gone.

Cuyler Jade appeared beside him even as he stood there, paralyzed with shock. "Oh, God," she said. "Oh, God, I didn't think she'd react that badly."

Michael grabbed her arm. "Bring her back!" he shouted. "Do what you did for me. Bring her back."

The little vampire looked up at him, her huge eyes wet, and shook her head slowly. "I can't, Michael. Only certain people can become what we are. It's something to do with the blood. You'll know when you see one. You'll feel it right to your toes. She doesn't have it." She glanced at the bed again. "And besides, she's already dead."

He closed his eyes, regret drowning him. "It should have been me. If I'd stayed dead, she would still be alive. This is some kind of punishment. I cheated death, so it took her instead.''

Cuyler shook her head slowly. ''You're missing an awful lot, for a cop. Why do you think she had that loaded gun in here in the first place, Michael?''

Frowning, he looked more closely at the bedside stand. He saw the glass of wine, the photo of him in his uniform—and the sheet of paper with her handwriting on it. Trembling, he moved closer, until he could see what she'd written there. ''Don't mourn me. I've gone to join Michael.''

Chapter 1

Present Day, Bangor, Maine

He sat in the darkest corner of the smallish city's most popular "vampire bar," a place called The Crypt, and watched the mortals play at being gods. They amused him. Young people, most of them. Twenty-somethings who had barely lived long enough to taste life, much less immortality. The women wore skintight black velvet gowns or scarlet-red sequined ones. The men wore leather, or tailed tuxes and starched white cravats with cheap fake jewels glittering from their centers. They all wore cloaks of one kind or another: satin, velvet, lined in scarlet or white or fur. Some had the stand-up collar of Dracula in a style that had never existed outside Hollywood. Some were hooded. Many of the patrons wore fake fangs. A few who were, he thought, a bit too fixated and perhaps in need of mental help had actually had their own incisors filed to points. They listened to hard-driving rock bands whose lyrics focused on body counts, and they drank made-up mixed drinks from the creative menu: Type-O-Transfusion and Plasma Punch. White Cell Watusi and Platelet Power. Everyone who drank here knew the code—the real drink behind the morbid name. A screwdriver, for example, was known here as a "Cranial Drill." All of them contained alcohol, which was perfectly legal now. Most of them also came with brilliant red coloring added for effect, and stir sticks that looked like miniature wooden stakes.

Michael knew the code. But he didn't drink here. Or hadn't. Yet.

He enjoyed watching them play, though. It was interesting to see what the pop culture world of the twenty-first century really thought of his kind.

They were way off the mark, of course. Vampires didn't often wear black lipstick, and he'd only met one who still insisted on the cloak. As for the multiple piercings and the tattoos, those would be less than healthy for vampires, given their tendency toward bleeding out.

Of course, the costumed customers were not the reason he came here night after night. *She* was.

Mary McLean stood behind the bar, hustling drinks and handling drunks with a grace and good humor that belied her situation. She wore snug jeans and a shimmering jade blouse of brushed satin beneath an apron as pristine as any cravat in the place. Her hair was pulled back in a long sable ponytail that moved whenever she did and fascinated him. At her throat hung a small cross on a fine silver chain. That fascinated him, too. In fact, he was expending a great deal of effort trying not to be fascinated by her, drawn to her. He was here to do a job.

She glanced up in his direction, though there were too many bodies, too much smoke and too little light for her to have seen him there. She *felt* him, though. She felt his eyes on her, maybe his presence, as well. That probably wasn't a good thing. In fact, he knew it to be a bad thing. She shouldn't be that aware of him. Mortals rarely were, even her kind.

It had occurred to him that there were probably other ways he could go about watching her than to sit here, inside the vampire bar, where the thrumming pulse of healthy heartbeats vied with the pounding bass of the music for his attention. It was risky to do it this way, and yet he couldn't resist. He wanted her to see him, to notice him, to talk to him.

Stupid.

She was one of The Chosen. The rare belladonna antigen danced in her blood, and that meant that they were related, the two of them, in some distant and abstract way. Only the children of belladonna could become vampires. And every vampire had been one of them as a mortal. Cuyler Jade had taught him all that, long ago. She'd been a friend, one of few.

But this was different from anything she had spoken of, and from anything he'd felt before. Mary McLean's pull on his senses was powerful and keen. He'd felt the tug of The Chosen before. But never like this.

They tended to die young, her kind. But she wasn't yet weakening. She was strong, healthy, vibrant, alive.

For now.

She was going to be murdered soon. That was why he was here.

She looked up again as she poured whiskey into a blood-red shot glass, her eyes narrow, probing the shadows where he sat. He forced his gaze away, looking instead at the people who filled the space between them. Sweat-coated mortals, dressed—they thought— as vampires, gyrated in a dance that was little more than a mimicry of the sex act, while the speakers blasted the same refrain over and over again.

"Let the bodies hit the floor./Let the bodies hit the floor./Let the bodies hit the floor."

A blood-red shot glass landed on the far side of the table with a tap, then slid easily across to stop just in front of him. He lifted his head slowly, letting his gaze take its time climbing her body, from her hips, level with the table, to her waist, over her chest, tracing the shapes of her breasts, and moving very, *very* slowly over her throat. Finally he examined her face: chin, jaw, cheeks—God, she was surely sculpted by the hand of a master—and then he met her eyes. Jade green, like the silk blouse, and just as shimmery.

Her eyes did not flinch from his steady, probing stare. And he supposed one of them ought to break the silence soon. So he said, "I didn't order anything."

And she said, "It's on the house."

Pursing his lips, giving a nod, he wrapped his hand around the tiny shot glass. "Thank you."

"No need. Do you care if I sit down?" As she spoke, she was untying the white apron's strings, pulling it off over her head.

He thought about saying yes, but he couldn't resist the opportunity to spend a little time with her. Reminding himself that the bond was only that of the blood they shared, even if it was somehow magnified with this one, he nodded. She pulled out the chair opposite his and sat down.

"I'm Mary," she said.

"I know."

Her lips pulled just a little. "I thought, maybe. But that's not the response I was looking for."

He lifted his brows, unsure what she meant.

"I say, 'I'm Mary.' And then you say, 'Nice to meet you, Mary. I'm...'"

She held a hand toward him, palm up.

"Michael."

She nodded. "Well, Michael, you've been coming in here every single night for the past two weeks. You don't eat. You don't drink. You don't dance. Mostly you just sit here in the corner and watch me. And I have to tell you, it's starting to make me uncomfortable."

He blinked at her, a little bit surprised. "You're very direct, aren't you?"

"I don't believe in playing games. So why don't you just tell me what it is you're doing here, and then we can move on."

"Doing?"

She nodded.

"Mostly just sitting here in the corner and watching you." She averted her eyes, and that made him curious enough to probe her mind, eavesdrop on her thoughts and feelings. What he found was fear. She was afraid of him. It hit him where he lived, and he instantly regretted his teasing reply. "I would never hurt you, Mary."

She flinched a little when he said it. "I never thought you would."

"Yes, you did. What I'm having trouble figuring

out is why." She couldn't know what he was. It
couldn't be that. If she knew, then he would have
expected her to be afraid of him. And repulsed and
horrified and driven to—

"Look, it doesn't matter," she said, breaking into
his thoughts. "It's none of your business. But you
need to stop, all right? Stop coming here, stop watching me."

"I'm afraid I can't do that."

"Then you should probably be expecting a visit
from the police." She pulled out her order pad and
pen. "I'll need a last name, address and phone number."

He smiled a little at the irony of it. "You're going
to report me to the police?"

She nodded, never lifting her eyes from the pad,
holding the pen poised above it as if she fully expected him to start supplying personal information.

"Just because I come to this bar and happen to look
your way every once in a while?"

Another nod.

"Why would the police think that was anything
close to suspicious behavior? You're a beautiful
woman, Mary. I can't be the only man who enjoys
looking at you."

She met his eyes, held them, and her cheeks grew
pink with the rush of blood. There was something in
her eyes, the spark and heat of attraction. For a moment he read her thoughts and knew she felt the pull
as strongly as he did, but she squelched it with an
inflexible will, told herself it was not only stupid but
dangerous.

"If it were just that—you coming here, watching
me—they probably wouldn't find anything suspicious

about it at all. But combined with the phone calls, the person who's been following me and the break-in at my apartment—"

He held up a hand to silence her. "Wait. You've had a break-in?" Why hadn't he known about this?

"That's very good, Michael. I don't suppose you know anything about it, though. Or the phone calls, either?"

"I haven't phoned you. And I've never broken into your apartment."

She swallowed hard, laid down the pad and pen but kept her eyes on the table. He sensed conflict in her. Part of her wanted to believe him almost desperately. Part of her knew, instinctively, that he was telling the truth. And a third part was afraid to give in to the other two. Deathly afraid. And no wonder. He hadn't realized that she was aware she was being hunted. He should have. The others had all been aware of it.

"So I'm supposed to believe it's just a coincidence?" she said. "That I've picked up some kind of obsessed lunatic stalker and a harmless bar-bound admirer at exactly the same time?"

He reached across the table and, using just his forefinger, lifted her chin until her eyes met his. "I suppose that would be a lot to swallow. No. I'm not going to tell you it's a coincidence. It's not. The two things are related. But not in the way you think. I'm not your stalker, Mary. I came here to protect you from him."

She blinked rapidly. "If you *were* my stalker," she said softly, "that would be the best lie you could possibly use to get closer to me."

"It's not a lie."

"How can I know that?"

"Give me your hand."

"What?"

He didn't wait, just reached for her hand and closed his around it. She gasped a little, probably at the chill of his flesh—or maybe it was at the power of the contact. Touching her made his body come alive in ways it hadn't done in years. And maybe she felt that, too. She didn't pull her hand free. He didn't need to touch her to read her thoughts. It would enhance the ability, yes. But he *wanted* to touch her. He was burning to touch her.

A flash swept through his mind as he opened it more fully to hers, to her thoughts. He closed his eyes, the better to see it. The telephone ringing. Her picking it up, wary. Then smiling. Yes.

"Your Aunt Cherry…Cheryl…Sherry. Sherry. She phoned you yesterday morning, early. She said her dog had been ill."

She jerked her hand away. "Okay, I get it. You're some kind of psychic."

He nodded. "Some kind, yes."

"And you came here to protect me from a stalker."

He licked his lips. She didn't believe him in the least. She thought he was a fraud, a con man. "He's a little more than a stalker, actually. He's…he's a killer, Mary."

She blinked, her face going a shade lighter.

"He strikes on the full moon. I don't know why. I can't seem to…to read him. But I know you're the next victim. And I'm here to protect you."

She stared at him for a long moment. "Are you a cop?"

"I was once. Not anymore."

"Then why are you trying so hard to scare the hell out of me?"

He paused, studying her, feeling her thoughts. "You were already afraid—but of the wrong thing. I'm not the threat to you, Mary. He is. Fear is healthy. It can be a powerful weapon. Misplaced, though, it can get you killed."

"And trust is a beautiful thing," she countered. "But misplaced, it'll get you killed even faster."

It was a well-aimed shot, and it hit home. He wanted her to trust him. But he was pushing too quickly. Then again, there wasn't much time.

"So you had this vision," she said. "And you showed up here to watch over me?"

He nodded.

"Right."

"It's true."

She nodded at the whiskey. "You going to drink that?"

"Probably not."

With a sweep of her hand she took the glass and downed its contents. Then she set it down hard on the table. "I'm off duty in a half hour. I want you long gone before then. I'm going to have my cell phone and my boss's German shepherd with me, and if I see you lurking around anywhere, I'll turn the dog on you and dial 911 while you try to keep from becoming his bedtime snack. Understand?"

He studied her for a long moment. "How can I be sure you make it home safely if I don't watch over you?"

She suppressed a shiver—he felt it—then she glanced toward the window. "You should know, being the psychic. The moon's not full yet," she said, and she pushed her chair away from the table. "Even if you're telling the truth, I should be fine for tonight."

Chapter 2

Mary sighed in mild relief when the man who called himself Michael left the bar. She'd noticed him the first time he'd come in. Of course she'd noticed him. A woman would have to be dead not to notice him. He was pale, but God, he was beautiful. The most strikingly beautiful man she had ever seen. His hair was long, a deep shade of brown. He didn't tie it back or hack it off. He let it hang just as it grew, no apologies. He was lean but powerful. That sense of raw energy was more a palpable thing than a visible one. He didn't bulge with muscle. There was just this quiet strength about him that left no doubt about its presence.

But his eyes struck her most of all. The first time he had lifted his hooded gaze to look her way, she'd felt those eyes on her like brands, and when she'd looked back, she'd felt herself falling into them. They were black, his eyes, and hypnotic. They made her heart pound harder against her chest, and her breath come quick and shallow. They made her stomach knot and her hands tremble.

It was only when he'd broken the connection by looking away quickly that she'd realized he didn't want to make contact. He wasn't trying to pick her up. Throughout that night and the nights that followed, she had felt that penetrating gaze on her again and again, but each time she tried to return it, he looked away.

She was suffering the throes of an intense physical attraction to a complete stranger. She was not the kind of woman who lusted after men she'd never met. She didn't go to strip clubs or buy hunk calendars or pant for action heroes. But if this guy were on a calendar, she thought, she would buy a copy for every wall in her apartment.

She'd fantasized about him at night, when she was alone in her room. Fantasies so bold and so unlike her that they startled her. And yet she relished every forbidden image that raced through her mind and her dreams.

It wasn't until the policeman working on her break-in complaint had asked her if there were anyone new in her life, anyone strange hanging around, perhaps paying undue attention to her, that she'd even begun to suspect her dark stranger at the bar might be the one. The cop thought that the break-in, combined with her feeling of being followed home three nights in a row and the barrage of odd phone calls, added up to a possible stalker. And that frightened her.

Not as much as Michael had.

The phone calls had begun two weeks ago. At first the caller would just phone once or twice after the bar closed, wake her from a sound sleep and hang up. Then he started with the heavy breathing. And now he'd moved up to whispered threats. One-liners. "I'm watching you," he'd tell her, or "I'm coming for you soon."

She'd gotten her number changed—the phone company had taken forever, but that had been done yesterday. In the meantime, someone had broken into her apartment, though nothing had been taken. Nothing she noticed, anyway.

So now she had all new locks on the doors and windows, and the police had promised to keep an eye on the place, whatever that meant.

When she hustled the last customer out of the bar and locked the door, a chill rushed up her spine. Michael said the man was more than a stalker—that he was a killer. And that she was next on his list. She swallowed hard, quickly rinsed the remaining glasses and wiped down the bar.

Tommy came in from the kitchen, drying his hands on a towel. "Good night for you, Mare?" he asked. He slung the towel over his shoulder and moved from table to table, turning the chairs upside down and setting them on top.

She glanced at her tip jar. A one-hundred-dollar bill lay on top of the mounds of ones and fives and change. "Uh...yeah. Another good day." She wasn't surprised. There had been one in her jar every night for a while now. Ever since the stranger named Michael had started coming around.

Customers did not put money into the tip jar. They left it on their tables or handed it to her themselves. She kept the jar under the mahogany bar, on a shelf, and added her tips to it herself throughout the night.

She'd never seen Michael leave his table or come any-where near it. Not once. And yet, somehow she knew he was responsible for it.

She would return the money to him if she could afford to. But so far his tips had enabled her to fend off both the car-repo company and the landlord. She could not afford to be proud.

She put a cap on the jar and dropped it into her purse. "Walk me to my car?" she asked.

Tommy grinned at her. "You bet." He put up the last of the chairs, tossed his towel onto the bar and then moved behind it, toward the small closet hidden on one side of the mirrored wall. "You have a jacket in here?"

"The blue one," she told him.

He got it for her, helped her into it before putting on his own, which was denim. "Ready?"

"Ready."

Tommy opened the door. Mary turned out the lights and stepped outside, into a light rain and a pitch-black night, pulling the door closed behind her and double-checking the lock. Sealed. Good.

The parking lot in front was deserted. Only one car was in it, and that was her own. She looked up and down the street, craned her neck to see through the warm rain, around to the back of the building. There were other businesses on either side of the bar, of course, but they were all closed up tight at this time of night. There was no traffic whatsoever, and the streetlights did little to dispel the gloom.

"Where's your car, Tommy?"

"Left the headlights on last night," he said, with a sheepish shrug. "Battery was dead this morning. But it's okay. I only live five blocks away."

"You're walking?"

He nodded, flipping up his collar.

Swallowing hard, her keys in her hand by now, she argued with herself inside her head. Tommy had always had a crush on her. Could he be the one making the calls, harassing her? It was far-fetched, even more far-fetched if this stalker really was something far more dangerous. Tommy wouldn't hurt a fly.

Then again, what if she let him walk home alone and something happened to him? Could she live with herself then?

"Excuse me," said a voice from the darkness.

She knew that voice. It sent shivers of recognition dancing down her spine. Michael, her pale, wild-haired, potent-eyed admirer.

She turned and met his eyes, fell into them, felt her blood heat and her belly tighten. God, what was it about him that stirred her up this way? She licked her lips and saw his gaze shoot to them and stay there. "I…suppose you need a ride, too," she said. Part of her was hoping he would—and arguing with the part of her that hoped he wouldn't.

He nodded. "Only…five blocks."

Five blocks. He only wanted to ride as far as Tommy was going. Well, Tommy certainly couldn't try anything with Michael along. And Michael wouldn't murder her in front of Tommy, either. And that was exactly what the stranger intended, wasn't it? To make her feel perfectly safe? To let her know she wasn't in any danger?

Stupid. He was not some guardian come to watch over her. He *wasn't*.

And yet she let him. "Fine. Get in. Both of you." Tommy looked put out, but he moved toward the car.

Michael beat him to the front door, opened it and slid in without asking. When Tommy got into the back seat, he almost appeared to be sulking.

"Tommy," Mary said as she shoved the keys into the switch and started the car, "this is Michael. Michael, Tommy."

"Hey," Tommy said.

"Likewise," Michael replied.

Mary rolled her eyes and backed out of the parking lot. She didn't fasten her seat belt. Some insane primal fear told her she should be ready to throw herself out of the car and run for her life at a moment's notice. A seat belt would slow her down.

She drove. Her cell phone bleated. She picked it up without a thought, ignoring all the public service announcements suggesting it was a bad idea. She simply hadn't gotten around to buying a Madonna-mike for her head.

"Hello?"

"Are you afraid, Mary? You should be." The voice was the coarse whisper of her nightmares, and it was followed by a sharp, decisive *click*.

She jerked the phone away from her head and glanced at the panel, but no number showed on the screen to tell her where the call had come from. She set the phone down.

Michael was looking at her. Those probing eyes staring straight through her skin and reading every thought—she could feel it. He knew exactly what that call had been. Maybe even heard it through her ears somehow. No. Impossible.

"Mary? Anything wrong?" Tommy asked from the back seat.

She shook her head. "Wrong number," she lied.

Oh well. At least the culprit was neither of the two men sitting with her alone, in the dark, in her car.

And then it hit her, and the bottom seemed to fall out of her belly. Because if Michael wasn't the stalker, then he really had no reason she could think of to lie to her. Did he?

Sure he did, her practical mind argued. Plenty of reasons. Maybe he was trying to make his name as a psychic by meddling in criminal cases. He probably had a connection at the police department, who had put him on to her. Or maybe he just wanted to get into her pants. That would be reason enough to scare her half to death, right?

She shot him a sideways glance. His eyes were right there waiting, and he shook his head slowly left then right. "Wrong on both counts," he whispered.

She felt her eyes widen. How in the hell...?

"What's that?" Tommy asked, leaning forward. "I didn't hear you."

"Nothing. We're here." Mary hit the brake, brought the car to a jerky stop without even pulling over to the curb in front of Tommy's building.

"Yeah. Thanks for the ride, Mary." He opened his door, then frowned at Michael's back. "You coming?"

"Look at that, it's raining even harder now," Michael said, nodding at the tiny beads glistening on the windshield. "I only live a block farther up. Do you mind?"

Hell, he wasn't the stalker. But that didn't mean he wasn't dangerous.

Tommy glanced at her as he got out. "You okay with that, Mare?"

"You should be," Michael said. "That stun gun

tucked under the side of your seat is plenty to keep me in line.''

She jerked her hand back to the steering wheel. She'd been reaching below, just to make sure she could grab the little weapon quickly should she need it. How the hell did he know?

''Mare?''

''Fine, Tommy. Go ahead. See you tomorrow night.''

''Yeah, see you.'' He closed the door and hurried away.

She glanced toward her passenger. ''So do you really live a block away?''

He shook his head from side to side. ''I'm going home with you.''

She closed her eyes. ''Oh, for God's sake—''

''No, Mary. For your sake.''

She sighed, gripping the steering wheel until her knuckles were white. ''So what is it, Michael? Am I supposed to think you're some kind of knight in shining armor? Maybe leap into bed with you to thank you for rescuing me from the evil phone call guy?''

He lifted his eyebrows. ''He's more than an 'evil phone call guy,' Mary. He's a killer. He's struck before—I can prove it to you, if you'll give me an hour. I brought evidence.'' He patted the shoulder bag that hung over his worn gray trench coat. ''And he'll strike again unless we stop him. But he's *not* going to get you.''

She thought he was finished. He sounded reasonable, convincing and fairly sane. He also sounded like a man who only wanted to watch over and protect her. Which meant he was too good to be true.

Then he sent her a knowing smile and added, ''How you choose to thank me, on the other hand, is entirely up to you.''

Chapter 3

Michael was not the person who'd been harassing her.

She told herself that over and over again. She refused to think "He's not the killer" because she didn't want to believe there *was* a killer. Just a nutcase with an obsession.

Michael was not easily dissuaded, and she found herself absurdly, perhaps stupidly, glad of that. She wanted to see just what "evidence" he was carrying in the flat brown leather case.

She drove through the city with the wipers beating out a steady pulse and the rain cascading over the windshield, until she came to the turnoff for her apartment building. It had a parking lot in the back. No nice dry garage. No attendant. But it was well lit, had a gate with a lock, and only the tenants had keys. She pulled up to the gate, stopped the car and looked into the back seat for her umbrella.

"I'll get it," Michael said. She hated to admit she'd been hoping he would offer. But she got the feeling he already knew that. She handed him the key. He was out of the car before she could offer him the umbrella, and back almost as quickly. Frowning at him, she said, "What? You decide to take the umbrella after all?"

"It's done."

She looked from him to the gate. In between passes of the wiper blades, she saw the gate standing wide-open, waiting. "That was fast." She frowned harder. "You barely got wet."

"I...hurried."

"Right." She pulled the car through the gate and noticed that when Michael got out to close it again, he took a bit longer. When he got back into the car, raindrop spatters darkened his coat and glistened in his long hair. Her hand tensed, and she caught herself in the nick of time. She'd been about to reach up and brush the raindrops from his hair—an act that would be too intimate and familiar. It didn't feel too intimate, though. It felt as natural as making love to him would feel.

Oh, God.

He handed her the keys. His hand caressed hers as she took them, and she didn't think it was an accident.

"Thanks."

She drove across the lot into her parking slot, right in front of her ground-floor apartment. It had a tiny concrete patio in front of the door, no more than five by five. She had a huge potted palm sitting on it, a begonia in a hanging basket, a lawn chair, a set of wind chimes and a welcome mat. It was sheltered from the rain by the overhanging balcony of the apartment above, which was exactly the same size. And it sported an outdoor light.

"You leave these things out? And no one's stolen them?"

She shrugged. "Guess no one's interested in lifting a plant or a three-dollar lawn chair." She unlocked the door, reached inside to flip on the light and then stood very still, staring in at the mess that had been her neat-as-a-pin apartment. The sofa cushions were on the floor; books from the tiny bookshelves had been strewn about; the lamp was lying on its side. "Oh, hell, not again."

She started to go inside, but Michael's hand on her shoulder stopped her. "Don't. He could still be around."

"If he is, he's going to be one sorry freaking stalker." She reached into the umbrella stand just inside the door, pulled out her trusty baseball bat and stomped inside. "Come on out, you bastard. I've had about all of this I'm going to take."

She was halfway to the kitchenette when she heard Michael say, "It's all right. He's gone." Did he sound slightly amused? She glanced back at him. He was taking off his coat now, laying his brown case on the coffee table.

"How do you know?" she asked, watching him.

He tapped his head with his forefinger.

"Oh, right. You're a mind reader." She rolled her eyes. "If you don't mind, I'd just as soon back that up with a mundane look-see."

He smiled at her. She almost dropped the bat. His smile was potent, a killer smile, and it made her go weak in the knees. Damn him. She turned away, moving across the living room to the kitchenette, which was only separated by a breakfast bar, but it was enough for someone to crouch behind.

No one was there. But the cupboard doors were all open, every last one of them, and there were dishes and food out that hadn't been out before. She stepped back into the living room and looked at the only door off it, which led to her bedroom. Her hand tightened on the bat.

"Let me," Michael offered.

She nodded. There was no sense pretending to be brave when she was scared half to death. She held the bat toward him. He glanced at it and smiled again, but he didn't take it; just turned the knob and opened her bedroom door, stepped inside, looked around.

Some hero he was; he didn't even turn on the light. She crept in behind him, bat at the ready, flipped on the light switch, scanned the room.

She didn't see anyone. But her top dresser drawer was open, and her lacy delicates had been scattered around the room. He noticed them. She saw him notice them. His gaze lingered on the negligee she'd bought at a lingerie party just to be nice. It was sheer, sheer black, and tiny, and it lay across the bed. As if she'd planned to put it on.

"That wasn't there before." She said it almost defensively.

"I'm glad to know that. I'd have thought you were expecting someone."

"I wasn't. And I wouldn't wear that for anyone, anyway. I mean, for anyone I'm currently seeing, because I'm not. Seeing anyone, I mean...."

"I know." He strode to the closet, opened the door, poked around inside. Then he opened the remaining door, which led to the bathroom, where makeup and brushes were scattered all over the sink and inside it. He even moved the curtain and looked inside the shower.

"No one here," he said.

He hadn't checked under the bed. She bit her lip and wondered how silly she would look if she asked him to. But she didn't have to ask. He came back into the bedroom, walked straight to the bed, lifted up the covers and bent low to peer underneath. Then he rose again and smoothed the covers back in place. "Have I missed anything?"

"No."

"Good." He went to the dresser, bent down and began picking up the things on the floor, placing them back in the drawer. His big hands on her bras and panties made her stomach clench. Her mind whispered things she wouldn't want him overhearing, and her breath came shorter and faster than before.

She went to him and took the items. "Really, um, I'll get it."

"I want to help."

"Then...go start on the other rooms." She'd thought about insisting he let her do it all herself, but she knew, somehow, he wouldn't see that as a viable option. But she didn't want him handling her underwear, because she couldn't help but wish she was in them at the time, and that was a ridiculous thing for her to think about a man she had just met.

No matter what he looked like. Or how intense his eyes.

It felt as if she knew him intimately—as if she'd known him forever.

He held her gaze for a long time, until she squirmed.

Then, finally, he broke eye contact as if it were an effort, turned and left her alone in the bedroom.

Michael had to force himself to move slowly. He'd made a big mistake when he'd opened the gate. He'd instinctively darted through the rain, moving at pre-ternatural speeds no human could achieve. He was only glad it had been too dark for her to have observed his movements. She wouldn't have seen more than a streak, a blur of motion.

He put the cushions back on the sofa, righted the lamp, began picking up books and glancing at the ti-tles as he replaced them on the shelf. She read the classics. Shakespeare, the Brontës, T.S. Eliot. That was in keeping with what he had observed about her. He knew she was intelligent. He believed her to be shy and uncomfortable around people. She barely talked to the customers at the bar where she worked, but in a place that dark and that noisy, she didn't need to. When any of them paid her undue attention, she would start fidgeting with the cross she wore, sliding it back and forth on its chain. A nervous habit, as if the clientele really were vampires and the cross really would ward them off.

God, how frightened would she be if she knew what *he* really was?

She had surprised him, he thought, glancing through the open bedroom door to see that she had finished in there and was moving into the bathroom. When she'd grabbed the bat and challenged the intruder, he'd been surprised and pleased. He liked her even better for that. She'd been petrified, but ready to fight to protect her space. Fear wouldn't make her back down. It was a remarkable quality in a woman who kept to herself the way she did. And he wondered if he'd pegged her wrong. Maybe it wasn't that she was shy. Maybe she simply didn't like people.

She seemed to like him, though—a little too well, maybe, even though she thought it unwise.

He moved into the kitchenette and stacked the dishes in the dishwasher, knowing she wouldn't want to eat from anything the intruder had touched. He wasn't as certain about the food. Mary was not wealthy. Working a double shift at the bar to pay for rent and tuition, barely ever sleeping. She was majoring in English, hoped to teach one day. She baby-sat for some of the neighbors to earn extra cash, and when the bar's owner had been looking for someone to come in and clean the place on weekends, she'd taken that job, as well. Her degree was slow in coming— she was twenty-seven now, and getting closer to that goal. She took only what classes she could afford, one or two at a time, fitting them around her work schedule. She was between spring and summer sessions right now.

He knew a lot about her. He supposed he should have expected the courage, given the determination and drive she showed in pursuing her education. He hadn't. He'd found it both surprising and endearing. And, like everything else about her, arousing as hell.

She came out of the bedroom as he stood with a box of macaroni and cheese mix in his hand. He held it up, brows raised in question. "What about the food?"

She shrugged. "Can't you just mutter over it? Work your mojo? Find out if he messed with it or something?"

"I read people. Not food."

She crossed the room, joining him in the kitchen, and he heard her thinking how much smaller it seemed with him in it, and that she didn't mind it, and then she thought about his hair again. She'd been thinking about his hair a lot. It probably wasn't altogether wise for him to keep reading her thoughts, but he didn't want to stop. She pictured herself running her hands through his hair, and then she pictured it spread across her chest as he kissed her breasts. He almost groaned aloud. Then she forced her focus to the food on the counter.

"Let's throw away whatever's open, keep whatever's sealed," she said.

"Let's throw it all away just to be safe."

"I can't afford—"

"I can."

She lowered her head, wrestling with her values, telling herself she couldn't accept money from a man she didn't know. That it was wrong and somehow sleazy.

"Consider it payment for my room and board tonight."

Her head came up fast. "You really can't stay."

"Sure I can."

"You won't even fit on my sofa. You're too tall."

"Not an issue." He scooped the food into the wastebasket, then closed the cupboards. "Let's sit, so I can get rid of the doubts in your mind about me."

She shot him a look. "Reading my mind again, right?"

He felt a bit guilty. "I'm sorry. I can't seem to help myself. I'll stop if you tell me to."

She smiled at him. God, she really was a beautiful creature. No bigger than a breeze, with those big jade-green eyes, and cheekbones sculpted by a god. "You don't need to apologize, Michael. I'm a total skeptic about this, in case you hadn't picked up on that already. Despite the little demonstrations you've been tossing out."

"I know you don't believe me. That's the first thing we need to get out of the way. Come. Sit." He took her arm, led her into the living room and set her on the small, floral-patterned sofa. "Now, tell me to do something, but don't say it aloud. Just think it in your mind."

Her lips curved into a smile as the many voices of her own mind began to argue.

This could be fun.

Don't be an idiot. Tell him to get me a glass of water.

No, tell him to kiss me.

Honestly, it's not going to matter what I tell him. I could tell him to carry me to the bed and undress me with his teeth, but he isn't going to hear any of it.

He held up a hand. "That's enough."

"But I didn't—"

He met her eyes. "Yeah, you did." Then he went to the kitchen, got a glass from the cupboard, filled it with water from the bottle in the fridge. He brought it to her but he didn't put it in her hand. He set it down on the maple coffee table instead. Putting his hands on her shoulders, he drew her to her feet, slid his arms around her waist and bent his head until his lips touched hers.

She shivered. She was mortified, realizing he had heard every single thought, yet her entire body quivered in anticipation and need. He kissed her mouth. When she wished he would pull her closer, he did, and when she wished he would use his tongue, he did that, too. She was sweet and shy, embarrassed and eager, nervous and frightened, but mostly she was hungry—for him.

He was beginning to think this little game had been a bad idea, because this had not been his intent. He hadn't come here to make love to her, but that was exactly what he was going to do. And whether or not it was a good idea really didn't matter very much at this point.

He scooped her into his arms and carried her to the bedroom, still exploring her mouth with his. Then he lowered her to the bed and bent over her, dragging his mouth away from hers, over her neck, to the top button of the jade-colored silk blouse. He kissed her flesh there, then freed the top button of the blouse with his teeth. Kissed her again and undid another, then kissed her again there.

"No." She put her hands firmly on his shoulders and gave him a push.

Michael froze, fought down his rising passion and slowly straightened away from her. "It's what you wanted," he told her.

"It crossed my mind. That's not the same thing."

He nodded, conceding the point. "You're right. A passing thought is not the same thing as real wanting. But it felt like real wanting when you thought it."

She stared up at him. She was still lying on the bed, with her blouse unbuttoned and her desire shining in her eyes. "It was," she whispered. "I'm trying to balance it with common sense. This isn't me, Michael. I don't act this way."

"I never ever once thought you did."

She nodded. "It's too soon."

Leaning over her, he gently buttoned her blouse, gripped her shoulders and helped her sit up.

"For what it's worth, you've convinced me. I believe you now. And I'm going to take you up on that offer."

He lifted his brows. "To undress you with my teeth?" He knew that wasn't what she meant, but he couldn't resist.

"To stop eavesdropping on my every thought."

"I was afraid that was what you meant." He sighed, showing his disappointment. "All right. I knew better, I just—your thoughts were so flattering."

"It's not fair. I can't read yours."

And it was a good thing, because a second ago he'd been thinking things that would either have driven her wild or scared the hell out of her. And he didn't want to scare her. "Trust me," he said. "You'd find mine flattering, too."

She smoothed her hair and got to her feet. "So are you ready to show me what's in that briefcase of yours?"

He nodded, took her hand, drew her back into the living room. Even though leaving the bedroom was the last thing he wanted to do.

Chapter 4

Four missing-person reports—photocopies, taken from various police departments—lay across her breakfast bar. There were names typed across the tops, and they all had three-by-five snapshots attached with paperclips: Samantha Carlson, Vivian Marie Patinski, Kathy Somerfield, Cynthia Stone.

Mary looked at the typed pages and tried to ignore the pretty, smiling faces of the women, the life in their eyes. "New Jersey, Vermont, Massachusetts, Connecticut—they all vanished from different states."

"All in the northeast," he said. "As is Maine."

"Okay. So he's a traveling stalker?"

"Read the reports."

Swallowing hard, she tried to focus on the pages instead of on the intensity of Michael's gaze or the disturbing tingle generated by his nearness. And then she didn't have to, because he narrated for her, maybe too impatient to wait.

"All four of them reported anonymous phone calls and feelings of being watched for a week or two prior to their disappearances. Each of them reported a break-in. Each of them vanished during the full moon."

A little shiver raced up her spine.

"Did they find...any of them?"

He lowered his head. "He dumps them in various places. Samantha's body was found by some fishermen in Crosswicks Creek. Vivian turned up in a city dump, underneath a mound of trash. Kathy and Cynthia are still missing."

She pressed her lips together and looked again at the photos. Then she glanced at their birthdates. "All under thirty."

"That's not all they have in common, Mary."

She closed her eyes, not sure she wanted to know this, but certain that she had to.

"They all shared a very rare blood antigen, known as belladonna. You have it, too."

She looked up at him fast. "How do you know that?"

He held her gaze. "The same way I know so many things about you. I feel you, Mary. Sometimes it's like I'm inside you."

She closed her eyes, suppressing a shiver. She had expected his so-called evidence would expose him as a fraud, or maybe a sincere but misguided do-gooder. Instead, he was convincing her. "How were they...?"

She didn't have to finish the question. "It's not important how they died. Only that they were killed in the same manner."

"The two that were found, at least."

"All four," he said. "But there are only autopsy reports on the two that were found."

Her gaze shifted to the brown leather case, which lay on the counter, its flap open. The corner of a manila envelope was visible inside. Then Michael took the case, on the pretense of returning the police reports to it. He closed it and set it beside him. He really didn't want her to know how the women had died, which told her it must have been horrible.

"Did you try to warn them, too?" she asked.

He shook his head slowly. "I didn't know about them until after they were killed. And then not from a vision, but from casual conversation among…some of my peers."

"Your psychic friends?"

He tried to smile. "Something like that. I heard about these four women, murdered, all of them bearing the antigen. I don't expect you to understand why, and I can't explain it to you, but among people like me, this was a topic that generated a lot of discussion and concern."

"People like you…"

"And then I saw you—in a dream. I *felt* you. And I knew you would be next."

"How did you know where to find me?"

He looked at the floor, gave his head a shake. "It's difficult to explain. Besides, I'm afraid you already think I'm deluded."

"So you have nothing to lose."

He drew a breath. "Once I had seen your face, sensed your aura, even though it was only in a dream, I was able to home in and track you down."

"Kind of like a bloodhound once he gets the scent?"

"Something like that."

She licked her lips and wondered why she wasn't afraid of him. He could be the killer, for all she knew. But if he was, why was he trying to warn her? And how had he managed the trick of calling her on the cell phone while sitting beside her in the car?

Tricky. But not impossible. There were devices, recorders, timers. She'd seen her share of spy films.

And yet she wasn't afraid of him. He was odd. Different. She'd never met a man like him. But there was no sense of fear. Which might be exactly what he wanted. Want it or not, though, there was no way he could be held responsible for the storm of desire raging inside her. No way. That was all her. He couldn't have planned that.

He was watching her now, studying her face. Then he nodded toward his coat, which hung on a rack just inside the apartment door. "There's a gun in the left pocket of my trench coat. Extra bullets in the right. I brought them for you, to protect yourself."

She blinked. "I don't...like guns."

"I don't, either, but we're talking about your life here. Go on, take it. And while you're there, search the other pockets. Assure yourself that I'm not hiding any other weapons."

Pursing her lips, she slid off the stool and went to the coat, doing what he told her. The gun was a small black revolver. The bullets were in a red-and-white box. The other pockets were empty.

When she turned, he was standing beside her, though she hadn't heard him cross the room. He stood with his arms out from his sides. "Go on. I want you to be sure of me."

Swallowing hard, she set the gun and bullets down

and put her hands on either side of his left arm, drawing them along it slowly, all the way to his wrist. She repeated the action on the other arm. He turned so she could run her palms over his back and shoulders, and she wished to God the shirt wasn't in her way. Then, as she prayed he hadn't heard that thought, he turned again. She ran her palms across his chest and belly.

Her heart was pounding so hard she thought he had to hear it. He was reacting, too; she knew he was. His eyes had closed, and his jaw was clenched tight. She moved her hands to his sides, up and down them. Then she bent her knees, hunkered lower, to rub a path along his outer thighs, to his calves. She felt him shiver when she worked her way back up the inside.

Finally she straightened. "No weapons." The words came out hoarse; she had to clear her throat. "No deadly ones, anyway."

She looked away quickly. "What is this thing, Michael? Why do I feel so...?" She couldn't finish. She just let the words trail off into silence.

"I don't know. But it's...not just you."

She looked at him and saw it clearly in his eyes: he wanted her. As badly as she wanted him. But he broke eye contact to pick up the gun and bullets from where she had placed them, then put them into her hands. "Keep the gun with you," he said. "And keep it loaded. There's no safety to worry about, and it's fairly simple to operate."

She played with the catch on the side, because it was something to do to take her attention away from her body's demanding cries. He wouldn't say no if she invited him to her bed. She wouldn't even have to ask him. She could just take his hand, lead him into the bedroom. He would understand.

She made the gun's cylinder fall open, so she could see the holes where the bullets would go. Then she clapped it closed again and thought about loading it, where to keep it while she slept and whether or not she could shoot someone—thought about anything but having sex with Michael Gray.

"Between that and your stun gun, you should be able to defend yourself," he said.

She nodded.

"I wouldn't supply you with a gun if I meant to hurt you, Mary."

"You think I don't know that at this point?"

He nodded, glanced at the clock. "It'll be dawn soon. You should get some sleep."

He was right. It had been almost 3:00 a.m. by the time she left the bar. "So should you." *Go on, say it. Just invite him to stay!*

"I will. We have one more thing working in our favor, Mary. He always strikes at night. Always."

"So far, you mean."

He nodded.

"And how is that in our favor?"

"I can protect you by night."

She frowned, not sure what that could mean. Then she felt a lightbulb go on. "You have a day job." Then she sighed. "So you plan to work by day, then stay up all night watching my back? That's crazy, Michael. How long do you think you can keep up a schedule like that?"

"As long as I have to. And it's not as crazy as you think it is." Again he glanced at the clock. "But time is awfully short. I really do have to leave you now."

He got to his feet, went to the door. And suddenly

she felt panic nipping at her heart. She ran to the door behind him. "Michael—"

He stopped, turned and placed a gentle palm on her face. "He's nowhere near here. Not now. I'd know if he was."

She closed her eyes. "Besides," she said, "the moon's not full."

"Lock the door behind me."

"I will. But…when will you come back?"

"I'll be at the bar right after sundown. You make sure you get there before dark. That way you'll be safe. And keep your weapons with you."

She nodded. "All right." Swallowing hard, she took his hand in both of hers. "Thank you, Michael. I have no idea why you're doing this. Why you even care, but…thank you."

"I'm doing it," he told her, "because I can't *not* do it."

"I don't understand what that means."

He smiled gently. "Let's just say you have some kind of power over me. I don't think I could resist it even if I wanted to. And to be honest, I don't want to." He cupped her cheek with his palm and leaned down to brush his lips over hers. "Get some rest, Mary."

She nodded, and he stepped out the door. Mary closed it and turned the locks. Then she moved to the window and pushed the curtain aside to watch him go…but he was already gone.

As if he'd simply…vanished.

Mary slept until the ringing of the doorbell woke her. Her eyes didn't want to open, but the ringing was rapid and repetitive and stubborn as hell. She didn't want to get up. It didn't seem she was going to get a choice in the matter, though.

Rolling to one side, she pried her eyelids apart just enough to see the luminous red digits on her alarm clock—10:00 a.m. She'd been asleep for about five and a half hours—Michael had pulled his disappearing act around four-thirty. The doorbell was still firing away.

"I'm coming, already!"

She pushed back her covers and let gravity pull her legs until her feet hit the floor. Feeling around while yawning, she found her slippers with her toes and burrowed her feet into them. She stood up, finished the yawn, and then she went stiff as the fog in her brain finally thinned enough to let her fear shine through.

What if it was the killer at her door right now?

But Michael had said he only struck at night. And during the full moon. It was broad daylight now. Still…

She opened the drawer in the bedside stand and took out the revolver. She'd loaded it and put it there before going to sleep last night. Where the hell to carry it, though? There was no pocket in her flannel pajamas. Licking her lips, scanning the room, with the doorbell pinging the entire time, she spotted a bathrobe on the back of a chair and snatched it up. As she pulled it on and dropped the gun into its deep terry pocket, the doorbell changed to rapid pounding, and a voice yelled, "Open up, Ms. McLean. It's the police."

Police?

She frowned, tugged the sash around her waist and tied it as she scuffed to the door and peered through the peephole. Two men in police uniforms stood at her door. Beyond the parking-lot gate, she could see a black-and-white car with all the right emblems and lights attached.

She unlocked the door, but left the chain on, and opened it just a little. "Look, I don't want to piss you guys off, but I'm gonna need to call the station and verify that you're really cops, okay?"

One rolled his eyes. He was heavyset, with a face that reminded her of a panda, dark circles around the eyes and heavy on the jowls.

The other one was younger, a blue-eyed blonde who belonged on a tanning-oil commercial. "That's understandable, considering the nature of the complaint you filed last week, and then the break-in," he said.

She blinked. "Why are you here? You're not the cops who were handling that for me."

"Well, there have been some developments, ma'am. Your case might overlap another one we're working, so—"

"Do you know something about this maniac who's been stalking me?"

"Maybe. Do you?" asked the older one.

"Wait here." She closed the door, turned the locks, glanced again at the car to see that they were city cops, then flipped open the phone book and found the number for headquarters. She got a fast answer and a quick verification that yes, two officers by the names of Strickland and Dunst were currently standing at her door.

"Thank you," she said, and hung up the phone. Then she took the little gun from her pocket and tucked it beneath the huge leaves of a houseplant. Finally she opened the door.

"I'm Officer Dunst," said the beach boy. "This is

Officer Strickland. We need to ask you a few questions, ma'am. Do you mind if we come inside?''

"Of course not. Sorry about the delay. You'll be happy to know you're legit." Neither of them so much as cracked a smile at her little joke. She stepped aside and let them precede her in; then she closed the door again, not bothering with the locks. She shouldn't need locks with two cops and a gun in a potted plant nearby. She waved them toward the sofa and took a seat in the chair opposite them. "So what is this about?"

"Tommy Campbell," Strickland told her. "You know him?"

"Of course I know him. We work together at The Crypt—that's a bar, not an actual crypt, of course."

"We know." Dunst's voice was softer. "Can you tell us the nature of your relationship with him, ma'am?"

Little chills were racing up and down her nape. "What's going on here? Is Tommy in some kind of trouble?"

"Just answer the questions, ma'am. Are you involved with Tommy Campbell?"

"*Involved?* No, I'm not *involved* with Tommy. We're friends. We work together." She licked her lips, and the cops stared at her, waiting. As if they knew there was more. "He…he may be nursing a little crush on me."

"What makes you think so?"

She shrugged. "I don't know. He's never acted on it, never asked me out or anything, but he just gives off that vibe, you know?" Great, she thought. Now she sounded like Michael.

"When was the last time you saw him, Mary?" Dunst asked.

She frowned, a sudden fear gnawing at her gut. "Last night. I gave him a ride home from the bar. It was raining, and he didn't want to walk, so—what is going on?"

"What time did you drop him off?"

She closed her eyes, thought back. "We close at two. It probably took us twenty minutes or so to get the customers out of there, and then we had clean-up. He only lives a few blocks—I don't know. It must have been close to three."

"You're sure about that?"

"Yes."

"Anyone else who can verify that?"

She frowned. "Can't you just ask Tommy?"

The police officers exchanged a look. It was Dunst who finally spoke. "Ms. McLean, Tommy Campbell was murdered last night."

She felt herself go numb, and her mind seemed unwilling to process the words. It was if he'd spoken in some other language. Then they came clear, and she shook her head in denial. "No, that's not possible. Tommy is...Tommy is..."

"Dead, Ms. McLean," Strickland said.

She closed her eyes, squeezing them tightly as if to block out the man's words. "But how? Why?"

"Someone tied him to his bed, doused him with gasoline and set him on fire."

"Strickland, don't—" Dunst warned.

Too late, though. She'd heard the horror, and her stomach heaved. She shot to her feet, lunging through her bedroom into the bathroom, and vomited. She sank to her knees in front of the toilet.

Dunst came in behind her. "Are you all right?"

"I don't...understand this. Why? Why would any-one hurt Tommy? He's gentle—he's harmless."

He reached past her, flushed the toilet, and then he wet a cloth in the sink and handed it to her. Mary wiped her face and hands and got to her feet.

"You were the last one to see him alive, Mary," Officer Dunst said.

She met his eyes and shook her head side to side. "No, I wasn't. The person who killed him was." The man averted his gaze, and then she knew. "My God, do you think *I* had something to do with this?"

"We have to question you. It's standard proce-dure." He took her arm, led her back through the bed-room toward the living room, his eyes scanning, seem-ing to take in everything. "We need to know everything that happened last night, up to when you dropped Tommy off."

She stopped walking when she reached the living room. The other cop was on his feet, waiting. "I've told you everything. Tommy needed a ride. I gave him one. He got out and went into his building, and I came home."

"And that's all?"

She nodded.

"You didn't see anyone strange hanging around outside his place when you dropped him off?"

She shook her head slowly. "It was pouring rain. The streets were empty."

"What about at the bar?" Dunst asked. "Anyone new been hanging around? Maybe paying extra atten-tion to him?"

She thought of Michael. She should tell them about him. He could verify her story, confirm that Tommy had been alive when she had left him and account for her whereabouts for the rest of the night. But something told her that would be a mistake, so she just shook her head.

"After you came home, what did you do?"

She blinked slowly. "I went to bed. I didn't get up again until you two woke me just now."

"You didn't leave again? Say between four-thirty and 5:00 a.m.?"

She shook her head. "Is that…is that when it happened?"

They didn't reply. It occurred to her that telling them about Michael wouldn't do either of them any good, anyway. Tommy had been killed after Michael had left here.

Tommy was killed after Michael left here.

She sank onto the sofa and looked up at them. "Someone must have seen something. Someone must know who did this."

Dunst nodded. "If someone does, we'll find out."

She sighed and lowered her head. "I hope to God you do."

The cops looked at each other again. Dunst shrugged. "We may have more questions for you later on, once we learn more. Don't leave town for a while, all right?"

She lifted her head sharply. "I'm a suspect, aren't I?"

"Everyone's a suspect until we rule them out. We haven't ruled you out yet," Strickland said. He went to the door, opened it and stepped outside.

"I'll be right out," Dunst called. "I'm gonna get her alternate telephone numbers so we can reach her."

With a nod, Strickland left.

Officer Dunst knelt in front of the sofa. "Mary, this is between us, all right? We think Tommy might have been your stalker. Strickland thinks you found out and murdered him. I don't."

"I appreciate that."

"There was some evidence found at his place that links him to…some other cases. Unusual cases."

"You're being awfully vague, Officer Dunst."

"I'm sorry. I have to be." He took a card from his pocket and handed it to her. "These people can help sort all of this out. I know them. They're good people."

She glanced at the card. It had the stylized initials S.I.S. across the top, and underneath, in smaller type, it read Supernatural Investigations Services.

"Supernatural?"

"You didn't get it from me, understand? This conversation never happened."

She nodded slowly. "What the hell is going on, Officer Dunst?"

"I don't know." He averted his eyes when he said it, as if maybe he did know at least a little more than he was telling her. "Give me your other numbers in case Strickland calls me on it."

She recited her cell phone number, which he scribbled quickly. Then he gave her a reassuring smile and left. She stood in the doorway, shocked and trembling, until he got into the car with his partner and drove away.

Then she closed the door, turned the locks and sank to the floor, shaking.

Michael could have done this.

Michael didn't have anything to do with it, and you know it.

He had time, after leaving her. He hadn't seemed to like Tommy. But why? Why would he do such a horrible thing?

What if he were the stalker after all?

He's not. He can't be.

But there *was* a stalker, and it couldn't be Tommy. The police were wrong about that. What if the real maniac had killed Tommy because he knew of Tommy's crush on her? Was it a jealous rage of some kind? Had this so-called evidence been planted at Tommy's place just to make him look guilty?

Her mind whirled with questions, and one gruesome image she couldn't erase from her mind—that of poor Tommy Campbell, burning alive in his bed.

Chapter 5

Something was wrong.

The bar was dark, only a single car in the parking lot beside his when he pulled in just after sundown. Mary's car. She tensed when his Jaguar's headlights illuminated her where she sat on the front step. He felt her fear rise up. It was palpable, even when he wasn't trying to read her thoughts. He quickly killed the engine and doused the lights, so she could see him.

Even then, though, her fear only eased a minute amount.

He opened the door and got out, and she got to her feet and came toward him. Her face was puffy, eyes red, as if she'd been crying.

"What's happened?"

She held his gaze. "Tommy. You remember Tommy, from last night?"

He nodded.

"He's dead. Someone killed him."

He went to her, put his arms around her to pull her close, the instinct to comfort her overriding his certainty that she was afraid of him all over again. But she didn't let him. She pulled away, and he let his arms fall to his sides as a cold dread settled over his heart. She suspected him.

"The police suspect me," she said.

It was the last thing he'd expected to hear. "What? Why on earth...?"

"He was killed around 5:00 a.m., they said. I was the last person to see him alive. The last they know of, at least."

"My God."

She kept her eyes on her shoes. He looked past her, noticing the sign taped to the entrance. "Closed due to death in the family." He shook his head in disgust. Tommy had been young, early twenties at most. And while Michael had found the boy mildly annoying, he was certain the kid had done nothing to deserve this.

He looked at Mary again. She was barely holding herself together.

"How did it happen?"

"He was tied to his bed and set on fire." She met his eyes briefly. "You're supposed to be some kind of psychic. Why didn't you see this coming?"

He shook his head. "I don't see everything, Mary. I didn't have any connection to Tommy."

"You don't have any connection to me, either."

"Yes, I do. You know good and well I do. You feel it just as strongly as I do, Mary. Don't deny that. Not now."

She lifted her brows. "Why shouldn't I deny it, when you refuse to explain it to me! I know you aren't telling me everything, Michael."

He was silent for a moment. She wanted to know everything. The last mortal woman he'd trusted enough to tell everything to had blasted a hole through her own head in reply. Mary might not react as badly as that. But she would certainly pull away from him, and if she did, the killer would find her alone, unprotected.

He couldn't tell her everything. But clearly, he had to tell her something. "The bond we share is one of blood," he told her, choosing every word with care. "The antigen."

"You have it, too?"

He only nodded. He would not tell her the rest…what he was. "Mary, I had no reason to want to harm Tommy."

She licked her lips.

"You shouldn't have come here, alone like this," he went on. "You could be in danger, you know that."

She shrugged. "I brought the gun. I knew you'd be looking for me here. And I needed to see you. Besides, the police think Tommy might have been the stalker. Apparently that's my motive for killing him."

"What makes them think that?"

She shook her head. "They wouldn't say. I'm not even supposed to know that much." Clearing her throat, she walked toward her car, parked beside his black Jag. "The police wanted to know if anyone was with me when I dropped Tommy off last night. Anyone who could verify that he was alive when I left him. But I didn't tell them about you."

It was good that she hadn't told them. He didn't need the kind of snooping and investigation that would have resulted if she had. But if it would clear her of suspicion...

"It wouldn't have mattered, anyway. He was killed after you left my place. You couldn't swear that I hadn't gone back and done this thing...any more than I could swear you hadn't."

He chose to ignore the latter comment. "What evidence do they have against you?" he asked.

"I already told you, I was the last person to see him alive, and if he was the stalker, then..."

"That's circumstantial. Is there anything physical?"

She frowned. "I don't know. How could there be, Michael? I was never there."

"Never mind. I'll find out. But first, we need to get you somewhere safe."

She was dangerously close to tears. "I'm not supposed to leave town."

He thought about that a moment. If he took her away and the police couldn't reach her, their suspicion would increase exponentially. "Do you have a cell phone?" She nodded. "And did you give the police the number?"

"Yeah."

"Good. I want you to get into your car and follow me back to your apartment, all right? We'll leave your car there, and you can come with me."

She shook her head. "I'm not going anywhere with you, Michael."

He held her gaze for a long time, then finally sighed, giving up. "You think it's me. You think I killed Tommy, don't you?"

"No. I don't think that at all, but part of me thinks that maybe I should—that maybe this...this...chemistry between us is clouding my judgment.'' She sighed, shaking her head in frustration. ''Hell, I don't know what to think. I only know that you're a stranger. As much as it feels like I've known you forever, you're a stranger to me, Michael. I don't even know your last name.''

He swallowed hard. Why her lack of trust in him should cause him pain was beyond knowing. That it did was beyond denying.

''I don't suppose I can blame you for being cautious. You're right. God, it seems to me that you know me better than anyone ever has, but that's just...that's just this.'' As he said it, he trailed the backs of his knuckles over her cheek, and she closed her eyes, pushing closer to his touch.

Then she opened them again and met his. ''It's powerful, Michael. Everything in me believes in you. But I have to be sure.'' She frowned. ''Isn't there some part of you that wonders if I might be guilty? If your feelings aren't clouding your judgment?''

His eyes probed hers. ''No. Not in the least. But then again, I'm more used to trusting my senses than you are. All of them tell me you're no killer. And they've rarely steered me wrong.'' He nodded slowly. ''We'll go back to your apartment. I'll see you safely inside and leave my cell phone number with you. Program it into your phone, so you can call me quickly if you need me. You can stay there, and I'll go see what I can find out about Tommy's murder, and then I'll come back and fill you in.''

She blinked, clearly uncertain. ''How do you think you can find anything out?''

He licked his lips, unsure how much to tell her. ''I was a cop, Mary. For ten years, I was a cop.''

"In New York?"

"Chicago."

"Why did you quit?"

He hesitated. "I was shot in the line of duty. The injuries were…life altering." He wasn't about to tell her that he'd been on the wrong end of a Capone-era tommy gun, or that he'd been pronounced dead in a hospital, only to wake up in its morgue forever changed.

He'd been offered a choice then—live or die. He'd chosen to live.

"I'm sorry. Is it still a painful memory for you?"

He shook his head. "It's in the past." Further in the past than she could ever imagine. "But I do know something about police work. I know where to look for the answers we need, and how to get them without anyone being the wiser." He'd visited a great many police departments since his change. There were always unsolved crimes—things he picked up on through his ability to read the thoughts of mortals, to move about almost silently. There were always wrongs he could help to right. And he did. Had for years. Evidence would turn up where none had been before; missing weapons would be located; witnesses would come forward. And the police never knew they'd had a helping hand—a cold, pale helping hand. In a lot of ways, he was a better cop now than he'd ever been before.

She pursed her lips, then nodded. "If you really think you can learn anything, then…then yes. Let's do it. Here, take my extra gate key so you can get back into my parking lot." She turned away, walking toward her car.

"Gray," he said to her back.

She stopped and turned to face him again. "What?"

"My name is Michael Gray."

"Oh." She smiled at him, weakly, shakily. "Thank you for that."

He nodded, and then she got into her car and he got into his.

After he left her, Michael went first to the building where Mary had dropped Tommy off the night before. There was no security, no key card required to get into the building, and it wasn't difficult to find the right apartment. Even without the yellow police tape marking the door, he would have known. He could still feel the lingering chill of death in the air. And there was the stench. Burning flesh did not emit a pleasant aroma.

The apartment door was locked. The lock gave without much resistance to the pressure of his hand, and he went inside and closed the door behind him. He didn't turn on the lights. He didn't have to.

The place reeked of smoke and charred flesh, but the only sign of fire was in the bedroom. A ring of black surrounded the bed—it had burned through the carpet and charred the floor underneath. The headboard had been destroyed, leaving only a bit of charred wood at its base. The wall behind it was blackened, as well, and the ceiling above. The mattress was missing, probably in a crime lab by now.

Oddly, the rest of the room showed very little damage. The firefighters must have arrived in time to contain the blaze, saving most of the apartment and the rest of the building. And probably a lot of lives in the process.

The room had been ransacked. Many items, he sensed, were missing.

He went to the bed, bracing himself for the onslaught of sensations the act would bring before he placed his hand on the bed springs.

He expected horror. Pain beyond endurance. Heat and searing torment. It wasn't what he got. He got nothing at all, other than an image of a body on fire. No thoughts. No sensations. Tommy hadn't been conscious when he'd gone up in flames.

Frowning, he searched the apartment but found no clues, got no other images. It wasn't until he left the building, on his way to the police department, that he felt that death energy again. Not from within, but from the alley just below Tommy's window.

He followed his senses into the garbage-strewn alley. Rats skittered from his approach. And then he smelled it.

Blood.

Moving closer, he located the source, a dark spatter on the brick outer wall of the building next to Tommy's. He pressed his hand to the stain and immediately felt a stunning blow to his forehead, right between the eyes, and what felt like an explosion at the back of his skull. He smelled the hot sulphur scent of gunpowder, and though he didn't hear a shot, his ears rang as if they had.

Someone had been shot in the head. Right here in this alley.

A young man. Early twenties, small and wiry, with brown hair.

God, Tommy had been shot right here. This was where he'd died.

It made no sense, Michael thought as he returned

to his car and drove away. Someone had lured or forced Tommy into the alley, only to then return him to his apartment. The risk of being seen carrying a body should have been enough reason not to do such a thing. And then to bind the boy to his own bed and burn the body—it was insane.

He was still no closer to learning what the police had found to implicate Mary, he realized. Whoever had done this had known where Tommy lived. Perhaps it was someone he knew, then. Or perhaps it was simply someone who had watched him enough to have learned that minor detail.

Hell, they could have figured that much out from the address on his driver's license.

But why? Why kill the boy at all, much less burn the body?

He found out more when he slipped into the police station and played mind games with the officers on duty to keep them away from the places where he needed to snoop. The place was no small-town PD, but it wasn't an overwhelmed, understaffed urban one, either. No, this was a wealthy community, and their police department was well funded.

There were the usual drawers full of paper files, but each folder had a pocket in the front, containing a CD-ROM. A quick check told him everything in the folder—from the crime scene photos on down—had been recorded on the CD. It couldn't have been any easier.

He found the box of unused CD-RWs and made a copy of the official records. Then he put everything back where he'd found it and slipped quietly out of the police department.

Easy. When you could plant thoughts in people's

minds, convince them they needed to be elsewhere and move too fast for human eyes to detect more than a blur of color, it was almost too easy.

He got into his Jag and drove back to Mary's apartment, eager to examine the evidence he'd found.

More eager, though, just to be close to her again.

Chapter 6

She paced, torn in two about what she should be doing right now. One tiny part of her brain told her she ought to be on the phone with the police, telling them everything she knew about Michael Gray—which was pathetically little. Every other part of her trusted him implicitly on nothing more than instinct.

But with her life?

Licking her lips, she picked up the business card that Officer Dunst had given her. She looked at the telephone number. Officer Dunst had said they were "good people."

Glancing outside just once, seeing no sign of Michael, she picked up the telephone and dialed the number.

"Supernatural Investigations Service."

Mary had second thoughts. She certainly didn't need to add any supernatural bent to what should be a simple background check. "I think I have the wrong number. Sorry."

"Don't you think you'd better make sure of that before you hang up?"

She sighed. "Look, I just need an ordinary P.I. for a routine background check on someone. There's nothing…supernatural about it. I shouldn't have called."

"How'd you get this number?" the woman asked.

"I…um…a cop gave it to me."

"Officer Dunst?"

"Yeah."

The woman said, "Well, he sends us a lot of business. I imagine he knew we'd be more than glad to take care of your routine background check for you, even if it's not precisely our usual area."

"You think so?"

"Either that or he has a feeling there's something supernatural about your case."

That was the feeling Mary had had when Dunst gave her the card. But she didn't want to explore that suspicion too deeply. "I just—look, there's this man who's shown up in my life. He seems to know things he shouldn't, claims to be some kind of a psychic. I just wanted someone to run a background check on him."

"We can usually do up a pretty thorough report within twenty-four hours. It'll cost you a hundred bucks. That's our special Dunst referral discount rate, by the way. Sound acceptable to you?"

"Yeah. Yes, that'll be fine. His name is Michael Gray. He's here in Bangor now, but he says he was a cop in Chicago, shot in the line of duty."

"Hell, girl, with that much to go on, we won't have any problem at all."

"Good." She heard a vehicle outside and jerked her head quickly toward the door. "Call me. Make sure you only talk to me though. My number is—"

"We have it, hon. Shows right up on our caller ID box. I'll talk to you tomorrow."

She hung up the phone, feeling guilty as hell and hoping to God Michael would keep his promise not to go poking around in her mind, reading things that were private. The call she'd just made felt to her like a deep and unforgivable betrayal. To keep her mind off it, just in case he snooped, she thought about Tommy, and the moment she did, the horror of the way he had died came flooding back to her. She didn't think she would have any problem keeping her focus on that—she might have a problem driving it from her mind later on, though.

Someone knocked on the door, and she knew it was Michael, could almost feel his presence, but she looked first, all the same. Then she opened the door and let him in, and forcibly resisted the impulse to slide her arms around him and press herself close to him and whisper that she'd missed him.

Maybe she was losing her mind.

He looked tired. Or it might have been worry that made his eyes seem so careworn, his face so tense.

"Did you find out anything?"

He nodded. "Many things. Still not everything. I think I ended up with more questions than I had before." He searched her face, and she almost squirmed with guilt, wondering what he could see there. "How are you doing?"

"I'm fine. And you'll have to take my word for it,

since you promised not to do any more trespassing in my private thoughts."

He smiled just a little. "I wasn't. I told you I wouldn't, Mary, and I won't. I promise."

"Just making sure. What did you learn about Tommy?"

"You want the good news or the bad news first?" He set his brown leather bag on the floor and shrugged out of the trench coat, then hung it up on the coatrack.

"You mean there's good news?"

He nodded, picking up the brown bag again, and walked through the apartment, taking a seat on one of the stools at the bar. "Yeah. There's good news. Tommy wasn't burned alive. He was shot in the head in the alley outside his apartment."

"But...but the police said he was tied to his bed and burned alive."

"He was tied to his bed and burned, but not alive. He was already dead."

As Michael spoke, he pulled a laptop computer out of his case, flipped it open and pushed the button that made it come on.

She wondered how the hell he could know any of that, then guessed. "You must have got a look at the autopsy report."

He shook his head as the computer went through its warm-up routine. "The autopsy hasn't been done yet."

"Then—"

"I went to the apartment. I touched the bed. I got nothing. But in the alley outside, I felt the bullet. It entered here." He poked a forefinger to the spot between his eyebrows. "Exited here." His palm open, he cupped the back of his head. "There was an explosion of blinding pain, but very brief. Like the flash of a camera. Then he was gone.''

She closed her eyes. ''You don't know how much I want to believe it happened that way, Michael, but—''

''I found the spray of blood on the alley wall. The police will find it, too. And when they do get their autopsy report, it will verify that Tommy was shot in the head and killed before his body was burned.''

''You're that good?'' she asked.

''I'm that good.'' He pushed a button on the computer, and the slender CD drive popped open. Then he dropped a shiny disk into it and closed it again. He hit a few keys. ''I stopped on the way back to take a look at this. It's gonna be hard to take, Mary.''

''So this would be the bad-news part?''

He nodded. ''The police were investigating Tommy.''

She frowned. ''For what?''

''He was their lead suspect in your break-in and the stalking.''

''They told me that. But I…I find it very hard to believe.''

''They were going to execute a search warrant at his place today. As it turned out, they didn't have to. The fire was pretty much contained in one part of the bedroom. The rest of his place only suffered smoke and water damage, and I imagine the fire department contaminated any forensic evidence that might have been there, but…well, they did find these.''

He flicked a button, nodded at the screen. There were rows and rows of thumbnail-size photographs— and they were all of her. She squinted.

He moved the mouse until its arrow pointed at one,

clicked it, and the photo appeared, full-size. It was her making drinks, standing behind the bar at The Crypt. Taken from behind. Michael closed it and clicked on another, then another and another.

In one she was walking through the front door of her apartment. In another she was in her bed, sound asleep. There were photos of her at the grocery store, at the bank, photos of her car, with close-ups of the license plate.

"He had an entire album full of these."

"He was that obsessed with me?" She stared at Michael, shaking her head in disbelief.

"No, Mary. I don't think he was obsessed with you at all. I think he was hunting you. These aren't the kind of photos a man with an obsession takes. These are surveillance shots. Every one has the date, time and place noted on the bottom. And there's more." He clicked on another image. Enlarged, it revealed a hand-drawn map.

She frowned and looked again. "That's my route home from work."

"He made maps of all your routes. To and from the gym, the store, anywhere you went regularly. Along with charts of the times and dates you visited those places."

"But...why?"

He licked his lips. "This is the work of a professional, Mary. Those phone calls—they weren't meant only to shake you up. They were probably also checks to see if you were home, or how much time you spent in the shower or the laundry room or whatever. He had your every movement charted and mapped."

She blinked slowly. "And the break-in?"

He sighed, clicked on another image. This one grew

large enough to fill most of the screen. It was her apartment, laid out like a blueprint, every item in it, including light switches, windows, doors, furniture and telephones, marked and labeled.

"The mess he left was just to cover what he was really doing here. Mapping the place so he'd know it backward and forward when he came to do the job."

She lifted her eyes to Michael's. "He...he was in the car when that phone call came. You were there, too. Remember?"

He nodded. "They found equipment at his place—a device that blocks any attempt to trace the call, another capable of being programmed to make a call and play a recording at a specific time before hanging up."

Mary couldn't believe what he was telling her. "Tommy...was going to kill me?"

He nodded. "I'm afraid so."

"But...but why?"

"I don't know. But I think it's the same reason he killed the other women with the antigen. They, uh, they found some photos of them at his place, too."

She tried to prevent the tears, but she felt so betrayed. So deceived. Tommy had seemed like an innocent, naive young man, little more than a boy nursing a crush. Not a cold, calculating murderer. He'd had her fooled.

Searching her reeling mind for answers, she hit on only one ray of hope. "At least I don't have to be worried anymore. He's dead. The full moon is the day after tomorrow, and I'll be able to go outside and look up at it if I want to, without worrying about some maniac attacking me."

She tried to force a lightness to her tone. Even a false smile to her lips. But Michael still looked grim.

"What? What is it?"

"I don't know. It's killing me that I don't know, but—Mary, I just don't get the feeling that the threat is gone. I still sense danger around you."

She searched her mind, wondering why on earth she might still be in danger. And then it hit her. "I know what it is. It's the police. If they know all this...?" She sent him a questioning look.

"They do. This all came from their files."

She sighed. "Then to them, it must look like I have the perfect motive for murdering Tommy. They'll assume I found out he was a serial killer, and that I killed him to keep him from killing me." She tapped a finger on her chin. "What I don't understand is why they haven't arrested me already."

"Because it's a far-fetched notion to think that a bartender without any special training could take out a professional killer like Tommy Campbell. That's why. They're searching for something in your background that would make it believable."

"Like what?"

"Like that you're an expert marksman, or you have a black belt in some martial art, or that you spent ten years working as a CIA operative or something."

"Or that I was a former cop?"

He looked at her sharply.

"Michael, you knew he'd killed before, and you knew he was coming after me next. I couldn't even blame you—not if you did it to protect me. Given the power of our feelings toward each other, I might have done the same."

He held her gaze for a long time. "I knew he had killed before, and I knew he was coming after you next. But I *didn't* know he was Tommy Campbell.

And I was a *cop,* Mary. A cop. Not a killer. If I had known, I'd have wanted him to do time for it. I'd have tipped off the police, exposed him somehow. I wouldn't have killed him unless he gave me no other choice. I'm not a murderer.''

She had to look away from his eyes. He seemed so wounded that she would suspect he had done such a thing. "I'm sorry," she said. "Please remember, Michael, I still don't know you very well."

He sighed, closed a hand around hers. "You know me inside and out. Just like I know you. I know you feel it, Mary."

Closing her eyes, she let herself admit it to him. "Yes. I do feel it. This odd sense of familiarity, as if you're my best friend. Someone I've loved, and who loved me in return, for all my life. Or maybe even longer than that."

Chapter 7

Michael made a halfhearted attempt to convince Mary that she didn't need to comb through the contents of the CD herself—that he could nutshell the important pieces of information for her. He knew before he suggested it that she would never agree. Odd, how well he knew her. As he'd expected, she insisted on seeing for herself. As she clicked through the files, the various reports, statements of witnesses, evidence lists, she didn't just skim. She read every word.

"The police knew about the other murders. And the blood connection, too. It's all right here." She pursed her lips, shaking her head as she scrolled down the screen. "There's a notation to keep me under surveillance for my own protection, but it says they saw no need to alarm me, since the chances that my stalker was the same man who'd murdered those other women were slim to none."

"I can't disagree with their decision on that," Michael said, trying to see the case from a cop's point of view. "If I didn't have this bond with you, then I wouldn't have known it, either. The fact that you happened to have the same rare blood marker as a handful of dead women in other states could have been a coincidence. At least they were taking precautions."

He took her mug from in front of her and refilled it with coffee, then replaced in on the counter. "We really should get you out of this apartment, Mary."

"I don't see the need. The killer is dead."

"But the danger is still there."

She frowned at him. "I don't know what you mean by that. How can it be, when Tommy's dead?"

He sighed, sliding onto a stool next to hers. "I don't know, either. It's there, that's all I can tell you. It's around you like a dark cloud. It hasn't changed in the least since Tommy's death. I know I'm right, Mary."

She pursed her lips. "There's no way you can be. My main goal now has to be to clear myself of suspicion in Tommy's murder. I can't do that if I go into hiding."

He searched her eyes. "If Tommy was the stalker, the murderer, then why is he dead? Who killed him?"

She shook her head slowly. "I don't know. A relative of one of his victims? Or maybe it was completely unrelated."

"I don't believe that."

"What else could it be?" She slid a hand over one of his. "Michael, he's dead. Maybe your…your feelings for me are messing with your reception on this."

He tried that theory on for size, but it didn't fit. He'd trusted his senses for too long to start doubting them now. So if it wasn't that, then what? "Mary, what if all the evidence is wrong? What if Tommy wasn't the stalker and someone planted all that stuff to make it look as if he was, then murdered him. It would certainly divert suspicion from themselves.''

Her eyes clouded so quickly, so suddenly, that he almost winced. "I thought of that, too. Then I told myself it was too far-fetched. The simplest answer is usually the right one, isn't that what they say?''

''That's what they say. But nothing about this has been simple.''

''Do you think it's possible?''

''It's the only explanation I can think of for what I'm sensing.''

She swallowed hard, and her chin rose a notch. ''Well, then…that's just one more reason for us to find the man who killed Tommy. We not only need to clear me of killing Tommy, but we need to clear Tommy of having been this psychopathic murderer. It's unfair to his memory.'' Lowering her eyes, she added, ''And if the killer *is* still out there, we need to get him before he gets me. Reason number three.''

''That would be reason number one,'' Michael corrected. ''And this apartment isn't essential to any of those goals.''

She searched his eyes, probing them. Was she wondering just what hidden motivations might be lying behind them? Did she still mistrust him? He stared back, unflinching, letting her probe as deeply as she wanted, stating without a word that he had nothing to hide. When in fact he did. Then the telephone shrilled, breaking the silence so abruptly that Mary jumped two inches off the floor.

Michael gripped her shoulders. ''All right?''

''Yeah, fine.''

''You want me to…?''

"No, no, I have it."

It rang again, and she went to the stand and picked it up. "Hello?"

Michael saw by the look in her eyes that there was no reply, and instantly, instinctively, slid inside her mind to listen through her ears.

"Hello?" she repeated. "Who is this?"

No answer. She closed her eyes, and Michael heard her thoughts. *This can't be happening. It can't be...* But the silence dragged on. And then there was a single word, drawn out and raspy.

"Soon."

Click. The phone went dead. Mary slammed her receiver down and spun to face Michael. "I'll go wherever you want."

"It was him." He made it a statement, not a question. And he withdrew from her mind, feeling guilty about having broken his earlier promise to her.

She faced him and nodded. "It's almost a relief, in a way. I didn't want to believe it was Tommy, anyway. It's going to be twice as satisfying to bring this bastard down, knowing he tried to make it look as if sweet little Tommy was responsible for his crimes." She was speaking quickly, too quickly, not pausing for a breath between words. "Talk about speaking ill of the dead. Bad enough he murdered Tommy, but to go to all that trouble to frame him, to try to ruin his memory like that, is just...is just..."

She'd run out of steam, he thought. Her rapid-fire words stopped. She closed her eyes, but the tears came through all the same, and when he pulled her close to him, this time she didn't resist. She seemed to soften in his arms, against his chest, buried her head there and let herself cry. He rubbed her back and shoulders, stroked her hair, wondered at the tightening of his throat and the burning in his eyes. It hurt him to see her in pain, and all he wanted at that moment was to ease her fear and her suffering.

"It's going to be all right, Mary. I'm not going to let anything happen to you. I promise you that. He won't get anywhere near you. You'll be safe with me. I'll keep you safe. Trust me. Believe me, Mary, I won't let him hurt you."

She nodded against him, sniffling. "I do believe you," she whispered.

"Why don't you pack a few things? I'll stow the laptop in the car, then come back in to carry your bags out for you. All right?"

"Okay." She straightened away, looked up at him.

It broke his heart to see her cheeks wet with tears. "Okay," he said again. It was an effort to let her go, but he managed to do so. She went into the bedroom to pack, and he popped the CD-ROM out of the laptop, shut the computer down and folded it shut. Then he slid it into his brown leather satchel and buckled it shut. He grabbed his coat and headed out to his car.

She waited until he'd stepped outside to call from the bedroom telephone. Her hands were shaking as she punched in the numbers. Her heart and soul and body were at war with her mind, ripping one another to shreds. She felt as if she were stabbing Michael in the heart by making this call. And yet some still small voice in her mind told her that someone, somewhere, ought to know where she was going and how to reach her.

The ringer sounded twice before anyone picked up.

"Supernatural Investigations Services, Stormy speaking."

"Hi, this is Mary McLean. I phoned you earlier?"

"Hi, Mary. Look, it's too soon to tell you anything yet, but—"

"No, no, it's not that. I just want to give you my cell phone number. I'll be away from the apartment, at Michael Gray's place. So you'll have to reach me on that."

"All right. Shoot."

She glanced out the window. Michael was walking back across the lot toward her door already. So strong, so beautiful and so utterly devoted to her. How could she still suspect him of anything?

She didn't, and that was the truth. She was head over heels for the guy. It wasn't Michael she didn't trust right now; it was her own judgment.

She recited the number quickly. Stormy read it back, getting the last digit wrong. Mary corrected her. Michael was opening the door.

"Got it?"

"Yes."

"Good." She hung up the phone just as he stepped inside and pulled the door closed behind him. "I'll only be a few more minutes," she called. As quickly as she could, she yanked a suitcase out of her closet, opened it and began tossing clothes inside. As she slammed it shut, she tried to slam the door on her guilty feelings, as well. But that wasn't so easily done.

Michael's home was not at all what she had expected. She wasn't certain just what she had expected—something that spoke of extreme wealth, she supposed, since he drove a Jaguar and dressed in expensive clothes. The place must be costing him a bundle, but it didn't advertise the fact. It was a beach house. Just one story, not tiny, but not sprawling, either. He took a side road off Route 1, north of Bangor. A few miles later he was pulling into the neat white gravel driveway that wound right up to the front doors, which were sliding glass, with heavy drapes behind them. Beyond the house was a beach, more rocks than sand, and plenty of frothing surf.

"This is where you live?"

He nodded. "Only since I came to Maine, looking for you. I found it the first night. I like the ocean."

"So do I."

They got out of the car and he handed his key ring to her. Then he opened the trunk to take out her suitcase, carrying it in one hand and his own case, with the laptop, in the other. Mary reached past him to close the trunk, then walked beside him over the flower-lined path to the door.

"It's the square-headed key," he told her. "The silver one."

She inserted the key in the lock, then slid the doors open and pushed the drapes aside to step in. The place was open and airy, its kitchen and dining room combined in one broad space, two steps down. Beyond them, the living room was two steps lower still, furnished with a brown velour sofa and chairs that looked as inviting as any she'd seen. His coffee and end tables were brass and glass, and another set of sliding doors stood at the far end. She dropped the keys on the table and went to them, pulling the drapes open, and then she took in the view.

Steep wooden stairs zigzagged from the back door down to the rocky beach. Not a soul was in sight this early in the season. But the sand and the rocks and the waves rolling gently in, one after the other, were a breathtaking sight. And soothing, somehow.

"This place is beautiful." She felt as if she really had found a haven.

"I'm glad you like it." He carried her bags through the living room to a door on the left. "This is the guest room. You'll be its first occupant."

"I can't imagine why. If I had a friend with a place like this, I'd be here so much they'd get sick of me." She said it with a teasing smile.

"You do have a friend with a place like this," he said. His tone wasn't light or teasing. "And I doubt I'd ever get sick of you."

She met his eyes, saw the tension, the passion, in them. She had to look away. "Michael, I...there's just so much going on now. I can't even think about—"

"I know. I wasn't trying to—" He licked his lips and started over. "No pressure, Mary. Not from me, and certainly not now. I just forgot to keep my feelings to myself for a second."

Her stomach tightened, and her face heated. "I want to explore this...this thing between us."

"So do I."

"I just need time."

He nodded.

Maybe...maybe when this was over and she knew more about him—God, she had to learn more about him—maybe then she would be ready to take this to the next level, see where it might lead.

But until then...until then she was going to be fighting every instinct and desire in her to keep herself in her own bed in the guest room and out of his.

He cleared his throat, breaking eye contact. "Look,

my schedule is a little crazy. I'll be gone before you wake in the morning and probably won't be able to get back until after dark. I don't want you to feel trapped here. But you *will* be safe. No one knows where to find you here. The locks are top-notch, and there's a security system, as well.''

She nodded. ''I don't feel trapped. I feel rescued. It made perfect sense to leave my car at my place so as not to alarm the police, and you'll need yours. I'll be fine as long as I can go down to the water, walk on the beach. And don't worry about your schedule, Michael. I'm used to sleeping by day and working by night, given my hours at The Crypt.''

He only smiled at her, opening the bedroom door and carrying her bags inside. The room was small and obviously unused. Still, it was carpeted in thick pile, and the bed was huge and comfy looking. A matching dresser and a bedside stand with a clock were the only other items inside.

''It's perfect. Thank you, Michael.''

''You're welcome.'' He looked around the room as if inspecting it for flaws.

''Stop. It's perfect, I told you.''

''I should have planned better,'' he said. ''I could have spruced the room up a little. And now that I think about it, there's probably not a crumb of food in the place.''

''What, you don't eat?''

He looked at her almost as if he were alarmed, but then he saw the teasing smile she sent him and returned it. ''There's a little store just a short walk from here. We can stock up tonight.'' He looked at his wristwatch. ''They're open for another hour yet.''

"Then we'd better get to that right now." He glanced at her suitcase.

"I can unpack when we get back."

"All right." He led her out of the bedroom, out the back doors and down the zigzag stairs to the beach below, then turned left, and they walked side by side in the sand. As they did, his hand brushed hers and turned, as if to enfold hers, but then he stopped himself.

She wanted him to hold her hand. She wanted far more than that. Mary slid her hand into his, and when he closed his around it, warmth suffused her entire being.

Something bright caught her eye, and she glanced out toward the sea. The moon was shining down on the ocean, its silver light spreading over the rippling waters.

She swallowed hard. "It's almost full."

"I know." He squeezed her hand. "I'll keep my promise, Mary. You're safe with me, I swear it."

A shiver went up her spine in spite of the warmth of being near him. It was a sudden rush of fear, of foreboding, almost a warning. She hoped to God he *could* keep his promise. But she wasn't certain that was possible if fate had other plans for her.

Chapter 8

He didn't *want* to feel the way he did about Mary.
He didn't want this power between them to be anything more than the undeniable awareness that always
came between her kind and his. She was one of what
vampires called The Chosen—a human with the belladonna antigen. They were linked by blood, the two
of them. The overwhelming urge to protect her was
to be expected.

And yet he couldn't deny that there was more than
that. He was compelled to walk close to her, stand
close to her, sit beside her, touch her at every opportunity, smell her.

Taste her…

No. Not that. He wouldn't do that. She must never
know what he was. The memory of Sally's reaction
to that knowledge was as fresh as if it had happened
yesterday.

They walked to the small store down the beach, and

he bought two bags of groceries. It was a difficult task, since it had been a long time since he'd had to shop for food, and the items offered today were foreign in comparison to what had filled the shelves in his own time.

He had to keep nudging her to make choices, and eventually she got over any feeling that he ought to be the one to choose and just did it. His relief must have shown on his face as the cashier rang them out.

"Not much of a shopper, are you?"

He shrugged. "I usually eat out."

She shook her head. "You don't know what you're missing."

He did know, but to be honest, he didn't miss it all that much. The appeal of food paled in comparison to the lust for blood. Of course, he couldn't tell her that. Or that while food might taste good going down, that was all it did. Blood came alive inside him, sparkling and sizzling through his veins like living energy. Electricity times a thousand. Life. It was life. Even the stale bagged blood he used as his sustenance, stolen from blood banks or hospitals, held the spark of that power. He was hungry. It had been days since he'd fed. Yet he wanted to be near her, to protect her his every waking moment. He couldn't take time away to scavenge for a meal.

He took the two paper grocery bags from the counter and, carrying one in each arm, left the store. Mary caught up quickly and took one of the bags from him. "You don't need to wait on me, you know."

"I wasn't." No. He was trying to keep her from seeing the glow of bloodlust in his eyes. He fought his hunger, wrestled it into submission, buried it and focused only on her.

She walked along the path beside him, warm and alive and beautiful. Her hair was long and loose tonight. The sea wind blew it around her face. In front of the store was a small parking area, and a road beyond it. Behind it, there was only a narrow, well-worn path that wound back to the beach.

"What is it you do?" she asked at length.

"Do?"

"Yeah. You said your work keeps you away most days, remember?"

"Oh. My...work."

She smiled at him a little nervously. "Must pay well. You drive a Jag. Live in a magnificent house on a private beach."

Plus, seventy years of careful investing had its benefits, he thought.

"Is it law-enforcement related?"

He glanced at her, realized he was expected to come up with an answer, one that made as much sense as her suggestion did. "Yeah, as a matter of fact, it is. I do consulting work for, uh, security companies. You know the kind that set up alarm systems and time locks for office buildings and banks and things like that?" He wondered if it sounded at all plausible and watched her face carefully for her reaction.

She nodded as if it made perfect sense. "Sounds exciting."

"I'd far rather be here with you," he told her.

She blushed in the darkness, lowered her eyes, didn't answer.

They arrived back at the beach house, and he insisted on taking the bag from her as they climbed the stairs. She couldn't know it was less than weightless to a man as powerful as he, and she argued.

"I'm just as capable of carrying a bag of groceries up the stairs as you are, you know," she said, trotting up the steps behind him.

"No, you aren't."

"Am so."

"Would you like me to carry you up, as well, Mary?"

She smacked him on the shoulder from behind. "Show-off."

He loved her when she was in a teasing, playful mood. It meant she wasn't dwelling on her fear. They reached the top, and he turned to face her. "Keys are still in my pocket." He nodded downward. "You want to reach in there and feel for them?"

She smirked at him. "You wish." Then she took one of the bags from him, freeing him to get his keys himself. She was more relaxed than he'd seen her since he'd first started going to the bar to watch over her at night, almost two weeks ago. The moon had been new then.

He opened the door, and she went inside, toed off her shoes and carried the grocery bags to the kitchen. Setting them on the table, she began unpacking. She turned to a cupboard to open it, then frowned and opened a couple more. "You weren't kidding about eating out a lot, were you?"

"I've only been living here a couple of weeks. I really haven't stocked the place yet."

"Been too busy being my guardian angel to worry about eating properly, I'll bet."

She couldn't possibly know how right she was about that. He shrugged, still nervous that the lack of food in the cupboards would cause her to ask questions, but Mary seemed to accept his explanation.

There were dishes in some of the cupboards. They'd been there when he'd moved into the place, and he'd washed them and put them right back—even though to him they were little more than props.

"You know, you're really roughing it here, Michael. No coffeemaker. No toaster. There's not even a microwave."

"Like I said—"

"Oh, don't explain. I've never yet known a member of your species to be overly concerned with nesting."

He went very still in the small kitchen. "My...*species?*"

"Yeah. Male."

He closed his eyes as his relief emerged in the form of a sigh and every tensed muscle relaxed. For a second he'd thought she might have known or guessed what he was.

But why would she guess? She probably didn't even believe creatures such as he existed.

When they finished emptying the grocery bags, she stretched her lovely arms, yawned and said, "It's after midnight. I think I'll get some sleep. I can't believe you're up this late when you have to get up before dawn."

"I rarely sleep much at night."

She shrugged. "Well, you should." She smiled at him. "You don't take very good care of yourself. You need to do better."

"I'll try my best."

Their eyes met and held for a long moment. Finally she sighed and looked away. "Good night, Michael."

"Good night."

Then she headed into her bedroom. Michael sat in the living room, listening to her. Sensing her. He could close his eyes and know where she was, what she was doing, just by opening his mind. He didn't even need to probe hers.

He heard the water in the bathroom, felt her peel away her clothes and step into the shower. He wanted her. It was a hunger, like the hunger for blood. And it was just as natural in his kind. Desire, in a vampire, wasn't a mere fancy or a passing impulse. It was a demanding, insatiable, driving need. He, for whatever reasons—and he didn't doubt their blood bond was one of them—desired her. He would know no peace until he had her.

He sighed and told himself that likely meant he would never know peace. Because he wasn't going to have her. The risk that he would lose himself to the need to taste her blood was too great. He knew that now as he'd never known it before. He was going to protect her until he knew she was safe, and then he was going to go on his way, long before she could learn what he was.

He continued sitting there, tuned in to her essence, if not her thoughts, for a long, long while. The shower stopped running, and she put on something slight. A T-shirt, perhaps. Then she slid into the bed and closed her eyes.

She slept. He felt her sinking into sleep rapidly, and he knew she hadn't been sleeping well since this entire thing had begun. She felt safe here, with him.

For a time he was content to sit there, feeling her sleep. Then he heard her, very clearly, whisper his name. *Michael.* At first he thought she had spoken it deliberately, called to him, and he was on his feet and at the bedroom door before it occurred to him that she was still asleep.

She'd said his name in her sleep.

He closed his hand on the doorknob, turned it, opened the door and stepped into the bedroom. She lay on her side, and he could see her face, serene, relaxed. Yes, she was asleep, hugging the pillow. She nuzzled its softness with her cheek, and again she muttered his name. This time her hips moved just a little as she did, and her arms clutched the pillow tighter to her breast.

She was dreaming. About him.

He shouldn't. He told himself he really shouldn't. She'd asked him not to pry into her mind, and he had honored that request, for the most part.

But he didn't think he knew any man, mortal or otherwise, who could have resisted just a tiny bit of exploration. He moved closer to the bed until he stood right beside it, his thighs touching the mattress. He lowered his hand, planning to lay it atop hers very lightly, to enhance their connection, let him view her thoughts more vividly and with less effort. But before he could make contact, her hand moved, turned and gripped his wrist hard. Her breathing quickened just a little. And still she slept.

He stared down at her face, then closed his eyes and focused on her mind, her thoughts, her touch.

And then he was there, inside her dream. He saw two nude people, writhing on the bed: himself and Mary. She was lying beneath him, her legs wrapped around his waist, linked at the ankles. His hips were snapping as he drove into her, and hers moved in time, receiving him. He felt her need mounting, her desire building, and yet she couldn't reach satisfaction. Not in her sleep. Not in a fantasy.

He burned with wanting her, wanting to assuage her

hunger—but he knew that would mean facing the temptation to assuage his own. And he needed her trust right now. He would lose it if she learned what he was, and if he lost her trust, she would die. Even with Tommy gone, he felt the menace surrounding her like a nimbus. She was still in danger.

He stroked her face and her hair, leaning closer, whispering to her mind with his, coaxing her dream along with erotic images projected into her mind and words spoken softly into her ear, until she shivered and trembled with the release his will had deemed inevitable. And then her arms curled around his neck, and her face turned up to his. He kissed her. He knew he shouldn't, but to deny himself even this brief taste of her was more than he could bear. He kissed her, and her mouth moved beneath his, lips parting, tongue tasting. Her fingers splayed in his hair as she kissed him, and he took full advantage of the opportunity to explore her mouth.

But she was sliding ever closer to lucidity, climbing slowly from the dream state, and he knew it had to end before she opened her eyes.

He eased into her mind with the command that she must sleep. That all this was just a pleasant dream and nothing more. He couldn't quite bring himself to tell her to forget. No, he wanted her to remember, because he would.

He felt her falling away into the depths of slumber, and he lifted his head from hers. Tucking the covers around her once more, brushing a stray coppery curl from her cheek, he forcibly ignored the soft, inviting rush of blood flowing just beneath her skin, the delicate, steady thrum of it pulsing there. Involuntarily he licked his lips.

Then he closed his eyes, and forcibly turned away from her, striding out of the room, and out of the house. He needed blood. It wouldn't take long.

When he crept back into the house a half hour before dawn, sated and warm thanks to the local blood bank's flimsy locks but no less hungry for her, he smelled something that made him slightly queasy. Following the aroma and his sense of Mary in the kitchen, he found her there, scooping yellow omelettes with flecks of green and brown and red onto plates. Two of them.

"Mary?" he asked. "Why are you up so early?"

She looked toward him, smiled brightly. The way she sparkled this morning took his breath away. "I set the alarm and got up early so I could make you a special breakfast before you had to leave for work."

He looked at the plate, then at her. His stomach twisted. "You shouldn't have gone to the trouble—"

"It's the least I could do, after all you've done for me." She shrugged. "You said you eat out most of the time. I thought a home-cooked breakfast would be a welcome change."

"That's...I don't know what to say." He truly didn't. He couldn't actually...eat that thing. Could he? And yet it touched him to his core that she wanted to do this for him. To take care of him—the way he wanted to take care of her.

She smiled again and pulled out his chair. "I'm going to go out walking today and if I should pass a shop that sells them, I'll buy you a coffeemaker. I don't know how you manage to start the day without coffee." She pulled out a chair and sat down. "Well? Dig in."

Licking his lips, he sat in the chair opposite her. The smell of the omelette wafted up to his nostrils, and his stomach rebelled again. He glanced at his wristwatch. "I'm not going to have time to do this luscious meal justice."

"I'm not gonna be offended if you have to eat and run. I know you have to get moving early."

He nodded and watched her eat a few bites. But she kept looking at him, and he knew damned well she was going to be wounded and offended and, worst of all, suspicious if he didn't eat the food. Bracing himself, he picked up the fork, squared his shoulders and shoved a bite into his mouth.

Solid food was a misnomer. It wasn't solid at all, but a mushy mass that only got more soggy as one attempted to grind it to a digestible consistency with one's teeth. He tried his best to turn the sounds of revulsion leaping up from his gut into moans of ecstasy. He almost gagged when he had to swallow, but he managed to force it down, and then he shoveled in another bite, and another.

He devoured fully half of the meal, then pushed his chair away from the table. Bits of the horrible thing still clung to his teeth and tongue, and hid in the crevices of his mouth. "That was the most delicious omelette I've ever had, Mary. Truly. Thank you. I'm so sorry I have to go."

"You're welcome. And don't apologize."

He was already halfway to the front door. His body was not designed to digest solid food. His liquid diet was absorbed into his blood stream directly from the stomach. The rest of the tract—hell, he didn't know, but he'd always assumed it was simply shut down. It certainly hadn't performed any noticeable function since he'd been transformed.

He closed the door behind him, and stumbled to the car, his keys in his hands as his stomach convulsed. His plan was to get into the car, drive out of sight and then—but no, it was too late for that. Dropping the keys on the car's front seat, he slammed the door and ran across the narrow side road and into a decorative copse of piñon pines. And then he fell to his knees as his stomach rejected the meal in terms so violent he thought his body was being torn apart from within.

When it finally stopped, he moved a few steps away, fell to the ground, and lay there, shaking, trembling, chilled through and oddly weak. He remained that way for several moments, until disgust forced him to get to his feet again and move farther. There was a stream a few yards away, runoff from the mountains leading into the sea. He went to it, dipped his hands full of icy cold water and filled his mouth with it, over and over, swishing, rinsing and spitting until he had rid his mouth of every crumb he could manage.

He needed a full bathroom, with a shower and sink and, most of all, a toothbrush. And floss. He shivered, and then he moved on into the scrubby excuse for a woodlot, over the narrow deer path.

The sun was on its way. He could already feel its touch on the air, though it had yet to peek over the ocean. He followed the trail, a shortcut to the cemetery, and emerged into the place from the rear. It was an old cemetery, with several family plots, each one consisting of one large stone and several smaller ones, all surrounded by a wrought-iron fence. They occurred in various sizes and styles, but nearly all the graves here were grouped that way.

A few more recent graves stood alone. Up the hill a bit were the crypts, including his own. His name was engraved at the top, chiseled into the granite, in all caps. He'd purchased it, allegedly for his father, even staged a fake funeral a month ago, in preparation for his move here, knowing he would need a safe backup shelter from the daylight.

The door was sealed and looked like all the others. But there was a hidden catch to release the lock from the outside. He did so, glancing around, opening his senses to be sure he wasn't observed. Then he opened the door and went inside. He closed it behind him and slid home the additional locks he'd installed on the inside of the crypt.

He sighed as he faced the four-by-eight rectangle and the stone slab upon which he was going to spend the day.

Chapter 9

The full moon was tonight.

No matter how else Mary tried to occupy herself through the day, that was one of the three thoughts that kept circulating through her mind.

The second was a question. Why hadn't Michael taken his car this morning? She liked to think he had decided at the last minute to leave it for her—except that she'd found the keys lying on the front seat and the car unlocked. Which just didn't seem in keeping with his past as a police officer.

He'd left in such a hurry—almost as if he were desperate to get out of her sight. She'd run to the window to wave him off, but he'd seemed...almost ill, suddenly. The way he stopped near the car, fumbled with the keys, dropped them, then went staggering off at an uneven run across the street and out of sight.

Had someone picked him up? Did he have a car pool he'd forgotten about or something?

No matter, she could just ask him when he got back home. She was sure there was some explanation.

The third thing on her mind was the dream she'd had last night. God, it had been so real. In the dream he'd made love to her, and it had been intense and incredible and the most erotic thing she'd ever experienced, real or imagined.

She cleaned up the kitchen, then took Michael's car out to do some shopping, a coffeemaker being at the top of her list. But all day long, erotic images and fluttering arousal gnawed at her, fighting for space beside the ice-cold fear in her mind. Shopping didn't help to alleviate either of the conflicting emotions. So when she returned to his place, she put her purchases away and tried to think of something else to occupy her mind.

She tried watching TV, but he didn't get many channels. She thought about planning an extravagant dinner, but she really didn't think he'd enjoyed breakfast all that much. So she sat on the sofa, and she gave in to the more pleasant of the barrage of thoughts. She let herself relive her exquisite dream of the night before. Her and Michael, making love. The things he'd whispered into her ear, the ways he'd made her feel, the places he'd touched her, the feeling of him inside her...

She shivered and closed her eyes. She had never had an experience like the one in her dream. She'd had sex, but never like that. It had been—like something beyond. And she wasn't sure, but she thought she'd climaxed in her sleep. Up until last night, she hadn't thought such a thing was possible.

Oh, hell, so now she was going to sit here and have sexual fantasies about Michael for the rest of the day?

Yeah, she realized, she just might at that. She'd wanted him from her very first glimpse of him, watching her in the bar, from the darkness. His eyes, so intent and appreciative. Almost hungry.

A delicious chill raced up her spine. She shook it away, even as she wondered if he could possibly feel as powerfully attracted to her as she did to him. She thought he did, and yet it didn't seem possible anyone could feel as strongly as she did about him.

But she shouldn't even be thinking along those lines, not now, when so much else was happening. The full moon was tonight.

She got to her feet and decided to explore the house. Surely that would keep her mind off sex with Michael. So she wandered. There wasn't much more to the place than what she had already seen. A laundry room in the back, with a nice jet-black washer and dryer. A garage on the side. She went into it, not expecting to find much of interest—it was a garage, after all. What would there be besides a few tools and car accessories, maybe some spare tires? But when she entered, she was surprised. There was a shiny midnight-blue motorcycle leaning on its kickstand.

And why did knowing he rode that thing make him even more attractive to her? She flashed on an image of the two of them riding it, her thighs framing his hips, her arms tight around his waist, her hair blowing in the wind.

Sighing, she wandered back into the house and went to the room she had been avoiding up to now. Michael's bedroom. Her hand closed on the doorknob, and she was almost surprised that it gave easily. Then again, why would he lock her out of his bedroom?

What surprised her even more than the unlocked door was the total and complete wall of darkness that greeted her on the other side. The place was black as pitch. She felt the wall for a light switch, found one and flipped it on.

But illuminated, the room was almost as grim as it had been in the dark. There was a bed, perfectly made, not a wrinkle or rumple in it. A dresser and matching stand flanked it, but aside from that, the room was empty. It looked as rarely used as the guest room had. And the windows! There were only two in the entire bedroom, and they were covered so tightly that not a droplet of light could penetrate.

She moved closer to inspect the thick, velvet drapes of dark burgundy. Behind them were black curtain panels in a cotton woven more densely than any she'd seen. They were heavy and thick. And behind *those* were blue window shades that must have been custom fitted, pulled down tight.

She pulled the window shade out just a little, to look beyond it. But the outside of the window was blocked, too, by shutters, closed tight.

"I guess he can't sleep with any light in the room," she muttered. Sighing, she carefully smoothed the layers of shade and fabric back into place and turned to go. But she paused when she saw that he had left his brown satchel on the bed.

The one with all the evidence of Tommy's murder in it, and the laptop computer, and...

Licking her lips, she wondered suddenly if he had the evidence from the other murders in that bag, as well. She glanced around almost guiltily, but that was silly. She was doing nothing wrong. Surely she had as much right to peruse those files as Michael did. More, even. Nodding hard, she snatched the satchel from the bed and darted from the room with it.

She chose to work in the little kitchen, because its sunny front window looked right out on the driveway, so she would see him if he came back. She could also see the back doors and the steps to the beach from there. If she was careful, she would see his approach and be able to shove the files back into the case, dash to his room, toss it on the bed and get back out before he opened the door.

As an afterthought, she turned the dead-bolt locks on both doors, just in case. Finally she extracted manila file folders from the bag and began to explore the records inside. Beginning with the one marked Samantha Carlson.

But before long she wished she hadn't snooped. Hell, she was fine reading the reports. The police report said that the woman's body had been found by fisherman in a New Jersey river, just as Michael had told her. But the police had found photographs, as well, taken by the killer and left behind at the woman's apartment. There were several snapshots, the instant kind, and she flipped through them one by one, growing colder and sicker with every shot.

The woman was nude, her body marred by stab wounds that the coroner said had not been the cause of death. She'd been bound at the ankles and suspended by them from a light fixture. Her throat was deeply cut, and a pool of blood covered the floor beneath her.

She'd been stabbed numerous times, then strung up, and finally her throat had been cut. Her arms were free and probably had never been bound. Mary guessed that from the close-up shot of the arms and hands, covered with blood, probably because the woman had tried to keep the precious fluid from escaping as she'd hung upside down and bled to death.

So that was how he killed them. And that was why Michael hadn't wanted her to know.

She finally found the ability to move again and returned to the written report. It claimed the woman had been stabbed numerous times, either in an effort to subdue her or from a desire to torture her. The killer apparently knew where he could drive the blade without causing immediately fatal injuries. The killer had some sick reason for wanting to keep the victims alive until they bled out.

She couldn't read any more. She closed the folder and returned everything to the brown bag. She glanced outside, seeing no sign of Michael, and then carried the bag back to his room, placing it on the bed just where she'd found it. She was tiptoeing out of his room, pulling the door gently closed behind her, when a sound shot through her head like an arrow through her heart.

But it was only the ringing of her cell phone.

Sighing, she ran through the house to her temporary bedroom, rummaged in her bag while the phone rang again and again, and finally found the thing, yanked it out, her heart still pounding, and hit the answer button.

"Mary McLean speaking."

"Hi, Ms. McLean, this is Stormy from S.I.S. We've finished your background check, and I thought you should probably know about it as soon as possible."

"What did you find?"

The woman sighed. "First, you should know that I contacted Officer Dunst and got the background on what's been going on with you. I told him nothing, just asked questions. Normally this isn't the kind of information I would pass on to a client I didn't know, but I think in your case, you need the full story. Can you come out here? I'd really rather tell you in person."

She glanced at the clock. "I don't know. Where are you?"

"Two hours north of you, in Easton. The address is on the card."

Mary shook her head. "No. There's no way I can go that far and get back in time, and I really can't wait. I need to know now."

The woman hesitated but finally began talking again. "All right. But this is gonna be a lot to swallow over the phone, especially if you don't already know about…some of the things I'm going to tell you. Michael Gray was indeed an officer in the Chicago Police Department, and he was indeed shot in the line of duty—by a member of the Capone gang in 1928."

"Excuse me?"

"Officer Michael Gray, Chicago PD, has been dead for more than seventy years."

She shook her head. "There's some kind of mistake. It was probably his father or grandfather, or someone else by the same name."

"He's the only Michael Gray who ever worked there. But given human imperfection, I got my hands on a photo just to make sure. Do you have a fax?"

"No." She recalled the laptop. "Uh, but there's a computer. Can you e-mail it to me?"

"Sure thing. What address?"

She rattled off the address of her online account, knowing she could access it from Michael's computer, but hating the idea that she was going to have to go back into his room and boot the thing up. It was getting late. He would be home soon.

"I'm sending it right now. Call me back if you want us to do anything further. But…Mary, you should prepare yourself to face some things you probably never believed in."

"Like what?"

The woman on the other end sighed. "Have you ever seen Michael during the day?"

"Well…no, but—"

"I didn't think so. Listen, this is going to sound far-fetched. But, Mary, there's a chance Michael Gray might be a vampire."

"Vampire?" She laughed, but the woman on the other end of the phone wasn't laughing, so her own died in her throat. "You *are* joking, right?"

"No. I know quite a few of them. They exist. And they're nothing like what most people think they are. They tend be driven to protect people like you."

"People like me?"

"It's got to do with your blood, Mary. Dunst told me you have the belladonna antigen. That's probably why he referred you to us in the first place."

She went cold inside, remembering how often Michael had mentioned that the antigen connected him to her. But surely this was complete and utter fantasy. Vampires? "Okay, sure. Whatever you say. You just send me that photo. I think I can handle this myself from here."

"Fine. If you change your mind—"

"I won't." She hung up the phone. Vampires.

Good grief, the woman was insane. And yet, even though she knew there were no such things, she thought it a pretty sick coincidence that she'd never seen Michael during the day. And his odd reaction to her meal this morning. As if he'd had to force himself to eat it. And the way he could read her mind. And how quickly and silently he managed to move.

And the things he'd said about the antigen creating a bond between them…

Sighing, Mary forced the ridiculous notion from her mind and walked back through the house, peering outside, seeing no one. But it was dimming. It would be dark soon. He'd said he should be back by dark.

Just another coincidence?

Hell. She would just have to be quick.

She went to his room, took the computer out of its case, booted it up right there on his bed. Seconds ticked by while she waited for it to go through the motions. Then she clicked on the wireless Internet connection button, and the thing logged on immediately. As fast as her fingers could move, she typed in her online server and brought up her private e-mail account. Then she waited, drumming her fingers, staring at the mailbox icon, waiting, waiting…there! The little flag popped up. She quickly accessed the e-mail, clicked on the paperclip icon and watched as, line by line, a photograph revealed itself on the screen. Hair, the top of a forehead, eyebrows, and finally eyes and the bridge of a nose….

"Oh, my God…"

Line by line, his cheeks, his mouth, his chin. All of Michael's face stared at her from beneath a dated policeman's hat. It was a photo ID, with his name and the date underneath. Michael Gray, born 5 February, 1899.

"This can't be…"

"Mary? Hey, Mary, are you here?" he called.

Mary stiffened and lifted her chin. And then his bedroom door opened, and he stood there, staring at her and at the computer. "Mary, what's going on?"

Shaking her head slowly from side to side, she said, "I don't know. But I think it's time you told me. Don't you?"

"I don't under—"

He stopped speaking as she turned the computer to face him, so he could see his own face filling the screen.

He didn't know what to say, what to do. If she could only have controlled her curiosity for one more day. But God, they couldn't deal with all of this—not tonight of all nights. Tonight was the full moon. If she ran from him now…

"I can ex—"

"How?"

He pursed his lips, shook his head. "All right. Look, I really didn't want to get into this so soon. Hell, I didn't want to get into it at all. I don't want to scare you away from me, Mary. I'm not evil. I'm only trying to protect you. You have to believe that."

She got up off the bed, backed up a few steps. He felt as if he were reliving his worst nightmare. "So is that you in the photo?"

He hesitated. "Mary, I'll tell you everything, but first—tell me where you put the gun I gave you."

She frowned. "Michael, what the hell does that have to do—"

"Please. Deep down, you trust me. You know me. Just answer the question."

She licked her lips. He knew she was afraid of him, yes, but she trusted him, too. "It's in the guest room, next to my bed."

"You swear?" He broke his promise, probed her mind, to be sure she was telling the truth.

"Yes. Now *you* answer *my* question. Is that you in the picture?"

"Yes."

"Then you're more than a hundred years old?"

He nodded.

"How can that be, Michael? You don't look a day over thirty."

"I shouldn't look a day over twenty-nine. That's how old I was when I was shot."

"By a member of the Capone gang?"

He closed his eyes. "There were two gangs doing the shooting. I got in between them."

He watched her face carefully. There was no sign of panic. No hint of the hysteria he'd seen in Sally's face that night. So far.

"Michael, I just got off the phone with some detective agency that told me you might be a...a...God, I can't even say it."

"Say it," he told her.

She held his eyes with hers. "She said you might be a vampire. Is that what you are, Michael?"

He chose his words with extreme care. "Mary, I'll tell you exactly what I am. I'm the man you see in front of you, the one who's been with you for days now, protecting you from a killer. I'm the man you know inside and out. Nothing about me is different from what you already know. But there are some things about me that you don't know yet. Things that are unique. They don't make me a freak or a monster or a demon. I'm still me.''

She nodded slowly. ''Go on.''

She wasn't losing it, not yet. ''I don't age. If I go out in the sunlight, I'll burst into flames. And in order to keep from going stark raving mad or dying of slow starvation, I have to feed on blood. Human is best, animal will do. But I don't kill. I never kill. I have never taken a human life. Never.''

She stared at him, then at the door behind him.

''I didn't want to tell you this, Mary. I didn't want to see the fear in your eyes the way I'm seeing it now. I'm not evil. I'm not a monster.''

''No, of course not,'' she said. But in her mind she was thinking she had to get away from him. That she couldn't think straight around him, that this was just too much to understand all at once. Humor him, she thought. Just keep him calm and get the hell out of here. He heard it all.

''I'm trying to protect you. That's all I'm trying to do.''

''And I'm…so grateful.'' She was only a few feet from the door. He was still by the bed. She was going to lunge fast to get past him.

He lowered his head, sighed, and let her see her chance while he wasn't looking at her. She ran for the door, but he moved, too, a burst of speed so fast that she collided with his chest.

''What? How did you…?''

He put his hands on her shoulders, steadying her, and also preventing her from backing away. Her mind was reeling, telling her there was no way he could be there. He hadn't moved.

"Everything is magnified in my kind, Mary. Speed and agility, physical strength and stamina, and all the senses."

She shook her head firmly. "No. I don't believe it. I *won't* believe it."

"What's the alternative, Mary? That I'm insane? Some kind of deluded madman? Have I done anything up to now to make you question my sanity?"

"Please, let me go. Just let me go, Michael."

Sighing, his heart breaking, he closed his eyes. "I can't let you go. It's the full moon. He's out there."

Great, she thought, so now she had to choose between taking her chances with a maniac or facing a killer. Unless...

"Don't. Don't even think it. You know I'm not a murderer."

"How? How could I possibly know that, Michael?" She was shivering now. The fear in her eyes, the hurt and confusion he felt beaming from them, was so real. And so was the caring. She felt so much for him—he could see it clearly in her eyes, in her mind. She didn't know why or how, but she cared about him. Deeply. Even now, after what he had confessed.

"I know," he whispered. "I know, Mary. It's the same for me."

She lowered her head. "Stop invading my mind!"

"Shhhh." His hand cupped her cheek, turned her face up to his, and he kissed her. His mouth covered hers, moving, caressing with his lips.

Heat pooled in his groin when her arms slid around his neck. He wrapped his around her waist, pulling her tight against his body, and his tongue parted her lips and explored her mouth. She tasted so good. His hips moved against her, and hers moved in reply. He burned for her, and though it made no sense to her, she wasn't even bothering to deny that she burned for him as well. She wanted him, and she didn't care what he was. His heart soared with that knowledge.

His hands cupped her buttocks, holding her even closer. Then he slid one hand up her back, beneath the blouse she wore, skimming her back. No bra strap blocked its path—she wasn't wearing one.

He pushed her legs with his own, walking her backward until she hit the bed. He lowered her onto it, breaking the kiss while his hands pushed her blouse up over her head and flung it aside. The laptop slipped off the other side, hitting the floor, and he didn't even look up. His attention was on her breasts. He bent to nurse at one and used his fingers to attend to the other. She lay there, writhing in response to his sucking, the gentle nips and pinches that he made steadily less playful, steadily more forceful. She was moving her head now, from side to side on the mattress. Her body was hot, on fire. He caught her hands in his, then lifted his head away, pressing her hands to her breasts, guiding her fingers to her own nipples, and pressing tighter and tighter until she whimpered. Then he slid lower, his mouth working its way over her waist and belly, his tongue dipping into her navel. He unfastened her jeans and tugged them off. Then he pulled off her panties, as well; his hands parted her thighs, and he kissed her there.

"Michael," she whispered.

"Shhh. Let me make you scream." He pressed her wide open with his thumbs and kissed her again. And then his tongue slid over her, teasingly, easily, before finally driving inside. He ravaged her with his mouth, tongue, teeth, driving her to the edge of ecstasy—and then he rose up over her again, naked, though she had no memory of him undressing, and he lowered himself atop her while his hands guided her knees apart. He slid into her, and a shudder moved through her from head to toe.

She locked her legs around his hips, arms around his shoulders. Her hands ran over his back, and he shivered at her touch. She was beautiful, and wonderful, and she was his. A fierce sense of possession overwhelmed him as he drove her higher. Her nails sank into his flesh as if she would never let him get up. She wanted him, all of him, something more than this physical joining. She told him so with her mind, with her body. It was a primal need, one that was foreign to her. She could no more identify it than prevent the flood of her climax from washing over her. He could identify it, though. He knew what she wanted. It was the same primal, instinctive urge that made her arch beneath him, tip her chin straight up and press his head to her throat. And he answered, parting his mouth over the skin there, and biting down.

The stab of pain was brief, the ecstasy that followed blinding both of them as he tasted her life and her essence, taking it into him, making them one.

When her mind returned from the stratosphere and her body finally stopped shuddering with aftershocks, Mary found herself lying naked in Michael's bed, held in his arms, her head pillowed by his shoulder and chest, while one of his hands rubbed lazy circles over her back. Gradually she realized he was speaking to her, his voice soft and somewhat coarse.

"I'll never hurt you. No one else will, either, I

promise you that. I'll die before I'll let anyone harm you. Know that, Mary. You have to know that."

She blinked slowly out of her state of bliss and took careful stock. She was in bed with Michael. He had just confessed to being a vampire, a theory that both the investigation agency and the local cop had apparently found to be perfectly believable. He could move so fast that her eyes couldn't follow the progress. He could read her mind. And she thought he might have bitten her neck.

Frowning, she lifted a hand to touch her neck. She felt the two tender spots in her skin.

Was it possible, she wondered, that she had just had sex with a vampire? Did she even care? She loved this man.

He was still talking, rubbing her and whispering assurances of his devotion. "I knew the blood, the antigen, connected us, but it's more than that. I swear it's more than that. I've never felt this drawn to anyone. Not ever. Belladonna antigen or not."

She blinked and lifted her head. "Michael, explain to me how this…this antigen connects me to you."

He met her eyes, his own seeming disappointed. And no wonder. She hadn't exactly responded to his pillow talk in kind. And he must be honoring her request that he stop reading her thoughts again, or he would have known what she was thinking. It was odd, but she was getting to the point where she could sense him when he was probing around inside her mind; it was almost visceral. But she didn't feel it then.

"Every vampire was once a mortal with the belladonna antigen," he told her.

She frowned. "So a person without the antigen…?"

"Can never become a vampire. Those with it have the choice. I was given that choice as I lay dying in a hospital bed, riddled with bullets, all those years ago. I chose life."

"And...how does one become a vampire?"

He stroked her hair away from her face. "Another vampire has to transform you. He would first drain the blood, and then—"

"Drain the blood," she repeated, going cold all over.

"It isn't as frightening as it sounds."

Perhaps not, but it was exactly the way the other women, all of whom shared the antigen, had been killed. By being drained of their blood. God, she felt as if she were being torn in half. How could she be so in love with him and yet so afraid of him? His power made him dangerous. But not to her. God, he could never be a danger to her.

"You shouldn't think about that, Mary. It's not something you need to even consider. Not now. You're strong, healthy. You will be for a long time yet."

"I hope you're right about that."

"I intend to make sure of it. It's the first night of the full moon," he told her. "And I plan to hold you close in my arms, safe and protected, until sunrise."

There was nothing she could do—and nothing she wanted to do more than spend the night in his arms. Her questions could wait.

She relaxed in his arms. And it felt so good, so safe and so perfect there, that she couldn't believe there could be any wrong in it. Being with Michael felt like being reunited with some part of herself that had been missing all her life.

They made love again. Then she needed a food break, and he admitted that he couldn't digest solid food, and that her breakfast had made him violently ill. That he'd forced himself to eat it, knowing how he would suffer, touched her deeply. No matter what else he was, Mary believed that his feelings for her were very real.

They spent the entire night talking, laughing, making love.

And then, finally, he rose and pulled on his clothes as he walked to the front door, gazed out the window.

She stood behind him, her hands sliding over his shoulders. Why couldn't he be an ordinary man? Why?

"I have to leave you, my love. It will be dawn very soon."

"Why can't you stay here?"

He lowered his eyes. "I—I can't. I don't want you to see me as I am when I sleep."

She decided not to argue, although she wanted to. "All right."

He turned, wrapped her up in his arms and kissed her deeply. "You don't know what it means to me, Mary, that you didn't run from me when I told you what I was. You can't know. Someday...someday I'll tell you. For now—just know that you have restored the pieces of a heart that was shattered. No one else could have done that, but you did."

Tears. There were tears welling up in his eyes. Swimming there, not spilling over—he had too much will to let them spill, she thought.

He stroked her hair. "Will you still be here when I come back?"

She nodded, looking him straight in the eyes. "I

will. I promise you, Michael, I will. I don't understand any of this, but I want to. And I'm not afraid of you. No matter what you are."

He averted his eyes, blinking rapidly. "Lock the door behind me." He glanced up at the sky. It was paling already. And yet he waited.

She knew he was delaying the moment when he would have to leave, to protect her right until he simply couldn't do it any longer. And finally, just as the first rays of the sun lit the sky, he kissed her once more, then opened the door and left at a brisk jog.

Mary watched as he crossed the road and vanished into the copse of woods just beyond. She tried to bank her curiosity, but she couldn't. She didn't fear him, didn't want to run from him. But she had to know. She had to know all of it.

He was long gone, of course, by the time she entered the woods. She already knew how fast he could move. It was no surprise. The woods were still dark; the early shafts of dawn didn't penetrate them. The warmth did, and as the dew-damp ground warmed, it released its moisture in the form of mists that rose from the ground, and swirled around her feet and ankles. There was a path. Difficult to see beyond the writhing silver mists, but there nonetheless.

Mary followed it. It meandered through the woodlot, then ended abruptly at a wide-open field that was dotted with shapes hiding in the fog. Too short to be trees. Perhaps shrubs of some kind. A sound drew her attention, like a door closing, and she whirled toward it but saw only the shape of what appeared to be a miniature house among the shadowy shapes.

Then she squinted as one shape seemed to come clearer. It had wings. Angel's wings. She moved closer, then went stock-still as the rays of the sun burned through the mist and it thinned, and she saw the stones all around her. Tombstones. Monuments. A stone angel. And the little house? The little house was a crypt.

She was standing in the middle of a cemetery. And unless she was very mistaken, her lover had just entered one of the crypts and closed the door behind him. Swallowing the urge to turn and run, she reminded herself that this was Michael, her Michael. She had to know where he spent his days.

She forced her feet to carry her closer…closer…to the crypt from whence the noise had come.

And then she stood right before it, staring up at the name engraved at the top. M I C H A E L G R A Y.

Chapter 10

Mary called ahead, then drove two hours to get to S.I.S., the investigations agency. She had expected an office in a building in a town. The place at which she arrived was none of those things. It was a huge Victorian manor, recently renovated and stunning.

The supernatural investigations racket must be a lucrative one, Mary thought, as she drove Michael's Jag into the driveway and brought it to a stop.

And then she sat there for a couple of minutes, doing what she'd been doing during the entire drive. Wondering if she had lost her mind.

When a person tells you he is a vampire, you should run away. Any sane person would have spent the day putting as many miles between herself and Michael Gray as humanly possible. But no. She must not be sane, because she was up here on a fact-finding mission instead. And she knew exactly what kinds of facts she was hoping to find: facts that would tell her that it was going to be okay. That there could be some kind of a future with Michael. That he'd told her everything now; there were no more secrets he was keeping from her. She wanted validation. She wanted to know everything about him.

Yes, she'd been thrown for a loop by what he claimed to be, and by seeing him a crypt with his name on it. And yes, she was scared to death by everything that had happened over the past few days. Not of Michael. Never of Michael. Nothing else that had happened was powerful enough to override the feelings that had been steadily growing inside her from the first time he'd walked into The Crypt.

Last night those feelings had filled her to overflowing. They made her fears and her rational mind tiny by comparison. She didn't *want* to run away from him. She wanted to stay. Maybe forever.

As she sat there, mulling all that over, the front door opened and a woman with short blond hair and a diamond stud in her nose stepped out onto the front porch, crossed her arms over her chest and tilted her head to one side.

Mary shut the car off and got out.

"Nice wheels," the woman said. "I'm Stormy. You must be Mary."

Mary nodded and walked up the steps to shake her hand. "Good to finally meet you."

"You look like hell. You okay?"

She ran her hand over her neck, where Michael's teeth had pierced her skin. It still tingled there. "I'm not sure. I think I was bitten by a vampire last night, but I have no idea what that means."

Stormy held her gaze. "Well, you're still alive, so I'm guessing it means you had a damn good night.

Lemme see.'' She pushed Mary's hand aside and peered at her neck. ''Hell, I can't be sure. The punctures heal the minute the sunlight hits them, but sometimes there's a tiny pink spot that gives it away.'' She squinted and leaned closer. ''Yeah, there's still a trace.''

Mary closed her eyes. The woman was as matter-of-fact as if she were talking about the weather. ''Then…?''

Stormy smiled at her. ''You really don't know anything about any of this, do you?''

Mary shook her head.

''Come on. Come inside and sit down. I'll fix you some tea. Max and Lou will be here any minute.'' She took Mary's arm and led her inside.

The foyer was spectacular. It took Mary's breath away, with the crystal chandelier, the antique furniture and the stunning staircase leading up to the second floor.

''We live in the main part of the house. The library serves as our office. Come on, it's right through here.''

She led Mary through a set of double doors and into a library. The room contained two desks. One was neat, shiny, nothing but a computer on top. The other held a computer but was strewn with file folders and papers and coffee rings, and had a miniature of the *Conspiracy Theory* movie poster taped to one side. There was a gas fireplace along one wall, and comfy-looking leather chairs, a settee and rows and rows and more rows of books lining the walls.

''Have a seat. I'll get the tea. And relax. You're not going to grow fangs or anything from one vamp bite. All right?''

She couldn't believe the amount of relief that

rushed through her at those words, that reassurance. God, to think she had actually been worried about something as far-fetched as—hell, everything she'd ever believed to be real and normal and ordinary had been turned inside out in the past few days. She didn't suppose anything was ridiculous at this point.

Stormy left her in the library, closing the doors behind her. Mary started toward a chair, as instructed, but paused, drawn to the bookshelves as she noticed the titles on some of the spines. *The Kybalion, The Tibetan Book of the Dead, The Key of Solomon the King*...

Every book on the shelf had some mystical title, and many appeared to be extremely old. There were illuminated manuscripts from medieval times, for heaven's sake.

"I see you appreciate our collection," a woman's voice said.

Mary turned to see her standing in the open doorway. She was petite, with short copper hair and huge green eyes. She reminded Mary of an imp or a wood sprite. She was standing beside a man who wore dress pants and a white shirt that seemed baggy on him. He was older than she was and had a tired look about him. Stormy walked in behind them and closed the doors.

"Mary McLean, meet Maxine Stuart and Lou Malone. The three of us are Supernatural Investigation Services. Officially, at least."

"Officially?"

Maxine smiled, coming forward, extending a hand. "Yeah. Unofficially we have a couple of silent but extremely helpful partners. Call me Max."

Mary shook her hand. "These books are incredible," she said.

"Thanks. There's a lot of incredible and accurate information in those books, stuff we need in this business. But you have to wade through a lot of superstitious bull and religious dogma to find it."

Mary didn't know whether to laugh or not.

"Have a seat," Lou said, "and let's hear what's been going on." He nodded her toward one of the leather chairs, so she took it. Stormy handed her a cup of steaming tea and sat down on the settee, while Maxine went behind the messy desk with the movie poster on it and sat there, booting up her computer. Lou took the remaining leather chair.

"I hardly know where to begin," Mary said.

"Start at the beginning," the man said. He had a gentle, easy way about him that made her feel both comfortable and safe.

"All right."

So Mary sipped her tea and told them everything from the very beginning. She told them about the phone calls and the break-in, about reporting both to the police. She told them about Michael, how he'd just started showing up at The Crypt, watching her, until he'd finally asked for a ride home so he could warn her that her stalker was a serial killer and that she was next on his hit list. And then she told them about Tommy's murder, the police suspecting her, and her going to Michael's place. And that was where she stopped.

Maxine, who had been clicking computer keys intermittently throughout the tale, and Lou, who had been patient and silent, both looked at her, waiting. She didn't say anything until Stormy prompted her.

"What happened last night, Mary? After I e-mailed you the photo of the cop named Michael Gray who was killed in Chicago seventy-some years ago?"

Mary sighed, licked her lips. She drank the last swallow of tea from the cup. "He walked in while I was looking at the photo. So I showed him, and I asked him to explain."

"And?"

She lowered her head, shaking it slowly. "He told me he was…a vampire." Unable to remain sitting, she got to her feet, paced a few steps, turned and paced back. "I don't know what the hell happened after that. My logical mind told me I should run, and yet I didn't. I didn't want to. I'm not afraid of him. I've got all these feelings for this guy that don't make any sense at all. He says it's partly because of my blood…something about the antigen, but it all sounds like science fiction to me. But he says there's more. And, I don't know…. He kissed me, and the next thing I knew, we were—I just…" She stopped pacing, pushed a hand through her hair. "We spent the night in bed together. And he…"

"He drank from her," Stormy filled in. "Not much, obviously. She's not even pale. Probably just got a little carried away in the height of…well, you know how it is with vamps."

"Hot-blooded little suckers, every last one of them," Maxine said with a wink and a grin at her own bad pun. "So what happened this morning? You guys resolve anything?"

She shook her head. "He reminded me tonight's the full moon. That's when this killer usually hits, and even though Tommy's dead and all evidence points to him, Michael says he can still sense danger around me. He made me promise to be there when he returned. And I did. And then he left.'' She looked at her feet. ''I followed him. He went to a cemetery, into a crypt, I think. It had his name across the top.'' She hugged herself and shivered.

''It's not as creepy as it sounds, Mary,'' Maxine said. ''I mean, some of them have the insides of those things fixed up nicer than a deluxe suite at the Ritz.''

She looked up slowly.

Lou said, ''You have to understand, they need to be careful. There are people who hunt them like animals. And God knows, if their existence ever became common knowledge, there would be no peace for them.''

''All they want,'' Stormy said, ''is to live their lives in peace. They aren't murderous maniacs, the way pop culture depicts them. They're just people. Just like us, with a few notable differences.''

She had gazed at each of them in turn. They were speaking so casually about something that, until very recently, she hadn't even believed in. Her knees went weak, and she bent them, landing in the chair behind her. ''You're telling me this isn't a unique situation here? Vampires are so common that you people know all about them?''

They nodded, all three of them. Maxine turned her computer monitor toward Mary. ''And so is the string of murders Michael's been telling you about. We've been following them ourselves. All the victims had the belladonna antigen. You have it, too, so his concern for your safety is valid.''

Mary nodded, letting all her breath escape her at once. ''I was so hoping you'd tell me just the opposite. I mean, I believe Michael. I've believed him all along. But it would be nice if someone could tell me he was overreacting—that I was never really in danger.''

"Sorry about that.''

Drawing a breath, Mary squared her shoulders. "Can you explain to me a little more about this...antigen in my blood? And the bond Michael says it creates between us?''

Nodding, Max glanced at Lou. He cleared his throat. "First, hon, let me just tell you that in all honesty, five years ago, I thought this was the most far-fetched pile of horse manure anyone had ever tried to dump on me. But I've seen the proof. I know it's true. It's a lot to digest all at once, but it's for real. It's important you not get hung up on that part of it, because you need to get by it in order to make much sense of the rest.''

"I'm trying, believe me.''

He smiled at her, reached across the space between them and patted her hand where it rested on the arm of her chair. "Some people have the belladonna antigen. It's a rare one. And those who have it have a few things in common. For one thing, they tend to bleed a lot when cut. Some to the point of hemophilia, but others not quite so bad as that. It's tough to find blood donors when they do, because so few people have the antigen.''

She nodded. "And what else?''

He lifted his brows.

"You said that was one of the few things we have in common. What are the others?''

He sent a look toward Maxine. She pursed her lips, moved her head almost imperceptibly from side to side. They were keeping something from her; she knew it then. Why so many secrets?

"Well, there's really a lot more than we can cover here today," Lou said. "But the main thing you need to know right now is this. The only people who can become vampires are people with the antigen."

"The Chosen," she whispered.

"Yeah. That's what the vamps call them. They know who has the antigen and who doesn't. They sense it somehow, and they have this instinctual urge to protect them. Some of them fight it, some embrace it, but it's extremely difficult for them to ignore. For a vampire to harm one of The Chosen is a rarity. It's almost impossible for them. I've only heard of one or two cases of it, and those both involved vamps with obvious mental illnesses."

"That means it's highly unlikely Michael could be the killer," Maxine said.

"Unlikely, hell," Lou added. "It's all but impossible."

Mary nodded. "I knew that about him, but it's good to have something more solid than my own feelings to base it on."

Max got up from behind the desk. "There's some lore that suggests each vampire will feel a bond with one of The Chosen more powerfully than with any other. It's supposed to hold true even if that person has been transformed before the two meet. The antigen remains, of course. I don't know if it's true. I think it was with Dante and Morgan, though. I've never seen anything like the power of the bond between the two of them."

"Dante and Morgan?" Mary asked.

"My sister and her husband. Our silent partners in the business. Hadn't you guessed by now? They're vampires."

Chapter 11

Vampires. Maxine Stuart's own twin sister—the award-winning, supposedly deceased screenwriter everyone had been talking about a few years back—was alive and well. Or undead and well.

And according to Max, vampires were very well depicted in her sister's films. They were not Stoker's murderous monsters or Whedon's soulless demons. They weren't even immortal. Not really. They could die by several methods, including incineration, blood loss and starvation. But they did have souls, feelings, and they were fully capable of every so-called human emotion.

Mary got so caught up in learning everything about Michael, what he was and what that meant, that she spent the entire day talking with Maxine, Lou and Stormy. They pulled out DVDs of Morgan DeSilva's vampire films, played them and narrated, answering Mary's questions while making judicious use of the pause function. In between the films, they told her tales of their own encounters with vampires in the five years since they'd first opened their agency. Mary lost track of how many times they told her their lives had been saved by one of the undead. They lamented that she couldn't meet Morgan and Dante to see for herself what they were like, but the couple were vacationing in Ireland, looking up one of Dante's oldest and dearest friends while they were there.

By the time she'd heard all they had to tell her, Mary was convinced that her instincts had been on target. There was no need for her to run away from Michael. There were issues the two of them would need to address. God, there were more challenges to this relationship than she could even begin to think about now. But he was exactly what he'd told her he was, exactly what she had known in her heart he was all along. He was the man she loved.

They were all in the comfortable living room, in the private section of the house now. The last video had ended, and the stories had wound down. Maxine had left the room briefly, and she returned now with a file folder in her hands, which she offered to Mary. "I think you should look at these records," she said. "This is just what's official. I have no way of knowing what he's done since he crossed over, but once I saw this stuff, I had no doubt about Michael Gray's character. I don't think you will, either. Not that you seem to anyway. But you said you wanted to know everything. Did you even know how he came to be shot?"

Shaking her head slowly, Mary opened the folder, skimming its contents. It held commendations, testimonials and a 1928 newspaper report headlined, Death of a Hero.

"There was a shootout between Capone's gang and a rival gang," Lou Malone said. And when she detected the catch in his voice, she remembered that he'd told her he had been a cop for twenty years before retiring and joining Maxine in this business.

Maxine sat down beside him, put a hand on his shoulder. It was a loving touch. He patted it with his own; a friendly gesture.

"A seven-year-old kid, confused and scared by all the noise, ran into the cross fire. Michael Gray ran out of a perfectly good cover position, into the storm of bullets, threw himself on the kid and acted as a human shield. The kid got nicked, nothing serious. Gray took nine bullets."

He went silent then, his lips pressed tight.

"A man like that doesn't turn bad," Stormy said. "He changed, physically, from a dying mortal to a powerful vampire. But inside, he's still the same guy. The hero cop who died saving a little boy."

Maxine nodded. "The official reports say that his wife, Sally, shot herself with Michael's service revolver the night after his death. I've been doing some digging, and rumor has it that he went to her after he was changed over. Told her what he was. She freaked out and blew herself away, right in front of him."

"Oh, God." Mary had tears streaming from her eyes now. She reached out to clasp Stormy's hands. "Thank you. Thank you all. I can't tell you how much you've helped me."

"Glad to hear it," Stormy said. She glanced at her watch, then shook her head. "We've been talking for-

ever. Why don't you join us for dinner and then
we'll—''

"What time is it?'' Mary asked. For the first time
she realized how long she must have been here, in the
company of these people. Three movies, hours of conversation—and the sky beyond the windows was already growing dim. "Oh, no.''

"What's wrong?''

"I…I promised Michael I would be there when he
came home tonight. If I'm not—he's going to
think—''

"Look, we'll call him,'' Maxine began.

"I have to go. I have to be there.'' She surged to
her feet and ran for the door over the protests of the
others. She couldn't bear the thought of Michael returning home and not finding her there. He would assume that, like his wife so long ago, she couldn't deal
with what he was. And it was the furthest thing from
the truth.

Maxine looked at Lou as the Jag squealed out of
the driveway and out of sight. "She said the killer
was dead. And Dunst agrees with that, right?''

"She also said Michael Gray sensed she was still
in danger,'' Lou said, and he pursed his lips, looking
up at the sky. "Moon's gonna be full tonight.''

"You're right. We'd better follow her. But it's
gonna be damned tough to keep up with her, given
what she's driving and the way she's driving it.''

"Then we'd better hurry.''

"I'll try to reach Michael Gray,'' Stormy said, as
Lou and Max ran to the car. "I'll let him know what's
going on, where she is, just in case.''

* * *

Michael emerged from the crypt at sundown and crept through the cemetery as the darkness gathered, until he reached the woods at the rear. Once on the path, out of sight, hidden by the trees and the night itself, he pushed for speed. But instead of feeling closer to Mary with every step, he felt only an eerie, ever-growing sense of emptiness. He knew before he even saw the vacant spot in the driveway that she wasn't there.

Mary was gone. She'd taken his car, and she'd left him.

He wasn't even surprised. Gut-wrenchingly disappointed, but not surprised. He ran around to the rear of the house, down the slope to the beach, searching the shoreline as if he expected to find her out there. But he didn't find her, and he had known he wouldn't.

He hadn't sensed any doubts from her as she'd made love with him all through the night. He hadn't tasted her fear in her blood. She hadn't fallen apart, hadn't been driven insane to the point of taking her own life, the way his wife had when faced with the knowledge of what he had become. Foolishly he had let himself believe that wouldn't change when she had time to mull it over by the cold light of day. Obviously it had.

He stood there on the shore as the waves washed up over his feet and the self-pity washed up over his soul. But not for very long. As the upper curve of the huge, silver moon crested the horizon and its light trickled toward shore on the rippled mirror of the ocean, he stopped feeling sorry for himself immediately. The beam of moonlight pierced the veil of his pain with the shattering reminder that tonight might very well be the last night of Mary's life.

He didn't panic. He'd been a cop for too long to panic. Instead, he ran for the house while his mind sought order within chaos. Where the hell could she be? How the hell could he find her in time? He tried sensing her, but she was either too far away or entirely closed off from him due to fear or revulsion or both.

A phone was ringing when he entered the beach house. And it wasn't his. It took him three full rings to realize it was her cell. Dammit, she'd been so eager to get away from him that she'd left her phone behind. As well as all her other belongings, he noted as he surged into the guest room and snatched up the phone.

"Mary?"

"No, I'm sorry," a man's voice said. "Is this Michael Gray?"

"Yes, who is this?"

"This is Officer Dunst. I've been working Mary McLean's case and the Tommy Campbell murder. I just got off the phone with an investigator who's been working with Mary. And I told her I'd contact you right after I phoned Mary. Is she there?"

Michael's head was spinning. "No. She left the cell phone behind. I don't know where she is."

"I might. Mr. Gray, Mary spent most of the day in Easton with those investigators, and now, if all is as it should be, she's on her way back..."

So many questions shot through his mind. He managed to ask them one at a time. What investigators? Where were they located? What time had Mary left? Was she alone? He made rapid notes, cutting the officer off every time he tried to interject anything extraneous. He had no time for narrative.

Once he knew Mary had left half an hour ago from

a place two hours north on Route 1, he started to hang up the phone.

"Wait, Mr. Gray. There's more. The reason I was calling in the first place."

"Make it fast. I have to get to Mary."

"The body we found in Tommy Campbell's apartment—it wasn't him. He apparently killed a vagrant, then burned the body to make us think it was him. We also learned that Tommy had a twin sister who died in a car accident at the age of ten. She bled to death. They couldn't find a donor in time to save her. She had the antigen, Gray."

"Tommy's still alive," Michael said softly. "And he's after Mary."

"I'm gonna take Route 9. You take Route 1. She could have gone either way."

Michael disconnected, walked rapidly from the house into the garage, hit the button to open the overhead door and swung one leg over the seat of his bike. Seconds later he was speeding through the night toward Mary.

And the moon kept on rising.

Mary drove the Jag for all it was worth, not an easy task on a highway that meandered through scenic areas and small towns and had posted speed limits all along the way. She never touched the brake pedal...not until she passed another car that was off the road, sitting at a cockeyed angle with one door open. A person was lying in the road, and she just barely managed to swerve and miss him. Then she skidded to a stop on the roadside, slammed the Jag into Reverse and backed up to the accident.

She was reaching for her cell phone to dial 911

before she remembered that she'd left it at Michael's place. Hell. She got out and ran back to the victim. A young man, lying very still, facedown.

Kneeling beside him, Mary touched his shoulders gently. "Hey, hey, are you all right?" No response, but he felt warm. She pressed her fingers to his neck and felt a pulse beating there, strong and steady. "Come on, wake up now. You have to wake up." She knew better than to move him, but damn, he was lying in the road. Another car could come along and…

He moaned and rolled very slowly onto his back.

"Wait, maybe you shouldn't move just yet. Hold on now." Then she saw his face and felt the blood drain from hers. *"Tommy?"*

He smiled very slowly and punched her in the belly. Pain lanced her, and she jerked backward, her hands going instinctively to her middle. Warm wetness coated them, and she looked down to see that he had a knife clutched in his fist. He hadn't punched her. He'd stabbed her.

"T-Tommy? Why? God, why?" She tried to get to her feet, stumbled, but managed to get upright. She managed two staggering steps toward Michael's Jag, and then he had her by the hair, pulling her backward as the blade plunged into her back.

A cry was driven from her lungs.

"You should have checked in with the police today, Mary. They finished the autopsy—found out that the body they found in my bed wasn't even mine."

Pain racked her, and she fell to her knees again.

"They had to wait for the autopsy or they would have told you that sooner. But it doesn't matter. I'll be in a new town, using a new name, by this time tomorrow."

He came around to stand in front of her, his knife, dripping with blood, still in his hand. She forced her eyes upward, away from the blade, to his face. Beyond his head, she saw the full moon rising ever higher in the sky. "Why, Tommy? Just tell me why?"

"You mean your precious vampire lover hasn't told you by now? About the vampire hunters? People who dedicate their lives to eradicating his kind from the planet? No?"

"But…but I'm not…not a vampire."

He smiled. "And you never will be. See, that's the beauty of doing it my way. I take your kind out before you can ever become like them. It's way more efficient."

"It's murder."

"To hell it is. You aren't going to live much longer anyway. Most of you never live to see thirty." She frowned, shaking her head in confusion. "What, he didn't tell you that, either? It's a handy little side effect of having the kind of blood you have, Mary. You get weak, you get sick and, unless they transform you, you die."

She closed her eyes. He crammed the knife into her shoulder, and her eyes flew open wide again with her scream.

"I'll admit, you probably had a few more years in you. But what the hell, now or later, it doesn't make any difference. All that matters is that I prevent any more of *them* from being made. You oughtta thank me, Mary. I'm about to save your soul."

She was fading fast. Her eyes fell closed again, and she thought of Michael, wished to God she had let him tell her his story instead of rushing off to find out for herself. She loved him, and yet she'd given in to her need to know all. Why hadn't she trusted her heart?

She knew what was coming next. She had read the autopsy reports on this man's other victims. He would stab her repeatedly, and then he would hang her by her feet and slit her throat while she was still alive, so that every ounce of blood would drain from her body.

"Why do you hate them so?" she managed.

"Why? Because they could have saved my sister," he told her. "But they didn't. Not one of them came around to help her when she needed it. If she couldn't live, then I'm gonna make damn sure none of you do."

He stabbed her again, in the side this time. She barely felt the pain, though. She was already losing consciousness, and she whispered a prayer of thanks for that.

Chapter 12

Maxine pointed when she saw the two vehicles on the roadside. "There! Over there!"

Lou swung the car off the road behind the other cars, and was out and running forward, his gun in his hand, almost before Max got the words out. She was right behind him, and she saw what their headlights illuminated. A young man, spattered in blood, leaning over a woman who was soaked in it, tying a rope around her ankles. As she ran, she saw that the other end of the rope was looped over the low-hanging branch of a nearby tree.

"Freeze, buddy, or you're history!" Lou, when he was in cop mode, had a voice that carried as if helped along by a bullhorn. "Back away from the lady."

The man, the killer, straightened. He had a knife in his hand as he took two steps backward; then he dropped it, turned and raced into the woods.

"Take care of Mary," Lou barked, and he raced off after him.

"God, I hate when he does that." Max knelt beside Mary McLean. "Ah, hell, look at this," she muttered, as she tore at the woman's blouse, trying to decide which hole to plug first. She'd already lost a great deal of blood. Max knew too well that there would probably be no donor close enough to help her. She ran to the car for the emergency first-aid kit she and Lou kept there. God knew they'd had to stop profuse bleeding enough times to know what to do. Pressure bandages, plenty of gauze. She punched 911 into her cell phone, then cradled it between her shoulder and ear, so she could use her hands to keep working on Mary as she spoke. Stormy had phoned to tell her that Dunst and Michael Gray were on the way, taking alternate routes. So Max told the 911 operator to let Officer Dunst know by radio what had happened and where. Then she hung up, despite the operator's insistent "stay on the line," and tossed the phone aside.

Even as she worked, plugging one knife wound after another, Max was painfully aware that while she might stop the bleeding, she could do nothing about any internal injuries, much less replace the blood the woman had already lost. She kept looking up, searching the dark woods for some sign of Lou and the killer. She didn't want her stubborn partner to be the bastard's next victim.

Then the sound of a motor drew her head up. A single headlight accompanied the sound, and by the time the motorcycle was close enough for her to make it out clearly, it was already skidding to a stop, crashing to its side as the rider leaped off and ran forward.

"I hope to God you're Michael Gray," Maxine said as he ran forward.

He proved he was by falling to his knees and shouting, "My God, no! Mary!"

Max gripped his shoulders hard, gave him a firm shake. "She's lost a lot of blood, Michael. He didn't cut her throat, but there are a lot of stab wounds, and we're miles from a hospital. I've called an ambulance, but they're half an hour out. I've done everything I can."

He stared into Max's eyes for a dozen heartbeats, and she thought he read her meaning perfectly well. Then he pulled free of her hands and gathered Mary to his chest, bending over her, stroking her hair.

"My partner's gone after Tommy. I've gotta go back him up," Max said. "This...this is up to you now. Do what you think is right."

Michael held Mary close to him, and he could feel the life ebbing slowly from her body. God, he didn't want to lose her.

"Michael..."

Her whisper came warm against his neck. He eased her back a little, enough so he could see her face. God forbid she be even more frightened at a time like this. But she might be afraid—of him. She'd fled from him, after all.

"It's all right. I won't hurt you, Mary. I could never hurt you."

"I know that." Weakly she lifted her hand to his cheek. "It doesn't hurt anymore," she whispered. "I think I'm dying, Michael."

"Hold on. We've called an ambulance. Help is on the way." God, once again his revelation of what he was had driven a woman he loved to her death. He couldn't bear it.

Mary's eyelids fell closed, but she popped them open again. "I have to tell you...to explain..."

"It's all right. Save your strength. You don't have to explain to me. I understand why you ran away."

She moved her head left, then right, and it seemed to take extreme effort. "No. I wasn't...running away. I just...I had to know."

He frowned, not understanding.

"I had to understand...what you are. What it means." She paused, seemed to force herself to breathe.

"So you went to...those investigators?" It hurt that she hadn't brought her questions to him. "You could have asked me, Mary. I'd have told you anything. Anything you wanted to know."

"And I'd have believed anything you told me." She was battling to keep her eyes open, clinging to consciousness with sheer will. "I had to talk to someone...someone I didn't love."

He closed his eyes in sheer anguish at her words. She loved him. My God, she loved him.

"I lost track of time. But I was coming back to you, Michael. I was coming back...."

Tears filled his eyes, blurring his vision, as he leaned closer, pressing his lips to hers. When he lifted his head away, he whispered, "I want to tell you that I love you, Mary. But those words don't begin to describe what I feel for you. It's beyond love—at least beyond what I thought love could be. It's a force more powerful than heaven and earth combined."

"I know," she said. Her voice was weaker now. So weak he had to bend closer to hear her words. "I feel it, too." She stopped there, breathing hard, as if even the mere whispered words were taking every bit of strength in her. "The ambulance...won't get here in time, will it, Michael?"

He could barely speak past the lump in his throat. "No." And then he forced himself to go on. "But I'm here. And, God help me, I don't want to let you go, Mary."

She stared into his eyes, her own fierce and determined, and with what had to be the last of her strength, she raised her head and forced out two final words in the strongest voice she could manage. "Then *don't*." Then her head fell back again, and her eyes closed.

Did she mean...? Oh, God, he couldn't be sure. Had the investigators explained this part to her? How could he commit this act without knowing for sure?

He was out of time. Mary was dying. Her heartbeat, which he could feel as if it were his own, began to skip and stutter. Her breathing stopped entirely.

He wasn't even certain he could save her at this point.

But he had to try.

The murderer's blade lay on the pavement near Mary's feet. Michael reached for it, took it, and made his decision. Using the tip, he pierced his own throat. And then he gathered Mary closer and pressed her lips to the tiny font. Closing his eyes, he willed her to swallow.

And finally, after what seemed an endless moment, she did.

Her body went rigid in his arms, and her teeth clamped down on his skin in reaction to the jolt of power she'd tasted. And then she relaxed, and she drank.

Suddenly she pulled her head away, her eyes open wide. "Oh, God, oh God, it *hurts!* Michael, it *hurts!*"

He held her against him. "I know. I'm sorry, my love, I'm sorry. We feel everything so much more than mortals do. Including pain."

She cried out, her head arching backward, the veins in her neck standing out. "H-how long?"

"Until dawn. Only until dawn. Then you'll sleep, and you'll heal."

The woman, Maxine, and the man he assumed was her partner emerged from the forest while Mary writhed and whimpered in agony. The man held Tommy in a firm grip. Maxine hurried forward, knelt beside Michael, her gaze going from him to Mary, who was grating her teeth against the pain.

"Michael, we can help you. Both of you. Get the medical kit and bring it here."

Michael looked where she pointed, spotted the large white box on the pavement on the other side of Mary and fetched it as quickly as he could. "I don't know what you can do for her," he said as he set the box beside Maxine. "I...she's..."

"She's one of you now. I can see that, Michael." She thrust a square bandage into his hand. "Put that on the cut in your neck. It's still bleeding."

He took it, did as she suggested and watched Maxine work. She pulled a cellophane-wrapped hypodermic needle from the box, tore off the wrapper and then pulled out a vial and inserted the needle into its end.

"What is that? What are you doing?"

She was intent on her work, tipping the bottle upside down, drawing the fluid into it. "You ever hear of DPI, Michael?"

He nodded. "They used to hunt us," he said.

"They also used you as guinea pigs. I got hold of some of their files several years ago. Their research has turned out to be damn useful. This stuff, for example." She pulled the needle from the vial, snapped her finger against the side a few times. "It's a tranquilizer they developed to keep their prisoners sedated—the only one in existence that works on vampires. I'm going to give her a small dose. She'll rest easy until sunrise comes."

Michael looked from the woman to the man. Could he trust them?

Mary cried out, and he knew her pain was beyond endurance. "All right," he said. "Do it."

Maxine nodded and leaned over Mary, injecting her quickly and expertly. Immediately Mary's face eased. She relaxed her body, breathed a heavy sigh. "Oh, thank you. Thank you," she whispered.

Maxine smiled as she stuck a Band-Aid over the injection site. "You're going to sleep in a few minutes. The next time you wake, you'll be fine. I promise. Okay?"

"Yes."

Max turned to Michael. "Get her somewhere safe. Watch those wounds until morning. If they start bleeding again, we could still lose her."

"I won't leave her for a minute."

"We'll take the bike back to our place," she went on. "You can pick it up tomorrow night. Mary knows where we are."

He nodded, more grateful than he could imagine.

Then he glanced at the prisoner. "What about Tommy?"

"Tommy's going to prison," Lou said. "Or maybe a mental hospital. Either way he'll never see daylight again. Mary's a missing person now, and the police are on their way as we speak. Even without a body, there's enough of Mary's blood here to convince them that she couldn't be alive. A lot of it is on Tommy-boy. It's not our fault if he refuses to tell us what he did with the body. He was stalking her, faked his own death. I've got no doubt further investigation will link him to the other murders, as well."

"You can't do this," Tommy muttered. "They can't live."

"Yes, they can, pal," Maxine said. "Happily ever after, if you ask me," She packed up her med kit and loaded it into the car as Lou put Tommy into the back seat. Then she went back to the motorcycle, stood it upright and climbed aboard. Lou pulled away with the car and prisoner, and Max followed on the bike, riding it as if she knew how.

As gently as he could, Michael scooped Mary up into his arms and carried her toward the Jag.

"I'll get your seats all bloody," she whispered. Her speech was slurred, and she was fading fast—not into death, like before, but only into sleep. Painless, restful sleep.

"I don't care about the seats, Mary." He opened the door and eased her down on the passenger side, then worked the control to lower the back of the seat, so she was reclining. "How's that?" he asked.

"Mmm." She sighed. "I feel so strange, Michael. Everything seems…different."

"Everything *is* different." He ran a hand through

her hair. "*You're* different now. Do you understand that, Mary?"

She nodded gently. "It's what I wanted."

"I wasn't sure."

Smiling very crookedly up at him she said, "I know. But I love you, Michael. And I'm not like she was…. I don't want to die rather than accept something new and different. I want to live. I want to love you for as long as the universe will let me. Forever, if that's possible."

"How did I ever find you?" he whispered, awe making him shake his head slowly. "How did I ever get so lucky as to find you?"

"I don't think luck had anything to do with it."

He kissed her, long, lingeringly. "Sleep, my love. When you wake, I'm going to show you a whole new world."

She smiled gently and let her eyes fall closed.

* * * * *

Turn the page for a classic tale from
WINGS IN THE NIGHT,

"Twilight Vows."

And when you've finished,
keep reading for a sneak preview of

"The Invisible Virgin"

coming in May 2003 as part of
Silhouette Books' thrilling anthology
BROKEN SILENCE.

TWILIGHT VOWS

Chapter 1

Irish countryside, 1808

I walked along the path that night, as I often did. Bone-tired from working in my father's fields, coated in a layer of good Irish soil spread fine on my skin and held fast by my sweat. My muscles ached, but 'twas a good sort of pain. The sort that came of relishing one's own strength and vigor. Of late, I hadn't done so any too often. I'd been taken with bouts of weakness, my head spinning sometimes until I passed out cold as a corpse. But today hadn't been like that at all. Today I'd felt good, certain whatever had plagued me was gone. And to prove it I'd worked like a horse in Da's fields. All the day through I'd put my brothers and cousins through their paces, darin' them to keep up with me, laughing when they couldn't. And I'd kept on wielding my hoe long after the others had called it a night.

So 'twas alone I was walking.

Autumn hung in the air, with the harvest beneath it and a big yellow moon hanging low in the sky. Leaves crackled under my feet and sent their aromas up to meet me as I walked by the squash patch, with its gray-blue hubbards as big as Ma's stew pot, and orange-yellow pumpkins clinging to their dying vines. We'd have to gather them in tomorrow. Gram said there would be a killing frost before next Sabbath.

A killing frost.

A little chill snaked up the back of my neck as the words repeated themselves, for some reason, in my mind. Foolishness, of course. I'd spent too many nights as a lad, curled on a braided rug before the hearth listenin' to Gram spin her yarns. This time of the year, her tales tended toward the frightening, with ghosties and ghoulies her favorite subjects. I supposed some of those tales had stuck in my mind. Though a man grown now, and all of twenty years plus three, I still got the shivers from Gram's tales. The way her voice would change as she told 'em, the way her ice-blue eyes would narrow as if she were sharing some dark secret while the firelight cast dancing shadows on her dear careworn face.

'Twas a night just like this one, boy. When all seemed peaceful and right. But any fool ought to know better than to walk alone after dark during the time of the harvest. For the veil between the world of the living and that of the dead is thinning…and parting…and…

"Hush, Gram," I whispered. But a chill breeze caressed my neck and goose bumps rose there to mark its passing. I thrust my hands into my pockets, hunching my shoulders, walking a little faster. Something skittered along the roadside, and my head jerked sharply to the right. "Only the wind," I said, and then I began to whistle.

Any fool ought to know better. Are you a fool, Donovan O'Roark?

I shook myself and walked still faster. There were eyes on me...someone watching from the crisp, black night. Or perhaps some*thing*. A wolf or even an owl. I told myself 'twas nothing, that I'd no reason to fear, but my breath began to hitch in my throat before puffing out in great clouds, and my heart to pound too quickly.

Then the dizziness came.

The ground buckled and heaved before me, though I know it never truly moved at all. I staggered sideways, would have fallen into the weeds along the edge of the path, had I not managed to brace my hand against a nearby tree. Palm flat to the warm, soft trunk, head hanging low, I fought to catch my breath, to cling to my consciousness.

The tree spoke.

"Alas, boy, I thought to wait...but I can see the deed must be done tonight."

I jerked my head up, then snatched my hand away, not from a tree, but from a man. Yet...not a man. His dark eyes swirled with the endless black of the very night, and his hair was black as soot, gleaming to midnight blue where the moon's rays alighted. His lips, cherry red, and full. Yet the pallor of his skin shocked me. Not sickly-looking, not like death. But fair, and fine, as if he were some fine work of art chiseled of pale granite. As if he were a part of the moonlight itself.

I took a step backward, leaves crunching, the breeze

picking up to tease my hair. The wind grew stronger all of a sudden...almost as if it knew something dire was about to take place this autumn night...

...the veil between the world of the living and the world of the dead is thinning...parting...

I backed away more quickly.

The creature only shook his head.

"Don't try to run. It will do you no good."

"Who are you?" I managed. "What do you want with me?"

His smile was sad, bitter. "Many things, Donovan. Many things. But for now...just the one." He reached out, though I never saw his hands move. They were simply there before him one moment, moving expressively as he spoke—and in the next instant they clasped the front of my homespun shirt. I struggled against him, but he pulled me easily to him, and my fighting amounted to nothing at all.

I am not a small man, nor a weak one, despite my recent illness. I stood fully a head taller than my da, and half that much above any other man in our village. My shoulders were broad and well formed by a lifetime of hard work. I'd never met a man I wasn't certain I could whip, should the need arise.

Yet this one, this *thing,* dragged me to him as if I were a child. Closer, inexorably closer, even as I twisted and tugged and fought for my freedom. He bent over me. Fear clutched at my heart, nearly stopping its frantic beat. Pain shot out through my chest, and down my left arm, and I couldn't draw air into my lungs.

Then I felt his mouth on my neck...lips parting, and the shocking pain as his teeth sank deeply into the skin of my throat, piercing me. Pain that faded almost as quickly as it appeared. And as it faded, so did everything else. Everything around me, from the soft singing of the crickets to the smell of the decaying leaves. I no longer felt the chill autumn air. There were three things of which I remained aware, three things that filled all my senses. Darkness. Silence. And the feel of his mouth on my throat, draining the very life from me.

Then even those things disappeared.

"Donovan! Donny-boy, wake up! Wake up!"

Someone shook my shoulders. Da's voice shouted in my ears, sounding like it never had. Raspy, panicky, afraid. There was a taste in my mouth, salty and rich. I wiped my lips with the back of my hand, as I fought to open my eyes. When I looked at my hand, I saw blood, glittering in the moonlight.

What had I done? What...?

Da scooped me up into old arms that shouldn't have had the strength to lift me. And staggering under my weight, he carried me toward the village, shouting for help. It was only moments before others came, my neighbors, my friends. Alicia with her flowing auburn curls and cat's eyes as green as Ireland itself, the girl I dreamed about at night. My ma, and sisters. My body was jostled as neighbor men relieved Da of the burden, and bore me swiftly into my home. They lowered me to a pallet, while Ma shouted questions. But no one could answer her. No one knew what had befallen me out there on the path this night. Only me, and one other soul. A monster, a creature of nightmares and Gram's tales.

Gram. Gram would know what had happened, what this meant. I listened for her voice among the others, but it was a long while before I heard it. And its grimness did nothing to reassure me.

"It can only be evil," she all but whispered. "'Tis the Eve of All Hallows. Foolish lad, out walking alone tonight of all nights!"

Ma hushed her impatiently, but I saw the way she stiffened at Gram's words. She snatched up a lamp, elbowing the men aside and leaning over me as if to see for herself. Then Ma gasped and drew slightly away, her loving eyes going wider.

"Lord a' mercy, there be blood on his lips."

"Aye," Da said. "But what does it mean?"

My mother said nothing. Gently, her hands pushed my shirt aside as she searched for injuries. I forced my eyes to remain open, though sleep…

Or is that death?

…called to me, drew me closer just as the stranger had done. I couldn't fight much longer.

Ma looked down at me, fear growing large in her eyes, though I could see her trying to keep it concealed from me. "You'll be all right, my boy. I'll see to that. You'll be—"

As she spoke, she pushed my hair aside. 'Twas long, my hair. Hung well past my shoulders, thick and darkest brown. My Ma lifted the heavy locks, and her eyes changed.

As if the light of love flickered…a guttering candle.

She snatched up a cloth, muttering a prayer in the old language as she dabbed the blood away from my throat with one hand and lifted her lamp higher with the other.

And then my mother screamed. "Devil! Demon spawn! Get the children out of this house, 'tis the mark of Satan!"

I felt my eyes widen as her face turned hateful. I lifted a hand toward her as she backed away. "Ma, what's wrong with you? 'Tis me, your son, Donovan—"

But she shook her head, her eyes fixed to the place on my throat where that creature had feasted, and she continued to back away. "Die, Lucifer," she whispered to me. Her son, her firstborn. And I couldn't believe she said it, couldn't believe the hatred in her eyes. "You're not my son, nor worthy to be there in his poor body. Die, or I vow I'll kill you myself."

I'd been fighting to hold on. But her words...the shock they sent through my body...'twas all it took to shake my tenuous grip on life. And I sank into darkness. Into death.

This time, the darkness lasted longer, though I was never aware of the passing of time. I only knew I felt clean when I began to surface toward life once more. My body, my clothing...were fresh. I smelled of heather and honeysuckle. The clothes I wore were not the scratchy, rough weave I wore every day, either. Ma had dressed me in a fine suit of clothes she'd made for me herself, and only allowed me to wear on the most important occasions.

I heard voices, smelled the familiar scent of tallow candles and lamps. And flowers. So many flowers. Someone played a fiddle, drawing the bow 'cross the strings in a slow and mournful wail. I heard the clink of glasses, and smelled good beer, and food.

Slowly, I managed to get my eyes open.

I never should have done that. For I found that I lay in a coffin. Homemade, likely by my da's own hand. The coffin had been set upon a table at O'Connor's tavern. Women walked past, heads low, tears damp on their cheeks. Men stood still, drinking beer from tin tankards. Sean Ryan stood in a corner with his fiddle tucked under his chin, eyes closed. Alicia, the girl I'd often kissed when her da wasn't looking, sat by herself in a chair, staring straight ahead, but seeing nothing.

Father Murphy stood up front, right beside the coffin, his back to me, his prayer book opened, and by clearing his throat he got everyone to look his way.

"Donovan O'Roark was a good man, but evil struck him down in the prime of his youth…"

Lord a' mercy, they were givin' me a funeral!

"No, Father," I cried as loud as I could manage. "I'm alive…Da, Ma, I'm…" I struggled to sit up.

Someone screamed, and then the room went dead silent. Father Murphy faced me, white as a specter, wide-eyed as he crossed himself. Alicia leapt to her feet and shouted, "Kill it! Kill it before it destroys us all!"

"No!" I cried. "I'm not evil! 'Tis me, Donovan O'Roark…won't someone listen…?"

"Get the women and children out," Father Murphy shouted, and for the first time I thought he sounded like some mighty prophet of old. His voice fairly shook the walls. Or perhaps 'twas my hearing that was altered, for indeed it seemed every voice was sharper, clearer to me. And the fiddle…

No time to dwell on that now, for my best friend Sean and some of the other young men began urging the women out of the tavern.

My ma stayed behind, glancing at me, then at my da. "You know what must be done."

Da nodded, and Ma fairly ran from the room then.

I braced my hands on the sides of the coffin, making

as if to get myself out, thinking how they'd all laugh once they realized how foolish they were being, and—

Da shoved me back. Hard. Cruel. Never had he handled me so roughly. I blinked in shock. Then froze— literally felt the ice creeping through my veins—as I saw Father Murphy take a wooden stake from somewhere nearby, muttering, "Your wife was right, O'Roark. 'Tis good we were prepared for this." He pressed the tip of the stake to my chest, and my da, *my own beloved da,* handed him the mallet.

From outside I could hear my mother sobbing softly and the girl I planned to marry one day shouting "Kill it! Kill it *now!*"

Father Murphy lifted the mallet.

I don't know where the strength came from—or, I didn't know then. I suppose I blamed it on panic or fear, rather than anything preternatural. But when I shoved against the hands that held me—my father's hands—I felt little resistance. I surged from that coffin with the force of a tidal wave, and landed on my feet beyond the two of them. My trusted confessor and my flesh-and-blood sire. My would-be executioners.

"Da, how can you do this? What have I done to deserve—"

"He's not your son," Father Murphy said. "He's evil, the same evil that took your son away. Do not heed him."

"But I *am* your son! Da, look at me!"

Da turned away. "Get thee behind me, Satan."

"Da, 'tis me, your firstborn…"

He faced me again with blood in his eyes. Yanking the stake and mallet from the priest's hands, my father surged at me, and suddenly there was no doubt in my mind he meant to do murder. I spun away and ran. Out the front door, the only door, and right through the midst of that crowd of mourners who'd called themselves my friends. My family. My woman.

"Get it!" someone cried. "It mustn't escape!"

And I fled. Shoving them aside easily, I ran, faster than I'd known I could run. I heard the pursuit. Some had fetched dogs, others had mounted their horses. I saw the flickering of yellow-orange torchlight coming closer as I ran for my very life. And they kept coming.

Someone yanked me off my feet and into the bushes alongside the path. I looked up, and saw the creature who'd brought all of this upon me, and I opened my mouth to curse his very existence. He easily covered it, stilling me and drawing me deep into the cover of the greenery. A second later the mob thundered past, shouting and cursing me, promising to destroy me in the most horrible ways imaginable. Calling me "Satan."

My captor no longer needed to hold me still, for I had no will to move. I relaxed to the ground, lowering my head as tears burned my eyes. My pursuers were gone. My assassin remained, but I no longer cared. "Kill me if you will," I offered. "I've no reason to wish to live."

"You have it all wrong, Donovan," he told me, and gripping my arms, he pulled me to my feet. Strong hands, gripping me hard, but no pain as a result. "You were dying before. The weakness, the dizziness, the blackouts."

I looked up sharply.

"Oh, yes, I've been watching you. You'd have been dead within a few more days, at most. But you…you didn't want death." He lowered his head, shook it.

"Rarely have I come upon a man as vividly alive and in love with life as you, my friend."

I frowned, shook my head. "Then why did you try to kill me?"

"I wasn't trying to kill you, Donovan. I was giving you life. You'll never die now. You can't."

"I...I can't...?"

"Well, there are ways, but...listen to me, lad. I took your blood, drained you to the point of death. And then I fed you from my own veins and filled you once again. It's how the dark gift is shared, how it's given."

"Dark gift. I don't know—"

"Immortality," he told me.

I stood there, blinking in confusion and staring up at this man. His dark head silhouetted by a Halloween moon, and bordered by the clawlike, leafless branches of slumbering trees. A pumpkin patch at his back. An owl singing of my death in the distance. And I think I sensed then, finally, just what he was about to say.

"My name is Dante, and I am a vampire."

I gasped, but he took my hand in a firm grip and shook it.

"Your name is Donovan," he told me, patient as if he were a teacher instructing a slow student. "And as of tonight, you are a vampire, too."

Chapter 2

Rachel Sullivan waltzed into O'Mallory's pub as if she'd never been gone, and ignored the hush that fell as she passed. Glasses stopped clinking, men stopped spinning their yarns. Eyes followed her when she sashayed to the back of the room and snatched a white apron from a hook. Behind the gleaming mahogany bar, Mary folded her arms over her plump middle and smiled. Rachel tied the apron on and turned around, eyeing the round, wooden tables and the familiar faces at each one.

"An' what's got you all so tongue-tied?" she asked, tossing her head. "I told you I'd come back, and now I have. So stop your gaping and drink your ale." She turned briskly back to the bar, snatching up a tray with two foaming pints on it, and then unerringly spotted the pair who had empty glasses before them, and delivered their refills.

The talk started up again. Mostly directed at her

now. Unshaven men who'd known her father, welcoming her home. Curly-headed women asking her about the States as she hustled back and forth with her laden tray. For the first time in what seemed like a long time, Rachel released a long, cleansing breath, and felt the tension drain from her spine. She was home, truly home. And it felt good. Better than the degree she'd worked so hard to earn. Better than anything had since...since before she'd left.

She'd been afraid, half expecting the locals to be wary of her now, but the rapid return to normalcy in the pub told her that fear had been unwarranted. The people of Dunkinny didn't like outsiders, that much was true. Oh, tourists occasionally found their way to the isolated village, particularly the ones with Irish surnames out to discover their roots. The locals were polite enough, but always reserved. Wary. Rachel, though, had been born and raised here. Orphaned here, and taken under the collective wing of these villagers. They'd been sad when she'd left them, but not angry. With one exception—Marney Neal, who'd been so determined to marry her. But he wasn't here tonight, she noted with relief. And the others welcomed her back into their midst without a second thought. Eight years away, but they didn't see her as an outsider.

"Welcome home, Rachel." Mary, who'd owned this place and the boarding house attached to it for as long as Rachel could remember, hugged her hard, slapping her back with enthusiastic blows. "I've kept your old room for you. I can already see you'll be takin' your old job back."

Rachel didn't have the heart to tell her it was only for a short time. Only until she got her thesis written, the final step in earning her doctorate. And then she'd...

What? Become the world's leading social anthropologist? Teach at an Ivy League university in the States?

She closed her eyes and inhaled the scent of Russell Finnegan's stale pipe smoke, fresh beer, and the sheep manure on Mitch Marley's boots. When she opened them again, she faced the window, and stared out at the worn track that passed for a road in this tiny village, and the rolling emerald hills, and the crumbling castle—Castle Dante—in the distance. It stood amid a ghostly mist as haunting as the tale that went along with the place—the tale she was basing her thesis on. Beyond the castle were the cliffs, and the green-blue sea far below.

And that was the other reason she'd come back. To see that castle one more time.

As a child, she'd believed in the tales. But in her heart, she'd never accepted the villagers' condemnation of the men who'd once lived there. One of them, she swore, had come to her. Twice in her childhood she'd met him, or so she'd believed for a long time. The first time had been when she'd nearly drowned in the river one night long ago. A dark stranger had pulled her from the water, breathed into her lungs, cradled her gently until others arrived, and then disappeared before she'd even had a chance to thank him. The second time was after her parents' deaths, when she'd lain awake and afraid in her bed, unable to sleep, feeling more alone than any being ever had. He'd come to her, held her hand, and told her she wasn't alone at all. That she had a guardian who would watch over her, protect her always, and that she must never fear. She'd barely seen his face in the darkness, but in her mind, she'd believed him to be Donovan O'Roark, or his ghost. And she'd loved him.

Always, she'd loved him. Even later, when she'd realized her childhood memories were only dreams, and that there were no such things as vampires, she'd nurtured a tender place for the fictional legend in her heart. And while she was home, she'd visit that castle once more...perhaps just to assure herself that he wasn't truly there, awaiting her return.

She'd been home for two weeks when he came.

The air was brisk, with the cold taste of winter on its lips when it kissed her face. But the doors of the pub were propped open all the same, to let the pipe smoke out and the fresh air in. And the fire snapping in Mary's cobblestone hearth kept the chill at bay.

When the silence fell this time, it was uneasy, rather than the friendly hush that had fallen upon Rachel's unexpected return. Then, she'd felt the smiling eyes, the welcome. Now she felt a frisson of something icy slipping up her spine. And when she turned to follow the curious gazes, she saw the stranger walking along the darkened road.

He paused, and stared off in the distance, toward the dark hulking silhouette of the castle. Mitch Marley gasped. Russell Finnegan gaped and his pipe dropped from his lax mouth to the table, unnoticed.

The tension that filled the room, filled *her,* was ridiculous, and unnecessary. "I'd forgot," she muttered, "just how superstitious you all are. Look at you, gawking at that fellow as if he's Donovan O'Roark come back from the dead!"

Mary crossed herself. "You saying you don't believe the old tales now that you're educated, Rachel Sullivan?''

''Old tales are just that. Old tales. Nothing more. I'll prove it, too.'' Rachel stepped into the open doorway, hands braced on either side, and leaned out. ''I don't know where you're going, stranger, but if it's food and a warm bed you're lookin' for, you won't find it anywhere but here.''

''Lord preserve us from that saucy girl,'' Mary murmured.

''Feisty as she ever was,'' someone agreed.

But Rachel ignored them, because the man was turning, looking at her. It was dark tonight, no moon to help her explore his face. She could only see dark eyes gleaming the reflection of the soft, muted light spilling out of the pub. Firelight and lamp glow. Mary detested bright electric lights at nighttime, though Rachel often suspected it was the bill she truly disliked.

''Come inside,'' Rachel said again, more softly this time because she sensed he could hear her very well. ''Warm yourself by the fire. And show these friends of mine that you're not the monster from their favorite folktale.''

I stood there, stunned to my bones. Amazed first that she'd spoken to me at all, for I knew the people of Dunkinny to be a superstitious lot, untrusting of strangers. Or they had been when I'd first left here, nigh on a hundred years ago, and they had been so still each time I'd returned since. But people in solitary villages like this one never tend to change overmuch. She was different, though. She'd always been different.

I fancied it ironic; I'd been one of them once, and

that wariness, that mistrust of strangers, was still with me. But I'd been betrayed too often to let it go. It was, in fact, stronger than ever.

So then, why did I stop? Why did I turn and look at her when she spoke to me, when my natural reaction would have been to keep walking, never so much as pausing in my gait.

But I did pause. Partly because of her voice, pure and silken, with the lilt of Ireland, of this very village to it. So familiar and dear to me, that accent. And frightening at the same time. 'Twas the voice of my own people, the ones who'd called me evil and tried to kill me. The ones who'd later murdered the best friend I'd ever had. But 'twas also the voice of the little girl I'd watched over long ago, but grown up now. And somehow, still the same.

She spoke again, her tone haughty, mischievous, almost taunting. And then I looked, and saw her silhouetted in the doorway, surrounded by a golden glow. Raven hair, long and wild. I'd seen Gypsies less mesmerizing.

She held out a hand to me. "Come," she said.

And as if her words held some sort of power over me, I went.

She clasped my hand as soon as I came within reach, and she drew me inside. She had long sharp nails. Red nails. I liked them, and the warmth of her small, strong hand. And the tingle of sensual awareness I felt passing through her body. I liked that, too. Knew better than to indulge it this close to what would soon be my home…again. But liked it all the same.

Over the years, I had changed, but not drastically. My skin was paler, yes. It hadn't felt the touch of the sun in nearly two centuries, after all. But its pink, healthy glow remained intact for several hours once I'd fed.

And I'd fed well tonight.

So when she drew me inside, there were no gasps of shock at my appearance. She settled me into a wooden chair near the fire, and that's when I realized this pub was in the exact place that other one had stood long ago. O'Connor's tavern. The site of my funeral. The place where my father had tried to murder me.

A lump came into my throat, but I forced it away.

"There, you see?" the girl was saying, hands on her hips, which moved enticingly whenever she did. She waved a hand toward me. "Just a tourist, not a legend come to life." She faced me again. "Tell us, stranger, what's your name?"

I cleared my throat. "O'Roark," I said, waiting, curious to see their reactions.

The plump woman dropped a tankard of ale and it crashed to the floor, spewing amber liquid and odorous foam around her feet.

The girl stared at me, searching my face with an intensity that shook me. But she couldn't recognize me. She'd never seen my face clearly enough to know it again now. And finally she grinned, a twinkle in her eye, and tilted her head to one side. "O'Roark, is it? Another one? Tell me, Mr. O'Roark, have you come travelin' from the States in search of your family history?"

I smiled very slightly, unable to help myself. Such a spirited girl, she was. "Has my accent faded so much that I sound like an American to you?" I asked her.

She gave me a sassy shrug. "I only know you're

not from Dunkinny. For I know everyone in this town.''

''You've lived here that long, have you?''

''Born here, as were my parents and theirs before them for five generations.''

''Mine, too.''

She frowned at me, and I took my time studying her face. Small features, fine bones. But her lips were full and her eyes large in that small face. ''You're saying you're descended from *our* O'Roarks?''

''So much so that I've inherited the castle.''

At last, I'd shaken her. The others had been uneasy from the moment I'd set foot inside, but not her. Now, though, I saw it. The widening of her deep green eyes, the loss of blood's glow in her cheeks.

''You're making it up,'' she accused, but softly.

I shook my head.

''He'll be wantin' to know about the legend then,'' Mary called.

''Aye, tell him the legend, Rachel! Stranger he may be, but no man ought to risk dallying about that place unwarned.''

Rachel. She'd grown into the name. A name as untamed and tempting as the woman she'd become.

She tilted her head to one side. ''He already knows,'' she ventured, studying me, watching my every reaction.

''How can you be sure?'' I asked her. ''Tell me, Rachel. What is this legend that seems to make everyone here so nervous? Everyone...but you, that is.''

She recovered quickly, regaining the bounce in her step as she snatched two steins of ale from the bar, and brought them to the table. One, she thumped to the table before me. The other, she drank from deeply, before wiping her mouth with the back of her hand and leaning back in the chair she'd taken.

Behind her the fire snapped and danced. "Long ago Donovan O'Roark, a farmer's son loved by all, was walking home from the fields. Alone, he walked, and well after dark, on the Eve of All Hallows."

I got a chill up my spine, and was reminded, briefly and vividly of my gram, and the way she'd spun her tales before the fire at night. Tales I'd never believed in.

"But poor Donovan never made it home unscathed that night, for a creature attacked him." She paused, looking around the room. I did likewise, seeing the rapt attention on every face—though they'd likely all heard the tale a hundred times by now. "A vampire," she said in a long, whispery breath.

I lifted my brows high, an attempt to show them my skepticism. "A vampire," I repeated.

"Indeed. The young man died that night, but he didn't stay dead long. He rose from his casket at his own funeral! No longer mortal, but a creature like the one who'd created him. The villagers tried to kill him, but he was too strong, and he escaped into the night and vanished."

I lifted the mug to my mouth, pretending to sip the beer, and licking the taste of it from my lips when I set the glass down again. "I still don't see what this has to do with the castle."

"Ah, so you're an impatient one, are you?"

I only shrugged and let her continue.

"Donovan wasn't seen again. Not for a hundred years. But everyone knew his tale. Then, something happened. The lord of that castle—" here she pointed in the castle's general direction "—was a rich Italian man, some said a nobleman. His name was Dante. Now how do you suppose his castle ended up in the hands of the family O'Roark?'' I smiled and said nothing. Rachel went on. ''No one had ever suspected Dante of anything evil. He simply kept to himself, and that was the way the villagers liked it.''

''He being an outsider, and all,'' I put in.

She gave me a curious glance. ''One night a young girl, who'd been hired to work sometimes at the castle, came running down from the cliffs, hysterical. Screaming and crying, she was. With blood runnin' down her neck in twin streams, and two tiny punctures in her pretty throat.''

I didn't interrupt her, though the words near choked me trying to escape. Dante had never harmed the girl. He'd adored her, loved her to distraction, and in the end, done the one thing he'd warned me over and over never to do.

He'd trusted her.

Rachel sipped her beer. ''The girl said Dante was a monster who slept in a coffin by day, and fed on livin' blood by night. He'd attacked her, tried to drain her dry, but she'd got away.''

''Did anyone wonder,'' I asked, unable to keep still any longer, ''how a young thing like that could get away from a creature like him?''

She frowned at me. ''You want to hear the rest or not?''

I nodded. She spoke. ''The girl said Dante wasn't alone up there. She said he had another with him, and that companion was none other than Donovan O'Roark.''

Around the room everyone nodded, muttering in agreement.

"The villagers discussed what needed to be done, while young Laura begged them to destroy the monsters. Finally, they agreed. At just before dawn they marched to the castle armed with torches and oil, and they set the place alight." When she said it, I thought she suppressed a shudder.

I remembered it all too well. The flames, the sickening realization that the woman Dante had loved had betrayed him in the worst possible way. His pained expression as he realized it, too. I knew that pain so well, because I'd felt it when my own family, and the girl I'd loved, had done the same to me.

"The vampires were forced to flee, and when they did, the sun was already coming up. And the castle has been owned by an O'Roark ever since." She stopped. I felt her hand on my arm. "Mister O'Roark?"

I opened my eyes, just realizing I had squeezed them shut.

"Are you all right?"

"It…it's a frightening tale. Gruesome."

"But just a tale, as I've been trying to tell these good people."

I nodded. "Go on, finish it. What became of the two victims?"

She tilted her head. "Victims?" Lowering her gaze, her voice softer, she said, "I never thought anyone else would see them that way. But you're right, 'tis exactly what they were." She met my eyes again, her voice more normal. "At any rate, they ran off in separate directions, but smoke could be seen curling from their clothes as they went. The villagers believed they both died, burned to cinders by the sun." She shook her head, almost sadly. "But not long after that, a crew of men arrived to begin working on the castle, and when they were questioned they would only say a man named O'Roark had hired them. The villagers believed it was Donovan, back from the dead a second time. They all said he'd return one day to seek vengeance on the people of Dunkinny for the murder of his friend.''

She sighed deeply, and for a long moment no one spoke, still under the spell of her story. But Rachel broke the silence a moment later. "I'm sure most of the locals are speculating as to whether you be him. Tell them your given name, O'Roark. Ease their superstitious minds.''

I smiled very gently, and laid money on the table to pay for my unfinished beer. Then got to my feet and turned for the door. "My given name,'' I said softly, "is Donovan.'' And then I stepped into the night, away from all of them and the dread on their faces.

Chapter 3

Someone was following me.

I slowed my pace slightly, keeping to the shadows, moving in utter silence. My mind open, probing, tracking the curious fool. Only one. No threat to me.

I never should've done it; taunted them the way I did. I knew better, and to this day I've no idea what possessed me to tell them my name, watch them go pale, and then walk away. I'd frightened the fools, deliberately frightened them. But it was no less than they deserved. They'd built themselves up a hefty debt over the generations. Turning on one of their own the way they'd turned on me so long ago. Murdering Dante…

I paused along the roadside where the heather bloomed its last and its scent was heavy in the air, lowered my head as the pain swept over me along with the autumn wind. They'd surrounded the castle, and brutally put their torches to our home, our sanctuary, forcing us to run for our lives. But we'd only found the rising sun awaiting our desperate flight. Its golden rays, so beautiful, so deadly. I remember the searing, the blistering of my flesh, the horror that surged within me as I saw thin tendrils of smoke rising up from my own body.

I'd been the lucky one that cold morn. By burrowing deep into a haystack in a field—a field I'd once worked at my father's side—I found shelter. But for Dante...I knew him to be dead. For I never saw him again after that day, and I've no doubt he'd have contacted me somehow if he'd survived.

Lifting my head, I sent my senses out, realizing that in the flood of memories this place evoked, I'd lost track of my follower.

But the stalker had stopped as well, and stood now several yards away, just watching, and thinking herself protected by the darkness. I almost smiled at her innocence, turned, and began walking again, wondering how far her courage would take her.

I'd left this place after the attack. Traveled, saw the world, lived in so many places I barely remember them all. But of people, of others like myself and mortals the same, I saw little. I can list the name of every person I've ever had words with in the past two hundred years, and that's how few they've been.

Dante drilled it into me, again and again. "Trust no one, Donovan. No one. And most especially, no mortal."

I could hear the sea in the distance now, and the road ran away from the farmers' fields and began to slope sharply upward, among rises too steep, and far too rocky, to be tilled. She was still following.

So long as we'd lived by Dante's words, we'd been

fine. A lonely life, it was. But safe, peaceful. Satisfying in so many other ways. The time we had, endless time—or so we believed then—to learn of music and art, to read and to write, to experience and to savor the things our mortal lifetimes would never have given us time to know.

But then Dante had fallen in love, and it had all ended. He'd told the girl the truth, and it seemed to me she must have run all the way back to that ignorant mass of villagers, so eager was she to tell our secret and see us destroyed.

Dante had been right from the start. Trust no one, and particularly, no mortal.

As I crested the hill, the wind blew in from the sea more fiercely, and I loved the feel of it. My wind, my sea. So familiar despite the bitterness I'd known here. I sat down amid a small outcropping of boulders along the roadside…not because I was tired.

The castle towered before me, no sign of the fire that had nearly killed me a century ago. Dante had willed the place to me, and I'd had it restored, or partially so. I kept it up, always, ready for his return. I'd long ago given up hope he'd ever come back…but somehow I couldn't let go of this place.

My good friend was gone, and I was alone in the world. There was no room to doubt that. And yet some foolish sentimental urge had drawn me back here to the very place where he'd been brutally murdered. Back to this place, to the castle, to my ancestral home—to her. I'd been drawn to see her again, to assure myself she was still safe and well.

She was nearly upon me now, the wind whipping her hair into wild chaos. Her eyes narrowing as she squinted into the darkness, trying to see where I'd gone. She thought she was stepping lightly, but I heard every footfall. Not that it would have mattered. She had a scent about her, one that was sharply different from the others—from any other mortal I'd encountered. Dante had told me that some did, and he'd told me what it meant.

Among other things, *vital* things, it meant that I was forbidden to harm her. By whose decree, I never knew. Never asked. Besides, I never was much for rules. But I couldn't have harmed her if I'd tried.

She came closer. Her long skirt snapped in the sea wind, whipping her ankles. Her blouse...sinfully snug-fitting, and molding to her breasts as if trying to squeeze them. She stood there a moment, so close I could feel her there. And after a fruitless search for me, she lowered her head in defeat. But still she remained, letting the wind buffet her body, and I do believe she was thoroughly enjoying its vicious embrace. But then she turned to go.

I stood slowly, silently. "Are you looking for someone?"

She sucked in a loud, violent gasp, spinning toward me, her hands flying to her chest as if to keep her heart from leaping out. Then she paused, blinking at me in the darkness, drawing several openmouthed breaths. "Lordy, you near scared the life out of me!"

I smiled then. Her accent was no longer as pronounced as it used to be, and I knew that was because she'd been away for a time. But it remained enchanting to me. My own had faded until it was barely discernible anymore.

"I was beginning to think," I told her, "that nothing frightened you."

She gave a tilt of her head and a shrug. "Well, it

takes a good deal more than an old folktale and a stranger showin' up in the village, claimin' to be a ghost.''

"I never claimed to be a ghost."

"You said you were Donovan O'Roark."

"Because I am."

She narrowed her emerald eyes on me. She had witch's eyes, Rachel Sullivan did. "Can you prove it?"

My gaze dipped to the pale, slender column of her throat, and impulsively, I put my fingers there and felt the blood churning beneath her skin. "I could..."

Her eyes sparkled. It was true, nothing frightened her. She smiled at me, and it took my breath away. "Goin' to bite my neck, are you?" she asked.

"If I did, would you run screaming to the villagers, and return with a mob bent on doing me in?"

Tipping her head back, she laughed softly, a deep husky sound. Her neck...so close, so smooth...

She brought her gaze level with mine, obviously amused. "I'd be more likely to bite you back, Donovan O'Roark, and don't you forget it."

I could say nothing. She robbed me of words, of the power of speech, of coherent thought, with that flippant reply.

"But the proof I had in mind," she went on, "was running more along the lines of paperwork. A driver's license, you know, or something of that sort."

Swallowing hard, I retrieved my wallet from my back pocket, extracted my identification and showed it to her. A man in my position did well to keep things such as these up-to-date, and there were many ways of doing so, none too complex. She took it, her fingers brushing mine, perhaps deliberately. She had to squint and finally pulled a cigarette lighter from her deep pocket and, turning her back to the wind, used it to see by.

Nodding sagely, she handed it back to me. "So you really are a descendant—named for your most infamous ancestor, no less." She bit her lower lip. "Is this your first visit to Dunkinny, then?"

She asked it as if trying to hide the question's importance to her. I thought it best not to answer. "Why were you following me, Rachel—it is Rachel, isn't it?"

"Indeed, Rachel Sullivan, with a few notorious ancestors of my own."

The back of my neck prickled to life at the mention of her ancestors. Treacherous women, women I'd known too well.

She went on. "The Sullivan women are somewhat known for scandals. Perhaps I ought to warn you of that right off. 'Twas one of my own who four generations ago screamed accusations against Lord Dante, and got him killed, or so the legends have it."

It was true, Laura Sullivan had been her name. My throat went dry.

"An' they say another Sullivan woman was promised to marry Donovan O'Roark himself—the first one, that is. But when he rose from his coffin, she cried for his blood."

"Yes," I said softly, hearing her shrill voice again in my mind, shouting, *"Kill it! Kill it before it destroys us all!"* "Alicia," I muttered.

"Really? I never heard her given name before."

I only shrugged. "So have you come to pick up where your forebears left off, Rachel? To destroy me?"

She slipped her arm through mine, and turned us toward the castle, walking slowly. "You're a funny man, Donovan. But you know as well as I those are only silly tales. No truth to 'em, or at least, so little 'tis barely recognizable anymore. No, I have a far different mission. But I'll be needin' your help."

"My help?" She had my curiosity piqued. And yet I feared her. It was too uncanny to be mere coincidence, and a shiver worked up my spine as I wondered if perhaps it was the destiny of the Sullivan women to destroy me—if they'd keep coming, generation after generation of them—until they saw the task completed.

And now I was thinking as foolishly and superstitiously as my people.

"Tell me of this mission, then. What is it?"

She looked up at me and smiled, eyes wide and green as the sea, full of innocence and mischief like the eyes of the child I remembered.

"I've come to learn all your secrets, Donovan. All the secrets of Castle Dante, and the truth behind the legend."

My heart tripped to a stop in my chest. My voice hoarse, I said, "If I told you all of that, pretty Rachel, I'm afraid I'd have to kill you."

Pressing closer to my side, clapping her hand to my arm and leaning her head on my shoulder, she laughed. A husky, deep sound, genuine amusement ringing in its voice. "I do love a man with a sense of humor," she said. "I can tell we're going to get along, Donovan. Why, we'll be best friends 'fore we're done."

She was warm at my side, and far too close to me.

And I relished her nearness...for the lack of human companionship wears a man down over the years.

She was here to destroy me. I had no doubt of that. And yet I couldn't bring myself to send her away. She couldn't force me to tell her anything, I told myself. She couldn't learn anything I didn't wish her to know. What harm would it do to let her accompany me to the castle?

Inside me, I heard Dante's dire warnings: *Don't do it, Donovan. Don't spend another second with her. She's dangerous! She's a Sullivan, dammit. Send her away, or kill her now and be done with it.*

We stopped, the wind blocked now by the towering mass of the castle itself. Before us two massive doors made of broad beams, and held together by black iron bands, stood like sentries awaiting the password.

"Ever since I was a little girl, I've wanted to see inside this castle," she said, so softly it was as if she were that little girl again, right now. "But my parents forbade it, and filled my head with so many foolish old tales that for a time I was frightened to death of sneaking up here the way the older ones did."

"For a time?"

"Aye. Later I changed my mind. He was no monster, the man who lived here. I crept around this place often, once I'd made up my mind to that. So childish, hopin' for a glimpse of a man long dead."

"But you didn't go inside?"

"I couldn't. I always felt..." She drew a deep breath, let it out all at once. "You'll laugh at me."

"No," I said. "I won't. Tell me."

She looked up, right into my eyes, and hers were honest, sincere, beautiful. "I always thought this place seemed...sacred, somehow. And...and it was my own blood kin that defiled it, ruined it. So to me, my setting foot inside would have been...a sacrilege.''

''And now?''

She eyed the castle doors, shivered a little. ''Maybe I was wrong. Maybe I'm the one who'll make it all right again, somehow.'' She lowered her head, sighing. ''I'm different from the others, you know.''

''Yes, I know.''

''They tell the tale, again and again, and they all shudder with fear of the creatures they claim lived here once.'' She placed a palm against the chiseled stone, closed her eyes. ''But not me. The first time I heard the tale I was all of three years old, and I cried. For hours, no one could comfort me. To me, it wasn't a horror story, it was a tragedy. One man, rising from the dead only to be driven out of the village by his own family. Another, murdered only because he dared to love.'' She met my eyes and smiled. ''To tell you the truth, back when I was still child enough to believe in the old tales, I thought of your ancestor as...as a friend. My own guardian angel.''

''And now?'' I asked her.

''And now I'm an adult, who knows better than to believe in fairy tales. But it does seem like Providence that you're here now. Just when I've returned home from the States. Just when I'm planning to write my thesis based on the legend, its sources, and its effects on the community to this day. Just when I'm wondering how I'll ever learn all I need to know about Castle Dante and the original Donovan O'Roark— here you are. I think it's a sign.''

She was enchanting me, mesmerizing me. Both with her scent, and with her beauty, but mostly with that enthusiasm and charm and slightly skewed view of the universe.

She had the belladonna antigen, and that was part of the attraction—had always been drawing me to her, urging me to watch over her. I could smell it in her blood, could sense it there. Every immortal had that antigen before they received the dark gift. If not, they wouldn't transform…they'd simply die. Dante had told me these things, and he'd warned me as well of the allure mortals with the antigen had for us…the attraction. And it was said to run both ways.

I knew all this. But knowing it did nothing to dampen its effect on me. As a child she'd been harmless, no threat to me at all, just a little girl in need of a protector. But now…

She stared up at me from emerald green eyes. "Will you take me inside, Donovan? With you fulfill my childhood dreams and show me your castle?"

And like a man held prisoner by a Gypsy enchantress's spell, I nodded, searched for my key, and opened my haven up to my enemy.

Chapter 4

There was something about him...

No, it was only her imagination playing games with her. Yes, he was pale, but only slightly so. And that grace about him, the way his every movement seemed as fluid as a part of a dance...it was simply his way. It didn't mean a thing.

He wasn't the guardian of her imagination. Her savior.

He gripped the iron ring and opened the doors, waiting and allowing her to enter first. Taking a single step into the looming, echoing blackness, she stopped, battling a shiver of unease that kept tickling at her spine.

"I can't see a thing," she said, reaching into her pocket for the lighter once again.

She felt him enter behind her. He stood close to her back as she fumbled in her pocket, and the deep moan of the door closing behind him made her heart skip a beat. Closing her hand around the lighter in her pocket, she pulled it out and promptly dropped it on the floor.

"It's all right," he said. "Wait here."

"As if I could do anything else," she replied, and hoped he didn't detect the tremor in her voice.

He moved past her then. She never heard his footsteps, and it seemed they should echo endlessly here, the way her every whisper did. There was a flare of light, a glow that illuminated his face for a moment, making it come alive with light and shadow as if he were some sort of undulating demon. But then he leaned over, and in a moment the glow spread as he touched the match to the tapers in a silver candelabra, lighting them one by one. And lifting it, he moved around the room, lighting others. It seemed to Rachel there must be candles everywhere in this place. By the time he returned to her side, the entire room glowed with them, shadows leaping and dancing, soft yellow light spilling over everything.

He took her hand. Drew her forward. Rachel went with him, her fear dispelled as her curiosity leapt to the fore. The room was as big as a barn, and high, high above her, she saw something glittering in the candleglow. "Is that a chandelier?"

Donovan looked up, then nodded. "The entire place is equipped with gas lights, but I'll need to connect the main line and open the valves before they'll be of any use."

"What I wouldn't give to see this place in the daylight," she breathed. She felt him tense and wondered why.

Twin fireplaces stood at opposite walls, each one laid ready, waiting only to be lit. Each one had a huge stone mantel, and above them tapestries hung. Breath-taking tapestries. She moved closer to the one nearest her, covering Donovan's hand with her own to lift the candelabra higher. "They must be ancient," she muttered.

"Quite old, medieval, or so Dante said."

Her spine prickled. "Dante said that, did he?"

Donovan looked down at her rather quickly. "Or so the story goes. I'm only repeating what's been told to me."

She tilted her head, studying his face in the soft glow. "Are you, now?"

Nodding, he moved her to the left of the fireplace, lifting the light again and nodding toward the wall, where two crossed swords hung. "The broadswords are medieval as well, but Irish, whereas the tapestries are Italian."

"This Dante must have been quite a collector."

Donovan shrugged and moved on, pointing out other relics fastened to the walls, a suit of armor standing in a corner, looking ridiculously short, and the furnishings. Large chairs with embroidered cushions and elaborately carved, utterly straight backs, were grouped around the fireplaces. A large, ornate table with smaller, less elaborate chairs surrounding it held the room's center, each of its legs the size of a small tree. And there were weapons everywhere. Lances, maces, shields with their crests emblazoned across the front.

And every so often, they'd pass an archway of darkness, leading off into some other part of the castle. Each time, she'd peer into the blackness, eyes narrow, eager to see more.

But each time, she saw nothing.

When they'd walked round the entire room, he led her to one of the cushioned chairs, setting the candles on a marble stand at its side. Then he turned and knelt before the fire, and a second later it blazed to life, though she'd never seen him strike a match.

She let the warmth rinse through her, chasing the chill of autumn away. And Donovan settled himself in the chair beside her.

"I'd offer you something to drink, but—"

"I know," she said. "You've only just arrived. I can't very well be expectin' your cupboards to be fully stocked so soon." She smiled at him. "'Twill be cold…lonely, living here in this place, don't you think?"

He nodded. "Yes. But there's a history here I needed to…touch. I had to come back."

"Come back? You have been here before, then?"

He blinked slowly, averting his eyes. "Long ago."

"In your childhood?"

"Something like that."

She nodded, not pushing him further, though she was fully aware he hadn't really answered her. He couldn't have been the man who saved her from the river. That was twenty years ago. He was far too young. "Is this—this great hall—the only room you're willing to show me, then, Donovan?"

"For now," he told her. "It wouldn't be safe to take you farther…" A long pause as his gaze burned into hers. "Without more light."

Her throat went dry. She tried to swallow, and found she couldn't. He had a hungry look about him, a predatory look that shook her.

"Perhaps I should go then. Leave you to get settled in."

"Perhaps," he said.

Nodding, she got to her feet. He rose as well. "I...I'd like to come back. To talk to you about the legend."

"I don't know much about that. You'll be disappointed."

"I get the feelin' you know more about it than anyone else, Donovan O'Roark." She turned and walked toward the door, and he trailed her. She sensed he was eager for her to go.

But when he pushed the huge door open, a blinding flash of lightning cut a jagged path across the sky. The rain slashed in at them, and thunder rumbled in the distance.

Closed within the huge stone walls, they hadn't even been aware of the change in the weather, and there wasn't a window to be seen in this room, she realized for the first time.

He stood motionless. Said nothing. Well, then, there was no way around it. She lowered her head and took a step out...only to feel his hands closing on her shoulders, drawing her back inside. She nearly sighed in relief.

"You can't walk back to the village in this." He said it as if he regretted it right to his bones.

"I could. I'm not sugar, Donovan, and I won't melt in a wee bit of rain."

He closed the door, lifted a hand and swiped the droplets from her face, and then her hair. "Not melt, but get soaked through and take sick, at the very least. Or worse, get crushed beneath a falling tree, or struck down in your tracks by a bolt of lightning. No, I can't let you leave."

"You sound sorry about that."

He nodded, surprising her by not denying it. "I like my privacy, Rachel. You'll do well to remember that about me."

"Oh."

He frowned at her. "What?"

Shrugging, she lifted her brows. "I guess I was thinkin' there might be some other reason my bein' here disturbed you so much. No matter though."

She was only half teasing him, and she thought he knew it. She was drawn to the man, in a way she didn't understand. It was as if some sort of spell were being worked on her, to make her....

She closed her eyes, gave her head a shake. "I believe I must be more sleepy than I realized."

"There should be some bedrooms made up," he said, his voice gentle. Did she detect a slight tremor in it?

"Lead the way, then."

He nodded, picking up the dancing candles once more "Best stay close to me, Rachel. I've no idea how safe the entire castle is, since only parts of it have been kept up. Besides, you could get lost very easily in these halls."

She nodded her assent, and as he led the way into the dark, vaulted corridors, she held tighter and tighter to his arm, aware that with every step she took she was leaving safety farther behind. Not that she feared him.

Oh, but she did.

The halls twisted, turned, veered off in countless directions. He took her up spiraling stairways that felt like tunnels, they were so narrow and dark. And then down more hallways.

"Donovan?"

He paused, and turned to look at her there in the darkness.

"Are you deliberately leading me round and round, only to keep me from knowing my way out?"

Solemnly, he shook his head. "Just the opposite, Rachel. The room is near a back exit. So you can leave first thing in the morning."

"And why would I wish to do that, when you could just as easily lead me out of here yourself?"

"I…I won't be here. I have a pressing engagement, I'm afraid. Very early. So by the time you wake up, I'll be gone."

Tipping her head back, she studied him. "Will you, now?"

"Yes. And Rachel, I want your promise that you'll do as I ask. Leave here in the morning. No snooping, or exploring. I've already told you, it could be dangerous."

Studying him a long moment, she said, "Is there something here you don't want me to see?"

He shook his head. "You have as big an imagination as those locals at the pub, don't you?"

She smiled. "Bigger. You wouldn't doubt it if you knew what I was thinkin' just now."

"And what was that?"

She lifted her brows and shoulders as one. "That perhaps the reason you won't be here in the morning is because you have an adverse reaction to daylight. And that perhaps the reason you don't want me snooping about, is so I won't stumble upon the coffin where you rest." She threw her head back and laughed at her own foolishness, and the sounds of it echoed endlessly, long after she stopped. "I guess I still have a bit of that gullible child in me after all. Or maybe 'tis simply livin' in Dunkinny that's made me so imaginative.''

But he only stared at her until her smile died.

She bit her lip, and her hand trembled slightly as she lifted it to touch his face. ''I've hurt your feelin's now, have I? I don't really think you're a vampire, Donovan. But just a man. A…a beautiful man.'' She lowered her gaze, not quite believing she was about to say what she was. ''I hope you don't think it bold of me to tell you this. But I—I'd like to see you again. Not because of the legend, but just…just because.'' And still he said nothing. Lowering her hand, she rolled her eyes ceilingward and drew a short, sharp breath. ''Landsakes, Donovan, say something, will you? Am I makin' a total fool of myself, or…''

''No.'' He reached out to brush a curl off her forehead. ''In fact, I've been trying very hard not to…feel anything toward you, all evening.''

She felt the blood rush to her face. ''Oh.'' Then, licking her lips, meeting his eyes again, she whispered, ''Why were you trying so hard not to feel that way, Donovan?''

''Because nothing can come of it.''

Her heart squeezed. ''You're married, then.''

''No. Of course not. It's just…'' He shook his head. ''You'll have to trust me, Rachel. Nothing can come of this. I…I probably won't even be here very long, and besides that, I—'' He sighed deeply. ''It doesn't matter. Here, this is your room.''

He pushed a door open and stepped inside.

Rachel followed, drawing a deep breath as the candlelight spilled on a canopied bed draped in sheer fabric of softest ivory. '''Tis beautiful.''

''It's been restored. This is the room Dante had

made ready for Laura Sullivan, the woman who betrayed him.''

"My...my heartless ancestor slept here?''

"No. No, she killed him before she ever saw it.''

Rachel turned toward him, a new idea creeping into her mind. "Are you puttin' me here, Donovan, so you won't forget whose blood runs in my veins?''

He didn't answer, only lowered his head.

"But you can't possibly blame me for what my forebears did.''

"No. And I don't. I simply thought...'' He shook his head. "I honestly don't know what I thought.''

She took a step closer, drawn to him beyond reason, and driven by more than her usual boldness. She felt as if she knew him, as if she'd always known him, and there was no hint of shyness, and no earthly reason to temper her actions. Simply being near him seemed to have stripped her inhibitions away. "I can tell you what I think, Donovan O'Roark,'' she said. And when he looked up, she moved still closer. "I think you haven't the nerve in you to kiss me goodnight.''

His lips quirked, as if he wanted to smile and was fighting it. "Do you? Is that meant as a challenge, Rachel Sullivan?''

"Indeed, it is. I don't like this idea of you fightin' so hard to dislike me. An' I know that if you kiss me once, you'll forget about all that nonsense my ancestors did to yours, and simply see me. Not Alicia, nor Laura, but me. Rachel Sullivan.''

He started to shake his head.

"I dare you,'' she whispered. "But I don't think you've the nerve.''

His eyes darkened and she knew she'd won. He set the candelabra down on a nightstand and he came toward her, a distinct purpose glowing in his midnight eyes.

Chapter 5

I moved closer to her, compelled by some force I couldn't begin to understand. But my lips merely brushed across hers, their touch light, fleeting. For her mouth was not my goal. Not yet. Part of me wished to frighten her, I think, but there was more. To taste her...I longed for it with a hunger more powerful than the preternatural bloodlust I'd lived with for so long. And for a moment—only a moment—perhaps I forgot where I was. Perhaps part of my mind slipped backward to the time when Dante and I lived like kings, feared by the villagers. The times when we dared walk among them at night, before they understood what we truly were. Those times when, should a maid strike our fancy, we were free to take her, to drink our fill from her pretty throat, and use the power of our vampiric minds to make her remember it only as a dream. Those times before we were fully aware just how dangerous it was to interact with mortals in any way.

I reverted, I think, in my mind that night. So my lips brushed across hers, and then across her cheek, and over her delicate jaw, and she knew. She knew on some level. Her head tipped back, to give me access to what I wanted. Her chin ceilingward as the breath shivered out of her. My lips found the skin of her neck; the spot where a river of blood rushed just beneath the surface. Its current thrummed louder, overwhelming my senses. Her scent, her texture...my head whirled. And my lips parted, and I tasted her then. The salt of her skin, warm on my tongue. Her pulse, throbbing faster against my lips. I drew the skin into my mouth, just a little, suckling her, allowing my teeth to press down ever so slightly.

Shuddering, she pushed herself closer to me, her body tight to mine—from the spot where my mouth teased her throat, to her breasts, straining against my chest, to her hips, arching forward, rubbing softly against mine and making me hard with wanting her.

My arms were around her, one hand cradling her upturned head, one cupping a softly rounded buttock and pulling her harder against me. Hers were on my head, fingers twisting and tugging at my hair as I sucked at her throat. I wanted to pierce her flesh. She wanted it too, I sensed that in everything she did, every soft sigh that whispered from her lips. But she didn't know what it was she was craving. She would though. She would.

I bit down harder, my incisors pinching, pushing against the soft flesh, preparing to break through that luscious surface to the nectar it concealed.

She gasped. A harsh, startled sound louder than the blast of a cannon to my ears, so focused was I on the taste of her. But it was enough to bring me back to myself, to make me realize what I'd been about to do.

The desire burned through me like a flame, and I trembled all over, a quake that utterly racked me as I forced myself to step away from her—to raise my head from her throat, and lower my arms to my sides and step away.

She didn't react immediately. And I knew too well why; could see it in the wide and slightly dazed look in her eyes. The allure of the vampire—and something more, too. Perhaps she'd felt the impact of this force between us as powerfully as I. Even I didn't understand it fully. To her, it would be even less comprehensible.

She came back to herself within a moment, blinking as if to clear her vision, and then staring up at me. "I don't think I've ever been...kissed...quite that way before." Lifting a hand, unaware she did so, she ran her fingertips slowly over the spot where my mouth had been.

"I...shouldn't have done that."

"Why did you?" she asked me.

I shook my head. "I'm not sure, Rachel. Perhaps for the same reason you allowed it."

Tilting her head to one side to study me, she frowned. Her hair slid away, revealing her neck to me again, and I felt a rush of renewed desire as I saw the redness forming there, and the moisture, and the way her fingers kept touching the spot and drawing away.

"Go to sleep," I whispered, but it was more than a whisper. I flexed the astral muscle, the one that didn't exist physically but was there all the same, the one that sent my wishes out to the minds of others. "Forget this happened." I caught her eyes with mine, sending the force out to her, the command that must be obeyed. "Forget the kiss, Rachel. It never happened. Go to sleep, and when you wake—"

"Oh, I doubt I'll sleep at all, Donovan O'Roark," she whispered with a soft, shaky smile. A bit of the mischief returned to her pretty eyes. "But forgettin' that kiss is certainly not an option whether I do or not. I'll either lie awake thinkin' about it, or go to sleep and dream it up again." Her smile broadened. "'Twas a rather nice kiss, you know."

I stepped backward, an instinctive act, rather like reeling in shock, I thought later. She didn't react to the mind control at all. It hadn't…it hadn't even given her pause.

I realized I was standing in the hall now, when she reached for the candelabra and offered it to me. "You should take this with you, to find your way."

"No," I blurted, still trying to puzzle out her lack of a reaction to my commands, too much so to censor myself, fool that I was. "I see perfectly well in the dark." I could have kicked myself the moment the words left my lips.

"Can you, now?" She drew the glowing tapers back to her side. "I'll leave you to it, then. Good night, Donovan."

And she closed the door.

I stood there, trembling. Never had I been so drawn to a mortal before. And never, not ever in two hundred years, had I been so ineffective in influencing the thoughts of one of them. Making them forget. This told me two things. That her will was very strong, and that she didn't *want* to forget.

And she was here, in my home, my haven. God, what if she learned more than she should? What then?

Rachel closed the door, leaned against it, lowered her head and closed her eyes. She was shaking so hard she could barely stand, and she'd been terrified he'd see it before he left. She'd hidden it, she thought. Pulled the mask into place in time. Assumed the demeanor of the flirtatious, irreverent, and slightly cocky barmaid to conceal the depth of her reactions to him.

My God. The way he'd kissed her...the way his mouth had, not just caressed, but devoured her...and then the feel of those...

Those teeth!

She stood bolt upright, still shaking, but no longer weak. Her hands flew to her neck once more, fingers searching, feeling, terror creeping over her soul. Had he...?

Diving into her deep pockets, she extracted a compact, struggled to open it, dropped it, and scrambled to snatch it up again. Finally, she leaned over the glowing candle flames, staring into the small, round mirror at the red mark on her neck. But there were no telltale puncture wounds, and there was no blood.

Just a small patch of bruised skin.

What her friends in the States called a hickey.

"Lord a' mercy," she breathed, snapping the compact shut, sagging once more. "I don't know whether to be weak with relief or to question my sanity for thinking..." Shaking her head, she drew herself upright, turned and went to the bed, taking the candles with her. She set them on a nightstand, and well away from the bed curtains that draped down from the canopy to swathe the thing in luxury. Beyond the sheer fabric, a red satin comforter swelled from the stacks of pillows beneath it, and when she pulled it back it was to find sheets of the same fabric, only black, not red.

The pulse in her throat beat a little harder.

She had no nightclothes here. But the bed hardly seemed made for such things.

Glancing quickly back toward the door, she saw the lock there, waiting to be turned. She saw it, licked her lips, and turned toward the bed once more. This time, to begin undressing.

And she slid naked into that decadent satin nest, felt its cool softness caressing her heated flesh, surrounding her in sensual pleasure. Cushioned and covered and enveloped within it. And when she fell asleep it was to dream of things more carnal than she'd ever done before.

She woke to the morning sunlight streaming through the window and bathing her face—and she was more curious about the man than ever before.

She flung the covers aside, got to her feet, naked in the chilly bedroom. Her clothes lay folded on a chair, just as she'd left them. She glanced at the unlocked door. He'd said he would be gone by the time she woke. But it was still early. Maybe...

She dressed quickly. Over and over his voice rang in her head. *Don't snoop. Leave by the back door as soon as you wake. I value my privacy.*

It would be wrong to go against his wishes, after he'd been so kind to her, letting her in when he obviously didn't want to. Letting her stay when he'd seemed almost afraid to.

Why?

She finished dressing, ran her fingers through her hair in lieu of a comb, and checked her appearance in

the compact mirror since there were none to be found
in the bedroom itself.

No mirrors?

She shook the thought away and examined her reflection. She looked storm-tossed. Wild. Hardly stu-
dious, much less virginal, and probably more like a
barmaid than she ever had.

Why?

Him. His kiss, and a night spent reliving it beneath
the caress of satin sheets that reminded her of his eyes.

"Damn," she whispered, and quickly made the bed
before heading out the door, into the hall. Light now.
Dim, for lack of windows, but enough light made its
way in to see by. The door that led out of here was
obvious. At the end of the hall to her right stood a
tall, wooden door, with light glowing from beyond its
thick pane of glass. Swallowing hard, stiffening her
spine, mustering her willpower, she marched toward
it, found it unlocked, and pulled it open.

Warm Irish sun bathed her face, her eyes. Stretching
before her, like the crooked, graying teeth of a very
old crocodile, were the crumbling stone steps, curving
intimately down this tower's outer wall and disappearing round its other side. From here she could see
the sea, glittering blue-green, with white froth roiling
as the waves crashed against the rocky shore. The
cliffs were almost directly below her.

The steps were probably perfectly safe.

"But he kept goin' on about the place perhaps bein'
dangerous," she muttered to herself. "No, I really do
believe he'd want me to go out the front way. Indeed,
if he were here, he'd likely insist."

She stepped back inside and closed the door. Then
she put her back to it, and faced a long, twisting cor-

ridor lined with doors, and open archways leading into other halls, or stairways going up or twisting downward. Shrugging her shoulders and battling an excited smile, she whispered, "I suppose I'll just have to search until I find a safer way out, won't I?"

Chapter 6

She got lost. Hopelessly, frighteningly lost. Lord, but she'd never realized how large this castle was, or how its corridors writhed about upon themselves like serpents in ecstasy. And so few windows! She no longer had any sense, even of what floor she might be wandering. Her only means of navigation was to try to go toward lighter areas, and away from the darker ones. But even this plan had its flaws, for she could only go so far before the light began to fade. Her choice then became, walk into the darkness or go back to where she'd already been. And going back would serve no purpose.

She made many discoveries that day. Some pleasant ones, but mostly unpleasant in the extreme. She discovered how thirsty she could become in a single day. How gruesome it was to walk face first into a sticky spider's web in the dark. How much she valued a good breakfast when one was unavailable.

Some of the more pleasant discoveries diverted her from her misery for short spans of time. She spent hours exploring rooms full of fascinating antiques, and when she was tired, took a nap on a satin chaise fit for a queen. Later, she stumbled upon the music room, where a harpsichord rested, dusty and old. The soft cushioned window seats built into the stone wall. She sat on one to rest, and caught her breath as she gazed out over what surely must be all of Ireland. She was up so high. She'd been up and down so many stairways that she'd lost track, and truly had no clue where she'd ended. Now she knew, though the knowledge did her little good, except to tell her she ought to be going down. And down some more. And doing it soon, for from this vantage point she could see that the sun now rested on the very edge of the horizon, and would soon sink out of sight. She must have napped longer than she realized.

She lingered there only a short time. She might have stayed longer, despite the late hour, but she made the mistake of leaning over the old instrument, her fingers just lightly caressing the keys. And it let out a belch of sound that nearly stopped her heart. After that she had to be out of the room. Ridiculous, the feeling that pervaded her senses then, but no use denying it. She had the distinct sense that she must get out before Donovan learned she was here. And that blast from the harpsichord might have given her away, even told him exactly where she was, had he heard it.

She ran from the room, back into the snakepit of corridors, and took the first set of stairs she found that led downward.

Only they led into darkness. Or perhaps it was that night was falling now. She kept going down, and the stairs twisted, circling and spiraling, lower and lower. She kept one hand pressed to the walls on either side to keep from falling as she continued endlessly downward. And yet there seemed no end. She began to feel stifled, constricted by the walls at her sides, and even imagined them narrowing. Tightening. Squeezing in on her as if she'd been dropped into a funnel.

The stone step beneath her foot crumbled, and she drew back quickly, listening as the bits of it clattered and echoed into the darkness. She could no longer see at all. And that might have meant full night had fallen, or perhaps it was only that no light could penetrate this narrow spiraling staircase, all encased in stone.

"Enough," she muttered. "I'm goin' back."

And she turned, but her foot slipped, as a still larger chunk of the stone step fell away. It bounded down, crashing like the feet of a giant. And then there was another sound. Soft at first, light. Like the gentle beat of wings and a timid cry...

And then louder.

Screaming.

The air above her filled with rapidly beating wings and piercing shrieks as the bats that falling stone had startled awake swarmed above and around her. Blind beasts! Her scream joined their unearthly voices as she flailed her arms, but they battered her, colliding with her one after another, only to bound off in another direction. She felt them hitting her. Their small, furry bodies wriggling, and those rubbery wings pumping madly. Tiny clawed feet, scraping her face and moving on. Wetness—God alone knew what that was.

She screamed and beat at them, turning in circles and covering her face with her arms.

And then she tumbled.

Head over heels, her body hurtled down the staircase, bounding up and crashing down onto the uneven stone again and again. Smashing against the curving wall, only to rebound from it and follow the downward spiral. No bats now. She'd fallen past them and their mad flight. And for a single moment she thought the fall would be endless.

She came to a stop some seconds before she realized it. Her head still spun and her body screamed in pain from a hundred bruises, each one throbbing as if it were being beaten anew. But gradually, the sense of motion faded, and she realized she was still. She lay on her side, more or less, though her limbs were twisted and bent in unnatural angles.

Slowly, she pulled herself upright, into a sitting position. Every movement hurt. Every spot on her body cried out in protest at her cruelty in moving it at all. But gradually, she did, getting her arms and legs into a more natural state, checking them to be sure they still functioned properly. Nothing seemed to be broken. At least, she could move everything.

God, but it hurt!

Slowly, inch by inch, her hands on the wall nearest her, she pulled herself to her feet. Her trouble, she realized, had not ended simply because her fall had. She still needed to find her way out of this castle. For the first time it occurred to her that she might be trapped here indefinitely. She could starve, or die of thirst before anyone found her.

And somehow the thought didn't frighten her as much as the thought of being found...

But that was foolish.

The stairs had ended, and she was now on a level floor, more or less, though there were chips and breaks in the stone that made walking precarious at best. Still, she made her way forward, wishing for nothing so much as a candle to see by…

The lighter.

She quickly dipped into her pocket and praised her lucky stars, it was still there. She lit it, held it out in front of her, and saw that she was in a long, wide corridor of stone and utter darkness—very much like a cave. But in the distance, doors stood, silent and closed. Perhaps one would lead to…to somewhere.

Her footsteps echoed—unevenly, since she was limping now—as she made her way down the hall, and paused before the first doorway. Pushing it open, she found only an empty room. So she moved on to the second. And of course, an empty room greeted her there, as well.

Only one door remained. Her heart in her throat, tears of frustration beginning to burn in her eyes, she touched the handle.

Locked.

A sob welled up to choke off her breath, and she lowered her head to the wood to cry.

But then there was a sound. A soft creaking sound…a sound that came from beyond that door.

Like another door of some kind, opening….slowly opening.

Straining to hear, she pressed closer, listening with everything in her. Gentle taps upon the floor. Someone moving around. Then a flare of light from beneath, one that grew brighter.

The steps came closer. And something…something made her back away.

The door opened with a deep, forbidding moan of protest.

She looked into the eyes of Donovan O'Roark, saw them widen with shock and something that might have been fear—perhaps even panic. And then she managed to tear her gaze from his to look past him into the room, where candles glowed now. There was nothing there…nothing except a large, gleaming coffin, its lid standing open, its satin lining aglow in the candlelight.

Black and red, the satin inside that box. Black and red like the satin in which she'd slept.

She backed away.

He reached for her.

She whirled, the lighter falling from her hands, and then she ran.

"Rachel! Rachel, wait!"

Panic bubbled in her chest, larger and larger, expanding until she felt the bubble would burst and she'd die, right there, from the force of the fear that possessed her. She fled, headlong, having no idea where she was going, what she would do.

But she knew he pursued her. She knew he'd catch her soon, and Lord help her, what would she do then? What?

The hallway ended. Abruptly, and without a hint of warning in the pitch blackness. She heard Donovan's voice shout a warning—one she ignored—and then she felt the solid, skin-razing wall of stone stopping her heedless flight with a single blow. Her head, her body, the impact rocked her to the teeth and to the bone. But the head was the worst, and she felt the warmth of blood running from the wound and stinging her eyes as she sank slowly to the floor.

"My God, Rachel…"

He was upon her like a wolf on an injured lamb,

and she knew she no longer had a chance. She'd die here in this dungeon or whatever it was. She'd die here, bloodless and pale, and the vampire would have his vengeance on the females of the Sullivan clan at last.

He knelt beside her, gathering her into his arms and leaning over her. She felt his breath on her face. His fingers, probing the pulsing wound on her forehead. "Damn fool woman, you could have got yourself killed!"

As if he wasn't planning to finish that job himself, she thought, groggy now, fading fast.

He got to his feet and carried her back down the hall, through one of the other doors, where she'd seen nothing, and right up to the wall. She tried weakly to leap from his embrace, which likely would have resulted in cracking her head again, this time on the floor, but his arms tightened around her. "Be still, Rachel."

"Let me go...let me go..." She twisted, pulled against him, but his arms were like steel. He paused there beside the wall, lifted one hand, holding her captive quite easily with the other. He touched something and the wall moved, backing away and leaving a two-foot gap on either side. Donovan carried her through that gap, and she caught her breath as the wall closed off again. He moved left, up a single flight of stairs, these ones broad and solid, rather than narrow and crumbling like the ones where she'd fallen. Then he touched another wall, this one at the top of the staircase, and it opened like a door.

He stepped out, and lowered her down onto a soft settee, and then he turned to a wall, and did something. Moments later a soft light suffused the room from above, growing brighter until the place was perfectly well lit.

The light above her was, she realized, the gas-powered chandelier. And the room around her was the great hall.

"So close...I was...so very close..."

"To what, Rachel? To escape?"

She closed her eyes, touched her throbbing head. He ignored her for the moment, intent on lighting first one fire and then the other as she lay there. She felt the heat, saw the light.

"If it was escape you wanted, why didn't you leave by the back door when you awoke this morning? Why did you insist on doing the one thing I asked you not to do?"

He turned to face her, she saw as she peered at him, but the sight of the flames in the fireplace, reflected in his dark hair and deep blue eyes, only made her head hurt more, so she quickly closed her eyes once again. "I wasn't snooping. I...the back stairs looked unsafe. I was only tryin' to find a saner way to leave this ruin."

He was closer now. Right beside her. "You're lying," he whispered.

"No—"

He gripped her shoulders, lifting her slightly, and readying, she thought, to do her in. But his hands closed on bruised flesh, and she winced in agony.

Donovan went utterly still. Then, frowning, he pushed her hair aside, eyeing her face, her neck. "My God, you're more injured than I realized."

That he was choosing to ignore the fact that she'd all but seen him rise from a coffin would have been amusing, if she hadn't been so certain her death was imminent. "I fell," she told him. "Down a long flight of stairs…the bats frightened me, and I lost my footing…" She bit her lip as the memory of it came up to choke off her words.

Sighing deeply, he gripped her shirt at its hem, and without even asking her consent, he tugged it over her head. Then he touched her, with his eyes as well as his hands, examining the bruises and scrapes she'd suffered.

"I'm all right," she told him. "Nothing's broken."

He nodded as if in agreement, but took a handkerchief, spotlessly white, from a pocket and pressed it to her wounded head. "I'll find some ice for this."

"I don't want ice. I just want to leave. Please…"

He shook his head slowly. "Why? I thought you wanted to know all my secrets."

She clamped her mouth closed, swallowing hard. His gaze moved, heating as it did, over her body. She felt naked, wearing no more than a bra and skirt. And the look in his eyes made her feel even more vulnerable and exposed.

"I've changed my mind. I'll find some other subject to write about. I just…just want to leave this place."

"And me, isn't that right, Rachel? Because you've discovered the monster of your nightmares. The demon of your childhood. The legend you refused to believe. All true, all real. All alive…in me."

She met his eyes. "It's true, isn't it?"

"What do you think?"

She only shook her head. "I never believed you were evil. Tell me I wasn't wrong."

He said nothing, just stared at her.

"Don't kill me," she whispered. "I swear, I'll never tell a soul."

His smile was slow, and almost sad. "I'm not going to kill you, Rachel. And I already know you won't tell my secret."

She blinked, hope washing over her like a flood of warmth and sunlight. "You can trust me. I swear it, Donovan—"

"No," he said. "I can't trust you. That's why you're going to have to stay here."

Her brows rose high, eyes widening. "Stay here? But...but..." She didn't understand, couldn't comprehend. "For how long?"

He said nothing, but she could see his meaning in his eyes, could hear his deep voice tingle up her spine even though he never spoke the word. She heard it, in her soul.

Forever.

Chapter 7

She was as bruised and battered as if I'd beaten her. I felt her pain, in spite of myself, as I bathed each spot in cool water.

But she drew away, her eyes partly angry, but mostly afraid.

"Don't touch me. I won't stay, do you hear me? You have to let me go."

With my simple glance, an icy one, she stilled. And I resumed pressing the cool cloth to the bruises. "You will stay," I said.

"They'll worry about me in the village. They'll come looking."

Her breasts strained against the bra she wore. A small purple welt formed on one of them, and I pressed the cloth gently over it, not taking my hand away, but keeping it there. Feeling her warmth seeping into my palm. And the heat of desire flaring up from within.

She went utterly still, staring at my hand where it rested upon her breast. Her breaths coming shallow and quick.

"Be honest, Rachel. You didn't tell a soul where you were going."

She blinked, and I knew I was right.

"You'll send a note...to Mary at the pub, telling her you've gone traveling and don't know when you'll return."

"I'll do no such thing." And she pulled free of me, leaping to her feet, snatching her blouse from the settee and struggling into it.

"You will do exactly as I tell you, Rachel."

"Never." She surged toward the door, and I stood still, letting her make her foolish attempt. When she tugged, she found the entryway sealed tight. Locked. She went still, her back to me, hand still on the door, and her head slowly lowered. Softly, she whispered, "What are you, Donovan O'Roark? And what are you goin' to do with me?"

"I think you know what I am."

She turned very slowly, and I felt her gaze burning into me, searching my soul. "No. 'Tisn't possible. 'Tis...'tis some elaborate hoax."

"It's not only possible, but true. And I think you know it."

Her eyes narrowed, a little of the fear leaving them. She came nearer, studying me so closely I felt exposed to my bones. But she stopped before she reached me. "There are no such things as vampires," she whispered. "And the tale of Donovan O'Roark is but a legend. Not real."

I stood very still, wondering why I felt so vulnerable, why I was waiting in secret dread of her reaction when she finally realized the truth.

"That's it, isn't it? This is your idea of a joke. You're but tryin' to teach me a lesson." One step, then another, and she stood very close. "You're only trying to scare me, and for a time, you succeeded. But I've come to my senses now, Donovan. So why don't you simply tell me the truth rather than playing out this game and pretending you won't let me leave?"

Raising my hands, I let them rest gently on her shoulders. "It is no game, Rachel. Tell me, why should I let you go the way Dante let Laura Sullivan go a century past? So you can run screaming through the village the way she did? So you can lead a mob back here at the break of dawn to end my miserable life?" Closing my eyes very slowly, I whispered, "Perhaps if I were wise I'd do just that."

But I instantly regretted that impulsive declaration. When I opened my eyes again I saw her frowning at me. "I won't believe any of it. If you're a vampire, prove it to me."

Lowering my head, I shook it slowly. "You have the talk of the villagers. The way they look at me when I pass…as if the devil himself is in their midst. What more proof do you need, lass?"

She shrugged her shoulders. "Turn into a bat," she suggested.

I looked up quickly, sensing the edgy humor creeping into her voice. God, did she really believe this was all a joke? "I'm afraid that's not a skill I've mastered. I've heard that shape-shifting is possible to the truly ancient ones among us. But I'm only two centuries old."

"Barely old enough to drive," she mocked.

Closing my eyes, sighing deeply, I muttered, "Do you have a mirror, Rachel?"

"A mirror?"

I nodded, not looking at her. She hesitated. Then, "Look, d-don't you think you've carried this joke far enough? You knew I wouldn't leave as you told me, so you pulled that prank with the coffin, and your timing was perfect. Though how you could be sure I'd find you in this maze of crumbling stone—I mean, I could've been killed and it really wasn't all that amusing, and—"

"Get the mirror." I met her eyes, stared into them. "Get the mirror, Rachel, and let's get this part of it over with, shall we?"

"You're a lunatic." She dug into her pocket. "This isn't going to prove a thing. I swear, you've made your point. I learned my lesson, my snooping days are over, and I…" She drew a compact out of her pocket, fingered it slowly, and I knew her fear was coming back. She fought it, but it was returning in spite of her skepticism.

"Open it," I told her. "And then you can go back to hating me the way the rest of them do."

"Don't be silly," she said. "They don't even know you." She opened the compact.

"They've known me for two centuries," I said. "I was one of them once." I took the mirror from her hands, bit my lip slightly. "Look, Rachel. See me for the monster everyone else does." And I held the mirror before my face.

She drew a deep breath, and moved around beside me. And then she gasped, and backed away. "It can't be…it can't be true."

I only stood where I was, snapping the despicable mirror closed and tossing it to the settee.

"Oh, it's true."

"And the legend? The tale of how you sat up in your own coffin and the priest tried…"

"Tried to kill me. My own father handed him the mallet and stake. My own mother called me a demon. And the girl I'd planned to marry screamed for my blood."

I heard her try to swallow, and the way she struggled to breathe. "And the rest of it? The belief that you'd return one day to destroy the village and take revenge on the Sullivan women?"

I lowered my head. "Do you believe that's why I've come home, Rachel?"

She blinked, and looked up into my eyes. "You said I couldn't leave. What do you intend to do with me?"

"I don't know."

"Am I in danger here?"

"If I said no, would you believe me?"

Her throat convulsed. "Let me leave, Donovan."

"You weren't so eager to leave me last night, Rachel. Or have you forgotten that kiss in your chamber?"

"That was before…"

"Before what? Before you knew the truth? That I'm a monster, bent on destruction and revenge? You know nothing about me, and yet you readily believe the worst."

For a moment she was silent. Then sighing, she said, "You're right. I'm behaving just the way the others do. Judging you, when I swore I never would. Exactly the way you believe the worst about me."

And her words rocked me. "That I'd betray you simply because my ancestors did. That if you let me go, I'd shout your secrets to the world."

I lowered my head. She was right, that was exactly what I thought. "So we're at an impasse."

She huffed. Folded her arms across her chest. "Are you going to kill me?"

"No." Then I met her eyes. "Do you believe that?"

"I shouldn't, but for some reason I do."

"Good." I literally sighed in relief.

"Don't celebrate, Donovan. Part of the reason I believe it is because I want to. I'm only too aware that I'm likely kidding myself."

"I won't hurt you, Rachel, you have my word on that."

"Will you let me go?"

"I can't. Not…yet."

"When?"

"I don't know." I pressed both hands to my head and turned in a slow circle. "I have to think."

She stood still for a long moment. Then she blinked and looked at the ceiling. "I'm having some trouble believing all this. I should be screaming or running for my life, or fainting, shouldn't I?"

"You already did those things."

Her mouth quirked very slightly, a tremulous hint of a smile. "So how do most women react when you tell them you're a vampire?"

"I've never told another woman."

I didn't look at her when I said it. Instead I turned and walked toward the blazing fireplace, then lowered myself into a chair close to it, seeking the warmth. "But if I had, I imagine they'd have reacted the same way you did. First with horror, then disbelief, and now..." I turned to look back at her, where she still stood. "What are you feeling now, Rachel?"

She moved closer, taking the opposite chair. "I'm mad as hell at you, for keeping me here against my will. As for the other..." Shaking her head quickly side to side, she shrugged. "I'm not sure I know what to make of it. And there's one other thing I'm feeling, Donovan O'Roark."

A hint of panic tickled at my nape. "What?"

"Hunger."

She watched him, still battling an eerie sense of having fallen into some dream world. Dizzy with the weight of his revelations, not sure she believed what her own eyes had shown her, she was dazzled. But not terrified—or not as much as she had been at first.

He went away, leaving her to explore on her own, and she did, thumbing through the books in his bookcase, taking a closer look at the tapestries on his wall. She recalled last night. The kiss. The way his lips had trailed over her throat, and he'd tasted her skin there. The incredible sensations the touch of his mouth had evoked in her. Sensations she'd never felt before. Just at a kiss.

What had he been thinking? Was it the way it was depicted in fiction? Had he been battling some kind of mad bloodlust? Barely restraining himself from taking her life? And why wasn't she paralyzed with fear?

But she wasn't. She was curious now that the fear was beginning to ebb. And more. Still drawn to him as she'd always been. And only now beginning to realize that what she'd believed as a child...might very well be true. It was no longer impossible, was it?

She'd never feared the shadowy figure she saw as her protector when she'd been a child. And she wasn't afraid of him now. Nervous, uncertain, angry, curious. But not afraid.

She must be losing her grip on reality, for she certainly should be.

He appeared then, a bowl of soup steaming in his hands, a glass of something red beside it. As her gaze fell on the scarlet liquid and widened, she heard him mutter, "Wine," and immediately felt foolish.

Of course it was wine. What else would it be?

He set the soup on a marble stand, then moved it closer to her chair. She returned to her seat, eyeing the meal.

"It was the best I could do. The workers left a few supplies in the cupboards when they left this last time."

She tilted her head to one side. "And...what about you?"

He lowered his head. "Don't ask questions if you aren't prepared for the answers, Rachel."

"I don't think anyone can be prepared for something like this. Were you?"

His head came up quickly. "What do you mean?"

"Well...I mean, when you first...how did it happen to you?"

"Why do you want to know?"

She shrugged. "I...I just do. You're holding me prisoner here, the least you can do is make conversation."

"It isn't conversation, it's interrogation."

She scowled at him. "It's curiosity. Nothing more."

"It's a girl after a story. That paper, my secrets, as

you said." He cleared his throat, staring at a spot just past her. "However, maybe it's for the best that you still want to know. I believe I've come up with a solution to our mutual problem here. A compromise."

"Oh?" She sipped soup from her spoon, and dipped in for more. It was hot, tasty. "A bargain, you mean?"

"Yes."

"Well, this is interesting. How can you make a bargain with me when you've already made it clear I'm stuck here whether I like it or not?"

"At least this way you'll get something in return."

"What?"

"Everything you want to know, Rachel. Stay with me, give me time to make certain…arrangements. Do this, and I'll tell you my story. And when I've done the things I need to do, I'll let you go."

She tilted her head to one side. "What kinds of arrangements are you speaking of, Donovan?"

I shrugged, unable to take my eyes from hers, openly curious, the fear fading bit by bit. "I'll need to change my name, establish a new identity, prepare a place for myself to live, a new place, where no one has seen me before."

Shaking her head slowly from side to side, she whispered, "But why?"

"Because you'll know all my secrets. And when you write your paper, others will know. They'll flock here in droves, some merely curious, others…others intent on my destruction."

"I think you're overreacting. No one would even believe it was true…"

"The locals already believe it."

She lowered her head. "This isn't 1898, Donovan. The angry mobs you envision are in your imagination."

"No," I said softly. "They're in my memory. I saw the best friend I'd ever had driven to his death, Rachel. I have no intention of ending my life that way. I won't."

She lifted her gaze to mine, probed my eyes. "I don't suppose I blame you." Then she set her bowl aside, still half filled, as if she'd lost her appetite. "You seem to have given this a lot of thought."

"I have."

"I believe there's one thing you haven't considered, Donovan." I looked at her, waited. She rose and paced to the hearth. Bracing her arms on the mantel she stared into the flames. Their light bathed her face, gleamed in her eyes. "You haven't credited me with an ounce of humanity. So it will come as a surprise to you to learn I am, indeed, human, since you seem to believe I'm the same sort of monster you keep calling yourself."

"I never implied—"

"I would never write a paper that would drive a man from his home, force him to give up his entire life. Why would I? For a degree? 'Tis hardly a fair exchange."

I searched her eyes, looking for the lie. But I didn't find it.

"None of this is necessary, Donovan. I'll simply find another subject for my paper."

My eyes narrowed. I almost wanted to believe her.

"Lord, but you think I'm lyin' to ya, don't you, Donovan?"

I had to look away. "You might be lying," I said.

"Or you might be telling the truth. I can't be sure. And I'm afraid I can't risk taking you at your word."

"I've never broken my word in my life!"

She declared it with such fierceness it nearly shook my resolve. Lowering my head, unable to face her, I whispered, "I'm sorry."

She faced me, then glanced beyond me toward the door, and when I managed to look at her again, there were tears building in her eyes. "You really are going to keep me here—like a prisoner—aren't you?"

"I have no choice, Rachel."

"The hell you don't, Donovan O'Roark. The hell you don't. You've been right about one thing, I'll grant you that. You truly *are* a monster. And not because you're a vampire, but because you have no heart. No trust. Nor a care for anyone besides yourself. Make your arrangements if you must. An' when you're ready to set me free, come fetch me."

Her anger washed over me like a tempest, and I actually staggered backward under its force. Then she whirled and stomped up the stairs, intent, I was certain, on finding her room, slamming its door and throwing the lock. And it would have been a very dramatic exit, too, if she hadn't paused, panting, halfway up the stone staircase. Without looking back she said, "Kindly guide me back to my room, O'Roark. I've no desire to become lost in this mausoleum again."

I nodded, and slowly mounted the stairs. When I got to her, I touched her elbow, cupped it in my hand, and she pulled away. "I am the way I am because I have to be," I said slowly as we moved up the stairs. "It's a matter of self-preservation. If Dante didn't teach me another thing, he taught me this. We're meant to be alone. To live alone. To trust no one. It's the only way we can survive. He forgot his own most important lessons. And he died because of it.''

She'd stopped walking, and when I glanced down to see why, she was staring at me, still angry, but there was something else in her eyes as well. ''Alone,'' she whispered. ''An' just how long have you been living by those words, Donovan?''

''Ever since Dante died,'' I told her softly.

''A hundred years…''

I shrugged and started walking again, touching her elbow, propelling her upward. ''One gets used to it.''

''No, I don't believe one does. 'Tis little wonder you've no idea how to behave toward another.''

I turned at the head of the stairs, stopped before a large door. ''I think you'll like this room better, Rachel. I…I had it decorated myself.''

She blinked. ''For whom?''

I looked at her. ''I…for no one. It was a whim. A foolish whim.'' I pushed the door open, turned a knob affixed to the wall, and watched as the gaslights slowly came up. I'd connected the lines while she slept, ignited all the pilots, even cleaned the glass globes. I hadn't really expected her to leave as I'd ordered. But I hadn't expected her to find my resting place either.

She stepped past me into the room I'd had built for no imaginable reason. I remembered more than Dante's betrayal at the hands of a woman, and subsequent death. I also remembered my friend's happiness, the glow about him when he'd been in love, and believed himself loved in return. Even I had been hesitant to berate Dante or speak my doubts of Laura

Sullivan's loyalty aloud. There must be no other happiness in the world like that of love.

And while I'd existed in utter solitude all this time, my mind had opportunity to wander. To wonder. To dream. What would it be like? What if it happened for me?

And that fantastical dream had inspired me to build these rooms. The suite I'd created for a dream lover I would never know. The rooms I would give to her if she were real. The rooms we would share.

Empty. They stood empty and likely always would.

Except for Rachel. For a few nights, they'd be filled with a woman whose beauty was worthy of them.

"Lordy, but this is lovely..." She stepped inside, twirling in a slow circle to take in the sheer mauve fabric draped from the bed's canopy to form curtains. The carpet, a similar color and so thick her feet left imprints as she moved. The glass doors, that opened out onto a stone balcony fit for a princess. The elaborately hand-tooled woodwork, painted gold to match the trim on the velvety wallpaper, and the tiebacks for the mauve drapes.

Her smile came, despite the situation. And I secretly relished it. The rooms were wasted with no one to enjoy them. That they gave her pleasure pleased some secret part of me.

"There's more," I told her, taking her hand and drawing her toward one of two doors. "The bath, here." She gasped at the sunken tub, the golden fixtures. Plump towels in deep green lined every rack, and deep rugs the same shade covered the floor. Bottles of expensive oils and fragrances lined the shelves.

"Who did you dream of entertaining here, Donovan? A queen?"

My lover. The one I would never know. But I didn't tell her that.

"There's a sitting room as well," I said, going back to the bedroom and pushing open a second door to reveal a room lined with bookshelves, two window seats, a small pedestal table with a pair of cushioned chairs, and a settee, sofa, and rocker. A fireplace laid ready, but unlit, and gas lamps lined the stone walls.

But she wasn't looking at the room. She was looking at me. "Why all this?" she whispered. "Why go to all this trouble if you truly intended to live your life alone, Donovan O'Roark?"

I shook my head. "As I said, a foolish whim."

"No, I don't think so." She came closer, tipping her head back, searching my eyes. "You're lonely. And tired of being, I think."

"That has nothing to do with..." I lowered my eyes, my voice trailing off.

"With what? With why you're keeping me here?" She blinked and looked around her. "You might believe that, Donovan, but I don't think it's true. I think you built this room with every intention of bringing someone here to fill it. To fill...you."

I turned fully now, glancing at the fireplace as if it fascinated me and trying not to tremble in fear at her words. "Thinking that way will only confuse you, Rachel. I need no one. I share my life with *no one*. You're here because I cannot let you leave. But I will, the moment my arrangements are made and it's safe for me to do so. That's all. There is no more to it than that."

I felt her staring at my back. "All right. If you say so."

I turned to go. She stayed silent as I stepped into the hall and closed the door. And then I stood there, trembling.

God, could she be right?

Chapter 8

"All the modern conveniences," she muttered, alone in her suite of rooms. He'd gone, left her here on her own, and he probably believed she preferred it that way.

She didn't. This place was too large, too hollow and quiet. Like a tomb. She soaked in a tub brimming with steamy water, and sprinkled some of the aromatic oils in with her. Her bruises needed the pampering, and the heat did ease her aches somewhat.

But she'd have to put her torn, dirty clothes back on when she got out, and the idea didn't appeal. She didn't suppose he'd let her go long enough to rush back to her room above the pub and fetch her own things. So would he expect her to spend her entire time here in the same clothing?

Moreover, did he expect her to spend it alone, in these rooms?

He couldn't. She wouldn't stand for that.

When the water began to cool, she got out, wrapped herself in a thick green towel, and stepped back into the bedroom. The double doors of a built-in wardrobe beckoned, and she went slowly toward them, hesitantly reached out, and pulled them open.

"Lordy..." The closet nearly spilled over with clothing. Satins, silks and lace in a hundred shades cascaded from hangers.

To one side were drawers built into the wall, and as she tugged them open she found nightgowns almost too fragile to touch, and underthings.

"But why?" She touched the garments, pulled the hangers along the rack one by one, saw that the sizes varied as widely as the colors and fabrics did. She paused at a long full skirt, paired on the hanger with a white off-the-shoulder blouse. It looked like something a Gypsy might wear.

"Take anything you like."

She caught her breath and whirled, automatically clutching at the towel around her. "Donovan. I didn't hear you come in."

"I expected the door to be locked."

She blinked, saying nothing. But as she searched his eyes this time, she saw the pain there. The loneliness. He'd built these rooms on a whim, he'd said. But it was obvious to her he'd prepared them for a woman. Was she real? she wondered. Or only some distant wish he'd allowed himself to indulge in secretly?

When she still didn't speak, he took a step backward, his hand still on the doorknob. "I'm sorry. I'll leave you alone."

"No, don't go."

He stopped abruptly, looking at her. And she saw

his gaze dip beyond her face, very briefly touching on her body, covered only by a towel. And she knew her bruises showed, and her hair was damp and tangled, hanging over her shoulders. And still she felt some deep reaction to that gaze. As if it were truly admiration in his eyes, and not only surprise.

"You...want me to stay?"

She turned back to the closet, removing the clothes she'd been drawn to, not looking at him. "If you're going to keep me here, Donovan, the least you can do is entertain me. I'll go crazy if I'm to spend all my time in these rooms alone. Lovely though they are, I'd soon die of boredom."

He lowered his head. "I...thought you'd want to rest."

"It's too early to rest. Besides, if I'm to sleep all night and you're to sleep all day..." She blinked, and tilted her head to one side. "You do, don't you?"

He only nodded.

"Well, then how are you going to keep to our bargain? When will you have time to tell me all your secrets, Donovan?"

He brought his gaze level with hers quickly, and a frown marred his brow. "So you've decided to write the paper after all?"

She shrugged, draping the clothes over her arm and heading toward the bathroom. "You can believe what you wish. You will anyway. The truth is, I'm curious."

"That's all?" he asked.

She paused in the doorway to glance back at him. "Yes. That's all. I'll only be a minute." And she closed the door. Quickly, she donned the skirt, long and loose, and moving around her like a spring breeze.

Then the blouse, its sleeves dipping low on her shoulders, and the elastic waistline clinging high enough so that a bit of her midriff was visible. She ran a brush through her hair, frowning at the lack of a mirror in the room.

No mirrors. As if, even in his fondest fantasies, he hadn't allowed himself to imagine a mortal woman filling his loneliness. Only another creature like him.

She didn't fit the bill in the least, did she?

She blinked, and then frowned hard. It didn't matter! What made her think such a thing? Oh, but she knew. Was knowing more and more with each moment that passed. He was that gentle soul who'd pulled her from the river, he was that dark angel who'd comforted her when she'd cried in her bed, alone and afraid. And she'd loved him all her life.

He didn't trust her. She wasn't even certain she could blame him for that. She was a Sullivan.

But she was meant to set it right, she sensed that. She was meant for him.

Finally, clearing her throat and gathering her wits about her, she stepped back into the bedroom.

Donovan looked her up and down, blinking as if in surprise.

"It's hardly modern," she said, fingering the fabric of the skirt.

"It's lovely. *You're* lovely."

She averted her face, feeling the heat creeping into her cheeks. "These rooms are so different from the rest of the castle...so is the great hall."

"Actually, it's only the north wing that's still in disrepair. Unfortunately, that's where you ended up earlier. Most of the place has been restored, updated." He reached out to move her hair off her forehead, and gingerly examined the bump there, a result of her collision with the wall. "There's even electricity."

"But you use the gas lamps?"

"I prefer them. Are you hurting much, Rachel?"

"I'm sore, but only a wee bit. I'll be fine," she told him. She eyed the soft golden glow emanating from the fixtures in the room and nodded. "I agree, the gas lamps are far nicer. Will you show me around, then? Um…the restored parts, I mean. I've no interest in seeing the north wing again."

"That's good. I'm afraid that wing is off-limits while you're here, Rachel."

She searched his face. "So there are some secrets you won't be sharing with me?"

His eyes hooded, he shook his head. "The north wing is unsafe, as you've already learned. Stay out of it, Rachel."

Her curiosity rose to new heights. "All right," she said.

She didn't think he believed her.

"Come." He offered his arm.

She took it. Closed her hand around his upper arm, and felt him. Warm, not cold as one might expect. He felt real. He felt like a man. Not a monster.

He had, she mused, the deepest, bluest eyes she'd ever seen, and hair a soft, dark brown, nearly black. She'd been incredibly attracted to him at first. And she still was.

He led her through the main hall of this wing. Showing her other bedrooms, none in use, but many ready for company. Odd, for a man who expected to be alone forever. Then he guided her back down the stairs, where he showed her the library, a huge room lined with books on shelves that towered to the ceilings. Leather chairs sat in pairs by the towering windows.

"'Tis a sad room," she said, speaking in muted tones as if she were at a funeral.

"Sad? Why do you say so?"

She walked forward slowly, pausing between two chairs beside a tall window that was completely enshrouded by heavy velvet drapes. "The seats…they're in pairs. All of them. But you've no one to sit in them with you."

When she glanced back at him, he only shrugged. She turned forward again, and fingered the deep honey velvet. "It's as if the world is a place you'd rather not see. But it's too beautiful to shut out, you know."

Stepping forward, he pulled the cord and opened the drapes. "Yes, I know."

She glanced out, then drew a surprised breath. The windows looked out on a flagstone path that meandered amid lush shrubs and bushes she couldn't identify. In the center, the moonlight glistened on a fountain, ancient, but completely restored. A stone image of some pagan goddess stood on a pedestal, spilling clear water from her outspread palms to splash into the pool spreading below her.

"'Tis beautiful," she whispered, but then she drew her gaze away, staring in confusion at the other windows, their draperies drawn tight.

"They're only drawn by day, Rachel. As soon as darkness falls, I part them." He looked past her, into his garden. "I love the night."

"And the daylight?" she asked, in a voice that emerged as a bare whisper.

"It would kill me. The way it killed Dante." He

turned to face her. "Would you like to walk in my garden?"

"Yes. Yes, I'd like that very much."

He reached for her hand. He seemed to make a habit of doing that. She let him take it, though, and followed as he led her to the far end of the library, to yet another set of drapes. These parted to reveal French doors, that opened onto the garden.

"It's larger than I could tell from the window."

Nodding, he cradled her hand in his, perhaps unaware of doing so. Or maybe not. "It stretches out on this side, and around to the rear of the castle, reaching nearly to the cliffs."

She fingered a delicate-looking vine that clung to the castle wall. Narrow green buds nodded heavily from it. "I've never seen this before."

"Wait," he told her. "We'll sit. Here." He pointed to a stone bench with claw feet and lion's heads for arms. They went to it, sat down.

"Is that why you rest by day? Because you can't be exposed to sunlight?"

He turned toward her. "Not entirely."

She only waited, willing him to answer while he searched her face for...something. Her true evil intent, she imagined.

"As daylight approaches our functions begin to slow. By dawn we're usually unconscious, whether we want to be or not. And it's not the sort of sleep from which one can be roused."

"Like...death?"

"Not so deep as death, I imagine. But far deeper than any mortal's sleep."

"So if someone were to poke you, or shake you or shout in your ear..."

"Or set me aflame or drive a stake through my heart," he finished for her. "I'd be aware of it, but likely unable to react enough to defend myself."

"That must be frightening."

"It's the reason for the coffins, hidden in the bowels of the castle. I'm most vulnerable while I rest...and why I'm telling you any of this I can't say."

"Maybe you're starting to trust me?"

"I trust no one, Rachel. Beautiful mortal females least of all."

She blinked. "You...find me beautiful?"

He stared at her for a long moment, and his eyes seemed to heat as they moved lower, raking her before slowly meeting hers again. Then he simply turned away, facing the castle, and the curious vines.

"Look."

She looked. Then she caught her breath as one by one, the green buds seemed to split. Bit by bit they opened, milk-white petals unfurling, their faces turning up to the moon as if in welcome. Welcoming the night.

"I've never seen anything like them."

"They're very rare. Moon lilies. I had them imported."

"They're beautiful." As she looked around, she noticed other plants in bloom.

"I have no flower that closes up by night. Everything either remains open through the dark hours, or only blooms in darkness."

"It makes sense. Day lilies or morning glories would be wasted here."

He nodded.

Rachel yawned, quickly covering her mouth with her hand.

"It's late," he said. "You've had an exhausting day. You should rest now."

She tilted her head to one side. "I can always sleep late in the morning. 'Tis not as if I'll miss anything."

He nodded, getting to his feet as she did, and guiding her back along the paths. She trailed one hand through the water of the fountain as they passed, and he watched a little oddly as she did. Then they were at the doors, and he was ushering her inside.

He pulled the doors closed behind them. Reached for the lock, one that would have to be opened with a key.

"Donovan," she asked, and he paused, and turned to face her instead.

"Have you truly been alone all this time?"

He frowned. "I deal with others only when I'm forced to."

"Well, that's not exactly what I meant."

"What then?"

She lowered her gaze. "I...I mean...have you been...you know. Without a woman? All this time? An entire century?"

He blinked, gave his head a shake. "What odd questions you ask, Rachel," he said. "Why do you want to know?"

She shrugged, and realized she'd been breathlessly awaiting his answer. "I...perhaps I shouldn't have asked something so personal." She met his gaze, though, battling the turmoil in her belly. "But you did say you'd tell my anything I wanted to know."

"I did, didn't I?" His voice was no longer gentle. In fact he seemed angry. He gripped her arm, his touch careful, but firm and possessive, as he led her onward.

And she noticed that he seemed to have forgotten all
about locking that door.

But she wasn't sure what had replaced it in his
mind, and that frightened her more than anything ever
had.

Chapter 9

I knew what she was doing. Trying to get to me. Trying to make me feel something for her. Desire, and perhaps something more. Because if I did, I'd soften. I'd care. I'd let her go, despite the fact that it could cost me everything.

She was wrong, of course. I'd taught myself too well over the centuries I'd spent alone. I would not care. Not for her, nor anyone.

I did desire her. She'd succeeded in that regard. But not because of her clever ploys. I'd desired her from the moment I'd seen her again, grown into a beautiful woman, standing in the doorway of that pub and beckoning me inside.

I opened her chamber door, but didn't stand politely outside when she went in. Instead, I followed. And closed the door behind me.

She turned when she heard the thunk of the door

banging shut, and her eyes widened, though she quickly tried to hide her alarm.

"You didn't tell me, Rachel. Why did you ask what you did?"

She lifted her chin. "I apologized for that," she said. "I was only curious."

"I think it was something more than that." I took a step toward her, but stopped when she backed away.

"I don't know what you mean."

"Yes, you do. You're playing a dangerous game, Rachel. Perhaps you don't realize how dangerous."

She shook her head. "I didn't mean—"

"Since you're so curious about sex, I'll tell you. It's very different, sex with a vampire."

Lowering her head, her cheeks flaming, she closed her eyes. "I don't want to hear this."

"You asked. You'll hear the answer. Look at me, Rachel."

Her jaw tight, she did as I asked. And I sent my will into her mind, took control, as easily this time as flicking a switch. "Come here."

She opened her mouth as if to refuse, then blinked in shock as her body disobeyed. Her feet, scuffing the floor, propelled her forward. "Closer," I told her, and she came. She stood very close to me. Head tipped back, eyes frightened, but aroused, glistening with a titillating mixture of fear and desire as she waited. And I knew why she responded this time when she hadn't before. Because it was what she wanted.

I lifted a hand to her face, touched her cheek very lightly, and trailed my fingers downward. Over her jaw, and chin, and then gently down her neck, pausing to feel the heady beat of her pulse there. Desire rushed through me. It wasn't supposed to. I hadn't planned it this way.

My fingers trailed lower, touching delicate collarbones, tracing her sternum, and then flitting lightly over one breast. I felt her response, the soft breath she drew, the tightening of her nipple beneath my fingers. But more than that, I felt my own reaction. She'd angered me...her power over me, the danger that power represented. My own apparent inability to remain untouched by her, to resist her allure. I'd meant to frighten her away, to show her how dangerous I could be so she'd stop tempting me with her eyes, and her words, and every damned breath she drew. Instead, I was only making it worse.

"Please...."

It was a whisper, a plea. I drew my hand away, but my fingertips tingled still. I wanted her.

"Playing on my desires is a risky game, Rachel," I told her. "Because I can touch your mind with mine." I stared down into her eyes. "Kiss me, Rachel."

She leaned up, her lips trembling, but parting, as they touched mine. Then touched them again. I stood motionless for a moment, but then shuddered and bowed over her, taking her mouth, possessing it, invading it, as she pressed her body tight to mine.

She tasted like honey. Her effect was like that of some addictive drug, and my craving for her more powerful than anything I'd ever known.

When I finally lifted my mouth away from hers, I was breathless, my heart pounding. But hers was as well.

Drawing a steadying breath, I delivered the final lesson. "Do you want to know the worst of it, Rachel?

The bit of knowledge that will frighten you the most?"

She nodded, only once.

"Even with this power, I couldn't make you do anything you didn't truly want to do. Your will is too strong for that." And with that, I released her, closed my mind off again, broke the connection.

She stood there, staring at me, but the fire in her eyes came as much, I thought, from anger as from the desire that still lingered there.

"You...you bastard." It was a whisper.

"I thought I behaved with a great deal of restraint. I didn't want to, Rachel. I don't think you did either."

She looked away. "Are you enjoying this, Donovan? Trying to humiliate me?"

"I was only making a point. Don't try to seduce me into letting you go, Rachel. I won't be played that way. I won't be manipulated. I may desire you but I'll never care for you. Never. I'm incapable of it. But if you insist on arousing my desires, I won't be denied. I'll have you."

She glared at me, her eyes snapping with a fire I thought I'd extinguished by now. "If the only way you can have a woman is by taking control of her mind, then I pity you, Donovan O'Roark."

I opened my mouth to reply, only to find myself unable to find words.

"And if you think what you've accomplished is so impressive, you're a blind man." Without another word, she gripped the elastic waistband of her blouse and tugged it over her head. And then she stood there, breasts bared and perfect, plump and firm, swelling toward me like some forbidden fruit of Eden.

She moved closer to me. "Go on," she whispered.

"Touch me." She gripped my hand, and drew it upward, pressing my palm to her breast. I closed my eyes as the warmth of her filled my hand. Air hissed through my teeth, and I felt the heat stirring, bubbling up inside me like a volcano, long dormant, about to erupt. I told myself to turn away, to leave the room, but I couldn't. My hand moved, caressed, squeezed. And then my other hand rose to do likewise, and my eyes fell closed as the desire became overwhelming.

Her breath stuttered out of her, her head tipping backward. Exposing her neck, satin-soft and utterly tempting. Lying before me like an offering to a dark god. An offering I wanted to take.

"So you see?" she whispered. "This power you have over me…it isn't only you who wields it. I can as well. And if it was seduction I had on my mind, Donovan, I'd have done more than ask a simple question of you."

And with that she took a quick sharp step backward, away from me, and left me standing there, panting, aroused to a state near madness, wondering if she had a clue what she had done.

"You're a fool." I snagged her waist, and jerked her closer, one hand pushing her head backward as my mouth parted.

Her body crushed to mine, I bent over her and sank my teeth into her tender throat. She gasped, stiffened, but then as I suckled her, extracting the precious fluid from her body, she uncoiled. Her body melted in my arms, and her head fell back farther. She arched her neck, pushing against my mouth. "Yes," she whispered. "Oh, yessss…"

I drew away, not sated, only having sampled the

barest taste of her...wanting more. Panting with wanting more.

Her hand stroked me, caressing the throbbing hardness between my legs, and in spite of myself, I arched against her touch. But I couldn't do this. Couldn't take her the way my body was screaming for me to do.

Because there was something more than desire here, something that frightened me. This entire demonstration of mine had backfired, hadn't it? She was the one who was supposed to be frightened.

I gazed down into her eyes, and knew she wasn't. Not really. Oh, there was some fear in her eyes, but it only served to enhance the wanting there.

As if she could see the indecision, my hesitation and my need to leave this room, she reached for the skirt, unfastened it, began to push it lower.

I closed my eyes, turning my back to her. "This...is not going to happen."

"You want it, too."

"Yes. I want to pierce your body with mine and take you. Just as I want to drain every drop of blood from your succulent throat, Rachel."

"You wouldn't hurt me."

I spun around. "What if hurting you is exactly what I want to do?"

"You don't." She shoved the skirt to the floor, stepped out of the panties, and came to me again, her hands sliding up the front of my shirt.

I gripped her wrists and stared down at her. Naked, aroused, all but begging me to take her. So aroused she barely knew what she was doing. I stilled her hands when she started unbuttoning my shirt. "Stop it, Rachel."

She froze, blinking up at me. When I released her

hands she lowered them to her sides, and I noticed her trembling, head to toe.

She turned her back to me, and not knowing what else to do, I left the room.

What had she done?

Oh, God. Rachel flung herself onto the bed, hiding her face in the satin coverlet, battling tears of utter shame. "It was him," she muttered. "He *made* me behave that way. He..." But she knew it wasn't true. He hadn't forced anything on her. She'd acted on her own, except for that one brief interlude when he'd meant to demonstrate his alleged power over her. And she'd had to reciprocate—to salvage her pride by showing him that she had power, too. Feminine power to bend the man to *her* will.

And she had. Perhaps too much, because he'd lost control. She'd felt it, sensed it. And understood it because it had happened to her as well.

She'd behaved like a well-trained whore. Who *was* this woman in her body? Not her, not Rachel Sullivan. She'd never act that way with any man. Never.

But he wasn't any man. He was her guardian.

Wasn't he? What if she was wrong?

She had to get out of here. Now, tonight. She couldn't trust herself to remain near him, couldn't think straight this close to him. What was this thing she was feeling, this certainty that he was meant to be hers, now and forever? Was it foolishness? A childish dream?

She sat up slowly, wiping her eyes and scanning the room for her clothes. Heat flooded her face when she spied them thrown carelessly on the floor. She'd done that. Undressed for him, unashamed, brazen. No, it wasn't her, but some wild woman who'd been living silently inside her. Hiding, and choosing now to emerge—the worst possible time.

No, she had to leave. She tugged on her clothes, paced to the door and cracked it open, just slightly. He was nowhere in sight. But loud, crashing music came up from below—the great hall. Beethoven, she thought. Violent in its power.

She crept into the hall and toward the stairs, then down them only a bit. Just enough so she could see him in the great hall. He stood near the blazing hearth, head lowered, eyes closed. Utterly still as the music smashed over him.

Licking her dry lips, she moved lower, reaching the bottom of the stairs, not taking her eyes off him until she slipped around the corner. He never moved, never flinched, or even raised his head. She'd moved in near silence, but somehow she'd expected him to know. To be aware of her, as if crediting him with some sixth sense he couldn't possibly...

Or maybe he could. But he didn't notice her.

She'd planned to make her escape tomorrow while he...slept. But she couldn't wait, not now. He was too confusing...and too angry at her for her feelings.

Her hand rose to touch the spot where he'd fed at her throat, and she felt the tiny wounds there. Not sore, but tingling with erotic awareness, so tender now, so sensitized. Just touching them reawakened the memory of his kiss, his touch...his mouth working her there.

She had to pause, lean back against a cool stone wall and draw deep breaths into her lungs. She wanted him. She desired a man she truly didn't know, though it felt as if she'd always known him. A vampire, but that made no difference to her.

She couldn't stay, because Lord only knew what she might do if she stayed. If he came to her room again, kissed her again...

But he wouldn't. He didn't want to care for her, he'd made that clear. Straightening, she squared her shoulders, and followed the corridor to the library. Then with one last glance behind her, to confirm he hadn't followed, she went inside. The French doors remained as they'd been before. Closed, but unlocked, and a moment later she was outside the castle. Free, in his beautiful garden of night.

For a moment she hesitated. It was such a contradiction, a man like him, having a place like this. As if he was capable of appreciating pure beauty. As if he had the soul of a poet, and not a determined hermit.

Shaking that thought away, she walked around the castle, each step faster than the one before, until at last she was running. Her hair blowing in the night wind as she pushed her muscles to their limits, racing through the darkness along the path, ever farther from the castle and toward the road that led to it. A road that meandered among woods, and later fields, and the village itself.

Free. She was free at last.

And that was when she heard the hounds.

Chapter 10

Hounds? She didn't understand. Not at first. But then she heard the men's voices in the distance, village men. And then the hounds drowned them out. Crying, baying in a horrific cacophony of noise that chilled her blood.

Marney Neal's hounds, she thought vaguely, knowing the animals were trained hunters. But they didn't hunt game, they hunted men. Marney trained them for that purpose. So if they were out tonight they must be after some criminal.

Then why were they heading toward the castle?

Donovan?

She swallowed hard, but her throat was dry. And then she stood there, frozen in fear, as the hounds rounded a curve in the road and came into sight. Running, bearing down on her. A horde of galloping, baying death. She whirled, panic taking hold as she surged into the woods, even knowing they'd offer no protection. But the dogs were too fast, too determined. One leapt, and his forelegs clawed her back, propelling her forward. Instinctively she rolled to her back, but the beast was upon her, teeth flashing. And then, suddenly the dog was hurled away.

Donovan. He stood above her, surrounded by the dogs, wielding a club as they lunged and snapped at him. "Go," he shouted. "Run for the castle. Go!" One snatched his arm in horrible teeth. She heard fabric tearing, saw blood as Donovan clubbed the animal uselessly.

Shaking, dirty and terrified, she struggled to her feet. And then she staggered toward the road. But she stopped as Donovan went down and the dogs leapt in for the kill. Screaming, she crouched low, scooping up hands full of debris and hurling it at their tawny bodies to get their attention.

"Here, you filthy beasts! Here! Come!" One dog turned toward her snarling. "Come for me then," she cried, and then she turned to run, knowing they'd follow.

And they did. She made it to the road with the hounds on her heels, now. But the men were in sight, and she cried out to them. "Marney Neal, call off your hounds! Call them off!"

"Sakes, 'tis Rachel!" someone said. But then the dogs were on her, knocking her down once more.

One of the men raced forward, shouting commands at the dogs. Thankfully, they were trained well enough to obey at once. The dogs fell away from her as one, and sat as docile as pups, awaiting the word of their master. And then Marney himself, beer on his breath, was leaning over her, helping her to her feet.

"Rachel, fer the love of God, where've ye been?

We've been worried to death for you! Are you harmed, girl? Are you harmed?''

She let him help her to her feet. "What in the name of God were you thinking, turning those killers lose on me like that, Marney Neal! I should have you jailed!''

"Nay, 'twas for you I done it, child. You disappeared and we feared the murderin' O'Roark had taken you to his lair!''

"What utter foolishness!'' She brushed the dirt and twigs from her clothes, and sent a furtive glance toward the woods where Donovan must still by lying. Perhaps dead, already.

"Is it, Rachel?'' Marney eyed her suspiciously. "I take the hounds through these woods every night since that bastard has been in residence. Just to be sure he stays within his castle walls, and doesn't venture out to make victims of my neighbors.''

"You're a superstitious fool. Donovan O'Roark is harmless.''

"Then what are you doin' here wandering these godforsaken lands? And where have you been these past two nights, Rachel?''

She lifted her chin, met his eyes. "Had I agreed to wed you as you wanted, I'd feel that to be your business, Marney Neal, but since I turned you down I've nothing to say.''

"You've been at the castle. As his lover?'' he asked.

"As a guest, Marney. No more than that. Mary knows full well my interest in the legends associated with Donovan's ancestor. He's offered to help me with my research.''

"Indeed!'' Marney huffed, and eyed the castle as

if it were something demonic. "Well, you're found now. Come with me, back to the village. Mary will be relieved to see you there, and well."

She glanced again toward the woods, then quickly at Marney again. "No. I'll return to the castle tonight. Tell Mary I'm fine and will contact her shortly."

He set his feet, hands on his hips. "I'll not have it."

"*You* have no say in it. Now kindly take your hounds and go home, Marney, before I decide to inform the authorities about this deadly pack you set on me. They nearly killed me. No doubt the law would see them all shot just to preserve the safety of the citizens."

"You wouldn't—"

"I will, I swear on my mother's grave. Unless you leave now, I will."

His eyes held hers only for a moment. Then lowered. "You've changed, Rachel Sullivan. The States have done this to ya, no doubt. Or perhaps 'twas that monster in the castle."

"I've grown up. I won't have you or anyone running my life for me. Not anymore."

"Fine. Ye deserve whatever fate befalls ye. But mark my words, Rachel, the man of that castle is no human bein'. He's a monster, and more dangerous to you than my dogs ever could be."

He turned to go, with his dogs leaping up to follow, tails wagging. Harmless pets. Rachel waited until they were out of sight. Then she turned and ran back into the darkness of the trees, falling to her knees beside the dark shape on the ground.

"Donovan?"

He opened his eyes, his face pain-racked and pale

in the night. "You could have gone with him," he whispered.

"Aye, I could have." She tore strips from her skirt and tied them tight round the wounds to stanch the bleeding. She'd never seen so much bleeding. "Can you stand? Walk?"

He tried to get up, faltered, and Rachel gripped him quickly, helping him to his feet. Then, pulling his arm around her shoulders, she propelled him forward, through the woods toward the castle. The road would be easier, but she'd prefer they not be seen by prying eyes. Especially Marney Neal's.

"There's a trail to the left," he managed, though he spoke through gritted teeth. "A shortcut."

She took him that way, found the trail and followed it, but felt his eyes on her face. "Why?" he asked her, breathless, still bleeding.

"Don't ask foolish questions, Donovan O'Roark."

He leaned on her heavily, and when he spoke, his words were slurred. "Is it foolish to ask why? You were free. It's what you said you wanted."

"I wanted my freedom, yes," she said. "But not at the cost of your life." She shook her head. "You jumped into the midst of those hounds as if you thought yourself invincible. You could've been killed." He said nothing, and she tugged him faster. "Don't be telling me again how you can care for no one besides yourself, Donovan O'Roark, for 'tis a bald-faced lie an' you know it."

"No—"

"No? No, you say? Why, then, would you risk your own life to save mine?"

He shook his head. She couldn't see his face, because he kept it so low. Or perhaps he had no choice, too weak to hold it upright.

"You're no more selfish than you are a hermit," she said. "You're selfless, and more lonely than you even realize. An' I'll tolerate no more of your non-sensical lies. I've seen through this mask you wear, Donovan, and you can't don it again."

"You're seeing what you want to see."

Her hand felt damp, and she looked down to see the blood dripping from it where she clung to him. "Damnation, why do you bleed so?"

"It...it's part of what I am. Bleeding to death is one of the few ways I can die."

"That and sunlight," she whispered, glancing at the sky between the trees.

"There's plenty of time before dawn, Rachel. More's the pity. It is only with the day sleep these wounds will heal. Until then—"

"Until then I'll stay beside you and be sure you don't bleed to death," she told him.

It shocked me. Astounded me, really. But that was precisely what she did.

My unwilling captive vanished, the rebel was gone. Her stubborn determination, her boundless energy, was directed toward helping me now, rather than es-caping me. She eased me onto the settee in the great hall, then ran back toward the door. For the briefest of moments I thought she would run from me now that she'd seen me safely back to the castle. I was utterly bewildered when, instead, she turned the lock.

"What—"

"For Marney Neal and those narrow-minded fools like him," she said, back at my side now. "Those hounds were meant for you, not me, Donovan. You must know it. An' those men would have stood gladly by an' let them tear out your heart had it been you and not me on that road.'' She knelt on the floor beside me, shoving her hands through her hair, her cheeks pink with exertion, or frustration, or anger. ''Lordy, how do you live like this?''

It wasn't a question she expected me to answer. Already she knelt beside the settee, tugging my shirt away to reveal the jagged tear in my side. Tearing the skirt she wore, until little remained but shreds, she packed the wound, and wrapped strips around my waist, tying them so tightly I could scarcely breathe. Her every touch brought on the most intense pain—and the most excruciating pleasure—I'd ever known. I thrilled at her hands on me, no matter the reason.

''Why do you come back here at all, Donovan,'' she asked. ''There must be places in the world where you're safe.''

''There are.'' I looked around the hall, my gaze straying to the hearth where Dante and I used to sit and talk for hours on end, or read in companionable silence while the fire danced. ''But this place is…dear to me.''

''Then move it.''

I only frowned at her.

'''Tis done all the time. Rich folk buying castles and having them moved stone by stone to the place of their choice.''

I shook my head slowly. ''It wouldn't be Ireland.''

''No.''

''You came back, Rachel. Despite the narrow-mindedness, despite the unwanted attentions…''

Her head came up sharply. "An' what would you know of that?"

"I know. Marney Neal would do well to know when to give up." I smiled slightly, despite the burning pain in my side. "Before you do him bodily harm."

"Aye, an' he's lucky I didn't tonight." She eyed my skin, shaking her head at all the blood. "You've watched me, haven't you?"

So she knew. I'd sensed it before. That she was aware somehow of my presence those nights when I'd drawn near to her, pulled as if by some irresistible force.

"There was a time, long ago," she whispered, dabbing now at the blood with a dry bit of crumpled fabric, "when I nearly drowned in the river near my home. Someone plucked me out, breathed into my lungs, and brought me back. But even as I lay there, choking, he vanished." She stopped wiping and met my eyes. "'Twas you, wasn't it?"

I lowered my head.

"And later, after my folks passed on. When I lay awake, frightened and alone, someone came to me in the darkness. Just a dream, I thought when I was older. But 'twas no dream, was it, Donovan? 'Twas you, the man who told me he was my guardian angel, that I'd be safe, always."

I released a long, slow breath. "It was."

"Did you ever know what that meant to me? Did you know how I slept soundly, how I believed it, how I clung to it? My parents were gone, but I had someone, still. Someone watching over me as my dear ma had, protecting me as my da had done. 'Twas the second time you saved me, you know."

"No," I said. "I didn't know."

"Now you do. Quite a thing for a self-servin' monster to do, wasn't it, Donovan?"

"You don't understand," I began. But I wasn't certain I could explain. I didn't understand it either. Not fully.

"Make me understand then."

Nodding, I shifted to one side, so she could sit beside me on the edge of the settee. I saw her gaze shift quickly to the wound again, as if to assure herself my movement hadn't started the bleeding up again. "Dante told me of our nature, long ago. He told me that only certain mortals can become…what we are."

Her intense expression told him how interested she was in hearing more.

"As a mortal, I had a rare antigen in my blood. It's known as belladonna. That made me one of those few, one of the Chosen, as we call them."

"That's fascinating. I had no idea…"

"I know. Vampires are…aware of mortals with the antigen. We sense them, just as Dante sensed it in me. And there's more. There's a…a connection. For each vampire there's a mortal somewhere, one with the antigen, for whom that connection is stronger. So strong that we're drawn to them."

"And…were you that mortal for Dante?"

I nodded. "Yes. I never knew it, but he watched over me for most of my life. If trouble had come, he'd have protected me. And if I'd needed help, he'd have sensed it, wherever he might have been, and he'd have come."

She lowered her head, made a noise of disbelief in her throat.

"You don't believe me," I stated.

Slowly, she raised her eyes to mine. "If the legends are true, Donovan, he attacked you as you walked alone one night. He made you into what he was. If you call that protection, then—"

"I was dying."

She blinked fast. Her eyes widened.

"I didn't know it, of course, but Dante did. I'd been feeling the symptoms for weeks. Weakness, dizziness, blacking out for no reason. I had no idea what was wrong, and I'd thought it was something that would pass. But it wasn't."

"How do you know?"

I didn't answer that. Couldn't. Not yet. It would be too cruel to give her so much to deal with all at once. I couldn't tell her that mortals with the antigen always suffered the same fate—an early death. I'd been very close to my end.

"I simply do," I told her instead. "There's no doubt."

She stared down at me. "Then...you'd have died if he hadn't...done that to you."

"Without a doubt."

She nodded, deep in thought. "But he could have given you the choice. He never asked you to decide."

I smiled slightly, remembering. "Dante was never one to take time about acting. He was impulsive. Action first, thought later. But there were other reasons too. Had he told me, I likely would have repeated it to my parents, or the village priest. And some secrets simply must be kept, Rachel."

She drew my bloody shirt down over my body, deep in thought. I saw the moment she made the connection, because her eyes widened and met mine. "I have the antigen, don't I?"

I nodded. "You are the mortal I'm driven to watch over, Rachel. It's a part of who—of what I am. Don't go attaching any noble motivations to it. It's simply an irresistible urge. I couldn't ignore you if I tried."

"So saving me from the hounds…?"

"A reflex. Nothing more."

She lowered her eyes. "I'm not sure I believe you."

"Why not?"

She shrugged. "I think there's an element of choice involved, Donovan. You can't tell me that it was impossible for you to choose not to put yourself into the jaws of those hounds." She tilted her head to one side. "Or not to come back here at all. But you did. You came back because of me, didn't you, Donovan?"

I lowered my head. "Perhaps that was part of it. But I also came back because of Dante."

"Dante is dead."

"Yes. But I don't know where…"

Frowning, she studied me. "Where? Where he lies, you mean?"

Sighing, I absently ran one hand over the wound in my side. "When they came for us, put their torches to the castle walls, the sun was just beginning to rise. We had no choice but to run. Flames…devour our kind very quickly, you see. We both knew our only hope was to make for the relative shelter of the woods, where the sun's light wouldn't penetrate quite as quickly. And perhaps that would give us time to find shelter. A few minutes, at best, but perhaps enough." She nodded, urging me with her eyes to go on. "When we emerged, they were waiting. We could have stood and fought, and likely defeated them all."

"But…I thought there were dozens…"

I nodded. "We're very strong, Rachel. We could

have fought, but the sun allowed no time. We had to run. They pursued us, though, and we had no choice but to split up. I ran in one direction, Dante in another. The mob...they went after him.''

''And what happened to you?''

''I made it to the forest, and the hayfield beyond. I saved myself by burrowing deep into a haystack and remaining there until nightfall. It offered thin protection, but I survived. Weak, burned in many places, but I lived.''

''And Dante didn't,'' she said softly.

''I returned to the castle ruins by night...for weeks. Knowing that's where he would look for me if he were alive. Even after I left the country, I came back periodically to wait for him here. I had the place rebuilt, just in case. But he never came. Now I only want to know where he died.''

''Will you put a marker there?'' she asked, her voice quiet.

''A garden,'' I told her. ''Something as alive as he was.''

''You loved him very much. Yet you claim you care for no one.''

''I loved him,'' I said. ''He was the last person I ever let myself care for. The lesson his death taught me was too hard won to forget.''

I felt heavy. Tired.

''If you can't love,'' she asked, ''then how can you live?''

''It isn't so hard.''

She closed her eyes. ''I'm like you,'' she said. ''In more ways than I realized.''

''How?''

But she only shook her head as I slipped into slumber.

Chapter 11

She didn't realize the time until he went still, and his eyes fell closed. It wasn't like death, this slumber of his. More like a very deep sleep.

She'd told him she was like him. Only now did she realize how much. She hadn't loved, either. With one exception. Since her parents had died there had been only one being she'd truly loved. And as she'd grown older, she'd convinced herself that love had only been a dream. But the love for that dream angel had remained.

And now she knew he was real. Her savior, her dream, was real.

And damp with his own blood, in torn, dirty clothes. He'd watched over her as a child. Taken care of her more than once. She could do no less for him.

But she could never tell him. He must never know how much she'd loved him in her youth. The fantasies she'd had. Because he was afraid of love. She'd never known anyone so afraid.

Slowly, Rachel got up off the settee, and headed to her own rooms. She found clean washcloths and soft towels, and fetched a basin of warm water. Then she returned to Donovan. He'd object to her caring for him this way if he were awake. But he wasn't awake.

She took off his shirt, moving him carefully, half afraid doing so would jar him awake, or worse, start him bleeding again. She eyed the bandaged wound. No red trickle emerged. Good. But her gaze slid slowly upward, over his flat belly, and muscled chest. His dark nipples intrigued her.

Her throat went dry. She looked away. Dipping the soft cloth into the water, squeezing it out, she pressed it to his skin. But she could feel him underneath it. Taut and hard. Masculinity was like an aura emanating from his flesh. Almost a scent, it drew her.

She leaned closer, over his chest, her face near enough so she could feel the heat rising from him and touching her. Closing her eyes, she inhaled deeply. And something stirred down in the pit of her belly. Something she knew, recognized, because she'd felt it before. Whenever this man was near her she felt it.

But she had no business feeling desire for a man incapable of feeling anything beyond desire in return.

She felt it all the same.

"God, help me," she whispered. "But I do want you, Donovan O'Roark." She closed her eyes, tried to get herself under control. Dipping the cloth in the now pink-tinted water, she squeezed it out again, and carefully took away her makeshift bandages from his wound, to clean it properly.

Then she squinted, dabbed the blood away, and looked again.

It…it was smaller.

It was shrinking. Amazed, she watched as, in slow motion, the wound's edges pulled together like some kind of experiment in time-lapse photography. It took several minutes, but bit by bit the skin seemed to regenerate. Leaving a pucker, and then even that smoothed itself out and faded away.

Blinking in shock, she washed the spot clean, searching for traces of the tear, but it was gone. Gone. In something like awe, she drew her fingers over the new, healthy skin. "It's unbelievable," she whispered, and flattened her palm against his warm flesh.

When his hand fell atop hers, she jumped and quickly looked up at his face. But his eyes remained closed, his breathing shallow, barely discernible. But his hand closed around hers in his sleep. A sleep in which he'd told her he was beyond responding to any stimulus.

He'd been wrong.

And now the hand of this man, who claimed he didn't need or want anyone in his life, clung to her own, and for the life of her, she wouldn't have taken hers away.

I woke to a feeling of warmth spread upon my chest. And then as my senses sharpened, I knew that warmth was her.

Rachel was on the floor, her legs curled beneath her, while her head rested upon my chest. Her lips…barely touching the bared skin of it. One arm spanned me, hand on my shoulder. Her other hand was tucked beneath her, held tightly in my own.

I flexed and relaxed my fingers, to confirm what seemed unlikely. But it was true. I was the one holding *her* hand like a lover. Not the other way around.

I couldn't lie like this…not for much longer. Her soft breaths whispering over my skin were driving me to the edge of madness. I was hungry. And she was too near. Too…

Her fingers spread on my shoulder, then kneaded like a happy cat's claws. She moved her face, as if burrowing, only my chest didn't give, and her lips brushed over it like fire. The groan that rose up from the depths of me was a rumble. A warning. The same rumble one might hear from a volcano as the pressure within builds. An eruption was dangerously near.

She stirred, satin hair tickling my skin as she sat up, batting huge dark eyes at me, myopic until she blinked the sleep haze away and brought me into focus. Then she smiled.

"It healed," she told me.

"I told you it would."

"I know, but seeing it with my own eyes…'twas amazing, Donovan."

I nodded, trying to ignore the fresh-wakened glow in her cheeks and the moisture making her sleepy eyes gleam. The tousled hair. She must look just like this when she's been thoroughly satisfied by a skilled lover, I thought. Just like this.

I tried to sit up. She noticed, and got off me so I could, and I instantly regretted the loss of her so near. But when she got to her feet, it was to press her hands to the small of her back and arch. She grimaced, groaned and rubbed, so I realized she'd spent a horribly uncomfortable day on the floor when she'd had a bed fit for a queen only yards away. "Rachel, why on earth didn't you go to your room?"

She kept her hands where they were, fingers massaging herself. But her head came up fast. "An' leave you here by the front door, unconscious and unprotected? Not likely!"

I lowered my head. The smile that wanted to come to my lips was a dangerous one, I knew. No sense encouraging her foolish notions. "You'd already locked the door."

"Marney Neal could make quick work of that lock, and 'twouldn't be the first time."

I went still, sought her eyes, but she kept them averted. "You say that as if you know."

"Aye."

The bastard. "What lock was it he made quick work of, Rachel?"

"The one on my room at the pub. Eight years ago, before I left for the States."

Her voice didn't break at all. Mine would if I spoke again. It would break or emerge as the growl I felt building up. I'd kill the bastard. I'd rip out his heart and—

"You're lookin' rather murd'rous, Donovan," she said softly, studying my face. "An' truly, there's no need. Marney's a thorn in my side, but a harmless one. He'd never have gone so far if he hadn't had a wee bit too much ale. An' I daresay he sobered up some about the time I shoved him out my window."

I blinked, then slowly reached out, hooking one finger under her chin and tipping her head up so I could see her face. She seemed to be telling the truth. "You pushed him out your window?"

"'Twasn't hard. Marney didn't have much balance

that night anyway, as I recall. So he kicks in my door and starts groping at me like a ruttin' buck, goin' on about marriage and love and other such nonsense. I simply turned so his back was to the window, and gave him a bit of a shove."

I couldn't help it. I smiled. "But your room is on the second floor."

"Aye. He broke his arm in two places when he landed. Good for him our main road isn't paved, wouldn't you say?"

I felt an odd feeling welling up for Rachel Sullivan, in the center of my chest.

"No man alive ever got so much as a kiss from me without my consent, Donovan. 'Tis not something I'd tolerate."

My gaze faltered. "Are you trying now to take the blame for what I did before?"

"I'm only saying you spoke true when you said that if I hadn't wanted it to happen, it wouldn't have. And not only because I'd have prevented it, but because you would."

I met her eyes, my own narrowing. "Don't start again tonight crediting me with qualities I don't possess."

She shrugged. "I'm starving. Aren't y—" She broke off there, bit her lip, and sent me a quick, hot glance. Her trembling hand shot to her neck, but the wounds there were gone now. Would have healed with the daylight. As if they'd never been there.

"Do you...would you..."

"Don't." I looked away, forcibly, from her tender throat. "Why don't you go to your rooms, Rachel. You must want a shower, a change of clothes."

"But...how do you get... What I mean is, where do you...?"

I looked at her again, unable to help myself. "I don't kill, if that's what you're asking. I have stores. Cold, stale, sealed in plastic bags." I swallowed hard, as one of my hands rose up to stroke her hair, arranging it behind her shoulder. My fingers touched the soft skin there. Felt the pulse thudding endlessly, the river of her blood, flowing there. Warm, living blood.

"You...you drank from me...before."

"I shouldn't have done that."

"It was..." She swallowed hard, but her eyes heated, and the flame singed me.

"It was ecstasy," I finished for her. "I know. That's the danger, Rachel. That's the allure. What makes us so dangerous to you. You love it. You want it. You crave what could end in your own destruction."

She lifted her chin. "You'd never hurt me."

"Don't be so sure of that, Rachel." I turned away.

"But I *am* sure of it," she said to my back. I'd been walking toward the kitchens, but I stopped then and stood motionless. "Perhaps you're the one who needs convincin'." She moved forward very slowly. When she slid her palms slowly up the length of my back, curling her fingers on my shoulders, I stiffened, inhaled sharply. "I'm not afraid of you, Donovan. I've no reason to be and you know it, I think. But you're afraid of me, aren't you?"

"Don't be a fool."

"I'd only be a fool if I were askin' you to trust me," she said, and she moved her hands slowly, caressing my neck, fanning her fingers up into my hair.

"Or to love me. But I'm not, Donovan. I'm not askin' for anything like that."

She was, she knew she was. All her life she'd dreamed of this man. He was meant for her, she knew that. Somewhere deep inside her, she'd always known. She'd never been with a man. Even believing her guardian angel, her immortal Donovan O'Roark to be a fantasy, she'd saved herself for him. Only for him.

He didn't turn, didn't speak.

She lowered her hands to her sides. Defeated. Maybe her dreams were as foolish as she'd once convinced herself they'd been. Maybe she'd been wrong after all.

"I'm sorry. I thought…I thought you wanted me, too."

Turning away, she went to the stairs, climbed them slowly, and found the haven of the rooms he'd created for some fantasy woman—a woman he must have dreamed of. A woman he'd never let in.

I stood where I was for a full minute. No longer. I ached for her, craved her with a force beyond endurance. And she was right, I feared her too. She could destroy me, if I gave her the power.

I went to the foot of the stairs, gazing up them, wanting with everything in me to go after her. I wanted her. It wasn't love. It wasn't trust. It was only need…a need I knew she felt as well.

I put my foot on the first step. Closed my eyes, swallowed the trepidation welling up in my throat. Told myself this was a bad idea. Very bad. I took another step, and another. And I could hear the shower running now. In my mind, I could see her standing beneath it, wet and beautiful, utterly naked, mine for the taking.

What man alive would deny her?

"Not me," I whispered, and the words emerged deep and throaty. "No, not me."

I took the rest of the stairs by twos.

Chapter 12

Her door stood open...in invitation, I thought. Her clothes lay tattered on the floor, and I recalled the hounds surrounding her. The fear in her eyes. The courage that surged in spite of it.

My fingers fumbled with the trousers I wore, and I stepped out of them, and into the bathroom. Nothing between us now but the flimsy shower curtain. Her naked on one side, beneath the pounding spray. Me naked on the other.

Suddenly the water stopped flowing. Her fingers curled around the edge of the curtain, and it slid open. And then she stood there, still, silent. Wide eyes sliding up and down my body, before finally meeting mine, holding them.

She stepped out, one foot lifting over the edge of the tub, lowering to the floor, then the other. She didn't reach for the towels stacked nearby. Instead she merely stood there, head tilted back, eyes dark and stormy.

I stared back at her, drinking her in with my eyes. Water beaded on her skin, her shoulders and arms. Her tight belly. Rivulets formed, trickling from her long, wet hair down over slick, perfect breasts. She waited. Up to me, I knew. But did she really think I could turn away now?

Reaching out, I touched her. Ran one hand slowly over her hair, and followed the water downward, absorbing it into my palm as I skimmed her delicate throat, her tender breast, her narrow waist and rounded hip. I tugged her closer. And she came so easily, at the merest nudge of my hand. She pressed her body to mine with a soft sigh, twining her arms around my neck and tilting her head back for my kiss.

I shuddered in reaction to the feel of her in my arms, wet and so warm, as I touched my mouth to hers. My arms closed tight around her, one hand cupping her buttocks while the other cradled her head. When her lips parted, I tasted heaven, and the fire inside me flared hotter. With my tongue, I delved inside, to touch and stroke hers. I felt her shaking. Warming until her flesh was hot against my hands. Feverish. I arched hard against her, and she pushed back. No hesitation, no shyness. My hands slid up and down her shower-damp body, unable to get enough of the feel of her as I fed from her mouth. She was sweet. And my mind floated away, until all that remained was sensation. Desire. And the taste of her. I moved my lips away, licking the moisture from her jaw, and her throat. She arched backward, and I slid lower, drinking every droplet from her skin, from her breast. Taking the hard little nipple into my mouth and suckling, gently at first, but harder when her hands tangled in my hair. Scraping and nipping with my teeth, making her whimper in need, a sound that added fuel to the fire.

I wanted her...all of her, everywhere. Lower, I moved, dropping to my knees and kissing the wet path down her belly, nuzzling my face in the nest of damp curls, and then pushing deeper. Parting her secret folds with my tongue, I tasted her, and she cried out, fists clenching in my hair and tugging it. Hurting me so deliciously that my knees nearly buckled. Then she stepped back, just a little, urging me upward again, until I was standing. Her arms encircled my neck, and she lifted herself. I helped her, clasping the backs of her thighs and lifting them, positioning them around my waist. I felt her, warm and ready, teasing at the very tip of me, and closed my eyes at the flash of desire that nearly blinded me. And then she lowered her body over mine, took me slowly, so slowly inside her. Deeper...and deeper still, and when I felt the resistance, wondered at it, she pushed harder. A soft gasp, a small sound of pain.

I went still. Throbbing inside her, feeling her body's tightness pressing around me, holding me, I closed my eyes and knew the secret she hadn't told me. The gift she'd just given me. "Rachel..."

"Shh," she whispered, and then she moved over me, lifting away, lowering again. Slowly, excruciatingly, her breasts sliding against my chest as she did, taut nipples caressing my skin.

Slowly, I told myself. *Gently.*

She nestled her head in the crook of my neck, kissed me there, suckled me there. Moved faster. Her breaths hot and quick on my skin. I pushed her back to the wall, gripped her buttocks and held her there, thrusting into her deeply, again and again.

She gasped, and clung to me, head thrown back, mouth open. I kissed her, took her mouth as I took her body, but the need wasn't sated. Even as my passion neared release, I knew it wouldn't be.

And it was as if she knew, sensed it somehow, because she clasped my head and drew it lower, pressed my face to her neck, tilted her chin upward, so the tender skin pressed to my lips. I felt the pulse pounding there, tasted the warmth and salt of her skin, knew it would be as good for her as for me, told myself there was no reason to deny what she offered.

"Take me, Donovan," she whispered. "Taste me..."

I shivered. I hungered. I neared release more with every thrust, and craved as I'd never craved before.

With a trembling sigh, I parted my lips, closed them over her thudding pulse and, quickly, pierced her throat. She drew a harsh breath, but her hands pushed my head closer, clung to me and she pressed her neck to my greedy mouth. And I fed. Suckled, devoured the very essence of her, and heard her short staccato cries as she neared climax. And then I heard nothing but the thunder of my own heart beating in time with hers as I exploded inside her. She screamed my name, shuddered around me, and slowly went limp in my arms.

I lifted my head, kissed the wound I'd left in her neck, and then her cheek, and her hair, and her lips.

She opened heavy-lidded eyes, and stared up at me. And something about that look made me realize the enormity of my mistake.

It wasn't simple desire I felt for her. Not need, not

physical longing. I *felt* something for her. Something powerful and older than time. I always had.

I'd done it, then. I'd put the power to destroy me squarely into her hands. All that remained was to see what she would do with it.

But not now. Not yet.

As I lowered her gently to her feet, she stared up at me, and her deep green eyes gleamed like emeralds in moonlight. She whispered, "Come," and she took my hand. Drawing me with her back into the shower, turning on the water. Standing with me beneath the spray. She wrapped herself in my arms and kissed me. Lingeringly…almost…lovingly.

She couldn't tell him how she felt, wasn't sure there were words for it even if she tried. Completed, somehow. As if a goal she'd been striving for all her life had finally come within reach. As if the very essence of her had been touched, shared, poured out into another soul. She was happy, truly happy for the first time in her memory.

He didn't feel the same. Couldn't love her. Wouldn't trust her. But she refused to dwell on those things right now. There would be time. So much time.

She'd get her wish, her dream. The man she'd loved all her life. She lowered her eyes, tried to believe he would return that love. Eventually.

"What is it?" he whispered, stroking her hair as he held her. They'd moved from the shower to the bed, where they snuggled now like lovers. Tough to believe he felt nothing for her. Impossible, in fact.

She shook her head. "Nothing, Donovan. I was just thinking…"

"Thinking about what?"

Shrugging, she brushed away her doubts. "I'd like to walk outside," she told him. "In the moonlight."

"Were you always such a night person, Rachel?"

She smiled at him, ignoring the wariness, the uncertainty in his eyes. "'Tis growing on me." She sat up, sensing his growing discomfort with the intimacy of holding her in bed this way, now that the desire was spent. For her part, she'd have just as soon remained like that through the night, but...

She walked to the closet, pawed the clothes and chose carefully. A dress of white, so he couldn't help but focus on her out there in the darkness. With a full, soft skirt that would dance in the slightest breeze, and a plunging neckline to remind him of how much he still wanted her. She hoped.

"I've always wondered what lies beyond this fence of yours," she said as we walked side by side in the moonlit night. Her hair, dried during lovemaking and untouched by a comb, hung in natural, careless curls, giving her the look of a wild thing of the forests. A fairy, or a nymph. She enchanted me.

I should never have made love to her. Never.

"I can show you," I heard myself tell her.

"But...there's no gate."

Frowning, I tilted my head, watching her study the tall, sturdy fence. "And how do you know that, Rachel?"

She looked at me quickly, then averted her eyes. "I...used to come here. As a child."

"Often?"

Meeting my gaze, her own hooded, she shrugged. "As often as I could slip away. I knew 'twas you, even then, you see. My secret protector."

I lowered my head to hide my reaction to her words. My stomach clenched tight, twisted and pulled. "Do you still want to see inside?"

She nodded.

"Come here, then."

Frowning, she came closer. I scooped her up into my arms, bent at the knees, and leapt the tall fence. I heard her delighted squeak as I came down on the other side. And then she went silent, seemingly content to remain in my arms as she scanned the woods to her left, and the rolling meadow in which we stood. Well-worn paths meandered among the lush sweet grasses, and into the woodlot. "Look," I whispered, turning with her, pointing.

In the distance a doe lifted her head to glance our way briefly. Then she went back to nibbling. "Donovan, there. Beyond the doe," Rachel whispered.

"Yes," I said, "I see them." Twin fawns frolicked in the deep grasses. Gently, I set Rachel on her feet. "The fence keeps hunters—men like Marney Neal and his hounds—away. The deer can leap the fence easily though. Come and go as they please. Most of them seem content to stay here."

"So you've made a haven for the deer." She continued watching, laughing softly, a sound more disturbingly beautiful than a night bird's song, at the twins' antics.

"Not only the deer." I turned toward the fence, crouching low and pushing the deep grasses aside. "There are hidden places like this one, where the smaller creatures can get underneath. And the game birds fly over to find safety. Come," I said, extending my hand. Her delight in this place so pleased me, I couldn't resist showing her more.

When she closed her hand around mine, a feeling of warmth suffused me. And for a moment, it seemed perfect, natural. Until I reminded myself that it was fleeting. She'd leave here, one day soon.

I led her over the meadow, to the place where wildflowers spread like a patchwork carpet in every direction. And beyond that, to the pond, fed by two streams. It glittered in the moonlight. Geese swam on the silvery water, undisturbed by our intrusion. Rachel sank into the grass on the pond's bank, and in spite of myself, I sat down beside her. Closer than I needed to, and yet not close enough.

"It's as if they know you're no threat to them."

"They should," I told her. "They've been safe here for generations."

I felt her eyes on me. "Why, Donovan?"

I shrugged. "Why not?"

"Tell me."

I looked at her, half reclining now. Like a goddess in her paradise. "All right," I said softly. "I created this haven for the animals because I understand them." I looked again at the geese, who swam further from shore as a fox came slinking slowly to the water's edge for a sip. "I know how it feels to be hunted," I told her.

I met her eyes. She nodded as if she understood. But she couldn't. Or…I refused to believe she could.

"You're truly a special man, Donovan O'Roark."

I shook my head slowly, but as she curled into the cradle of my arm and rested her head upon my shoulder, I *felt* special. Cherished.

God, I was a fool to feel the things she made me feel.

We stayed there, in my own private paradise for

most of the night. Walking hand in hand, spotting and observing the wildlife. Like young mortals in love. Like some idealistic fantasy. And I relished every moment of it, in spite of the knowledge that doing so was a fool's dream. I only suggested we return to the castle when I knew dawn was on the rise, and Rachel still hadn't eaten.

But when we entered through the library doors, it was to the sound of urgent pounding, and shouts from the front. And even before I went to the great hall to answer the noisy summons, I sensed my brief time in paradise was coming to an end.

Mary O'Mallory stood at the door, breathless, red in the face. Her frantic gaze slid from me to Rachel, then relaxed slightly in relief. "Rachel," she sighed. "Lordy, girl, what took you so long?"

Rachel frowned, ushering her inside, one arm supporting the woman, and I knew she cared for Mary. Genuinely cared. I saw the worry in her eyes. "We were outside," Rachel explained. "Come, sit down before you faint dead away. Whatever is the matter?"

Mary sat, though on the edge of the settee. As if ready to spring and run should the need arise. "I need to speak with you, Rachel. Alone." She slid a sideways glance toward me, and I knew what she thought of me. That I was a monster. They all believed that. All...except for Rachel. She'd never seen me that way, had she?

"There's nothing you can't say to me in front of Donovan."

Mary pursed her lips.

"He's my friend, Mary."

"Never mind. I'll give you your privacy," I offered. But I slanted a long look Rachel's way. Would she run now? Should I lock the door?

No. No need sending Mary into a panic. They wouldn't be long.

"I'll call you when we've finished," Rachel said. And I knew it was her way of promising she wouldn't run off. But she would, eventually. It was inevitable. And it was going to hurt.

I only nodded and left the two alone.

Rachel sat beside Mary and clasped the older woman's hands. "Now tell me, what's wrong?"

"The very fact that yer here, with that...that—"

"He's a man, Mary. Just a man. And he's been nothing but kind to me."

"Lordy, child, tell me you're not in love with him!"

Rachel only lowered her eyes. "Why don't you simply tell me why you've come."

"'Tis the villagers, girl. Marney Neal, above all. He's stirred them up until I fear history is about to repeat itself. An' I want you safe away from this place before it does."

A bird of panic took wing in Rachel's chest. "What are you saying?"

"Marney claims the beast has you under some sort of spell, child. That you're his prisoner, but too enchanted to realize it. He's convinced them you're in need of rescue, Rachel, and even now the men are gathering at the pub. 'Twas all I could do to slip away unnoticed, to warn you."

Rachel lowered her head, closed her eyes. "So they'll come here."

"Aye," Mary said. "An' I fear violence will be

done this night, child. Ye must come away with me now."

Facing her squarely, Rachel nodded. "I'll come. But I'll speak with Donovan first."

"Rachel, you mustn't—"

"I must. I can't leave him here, unprepared. Unwarned. I can't go without telling him goodbye or explaining… No, you go on. I'll be along shortly, I promise."

Mary looked as if she were about to argue, but when she met Rachel's eyes, she seemed to change her mind. "I can see you're determined. What's between you two, Rachel?"

"Nothing that need concern you. Go, now. Try to hold the men off until I get there."

Sighing, Mary left. Rachel stood at the door, watching her go. Then she turned, wandered back to the hall that led to the library, and called Donovan's name. She heard his steps coming toward her, felt his essence touching her even before he came into sight. He only looked into her eyes, standing very still, then nodded. "You're leaving tonight, aren't you Rachel?"

"I must. You have to let me go, Donovan. It's—"

He held up a hand. "I won't stop you. My… arrangements are in place, for the most part. I can leave here right after you do."

She tilted her head, frowning hard at him. "My God, Donovan, do you still believe that's necessary? After what we've shared? The way we've talked…you really think I'd leave here only to tell your secrets to the world?"

He lowered his head. "What I believe," he whispered, "is that I'm as big a fool as Dante was. But I've no wish to suffer the same fate."

She looked up at him, stared deeply into his eyes, and what she saw there was pain. "If you leave…I'll never be able to find you again. Will I?"

He averted his eyes. "That's the entire point."

"No," she said softly. "It's not even close to the point."

"Then what is?"

She stepped closer, gripped the front of his shirt in trembling fists. "Must I throw my heart at your feet and wait for you to kick it aside? I will then. You mean more to me than my pride."

"Don't, Rachel—"

"I love you, Donovan O'Roark. I've loved you all my life, and I will until I die."

His face seemed to crumple in pain.

"I'm leavin' you tonight, yes. Because I must. But only tonight. I'd have come back. I'd have come back here, for you."

"Rachel…"

"You'd do well to leave, too, Donovan, for there's danger to you here tonight. But it's up to you where you go. Far away, where I can never set eyes on you again. Or close by…close enough so that I can find you…or you can find me."

Slowly, he shook his head. "You don't understand. It's the curse of my kind to live our lives alone, Rachel. It's how it has to be."

"No. 'Tis how you've made it. You have a choice now, Donovan. But it's up to you." Tears choked her. God, she didn't want to leave him. To lose him. To never see him again. But if she didn't, she might lose him anyway. To an angry mob, just the way he'd lost

Dante. Impulsively, tears streaming over her cheeks, she pressed her lips to his, clung to his neck for a brief, passionate kiss. Then she turned and fled, through the front door and into the waning night.

Chapter 13

When she left it was as if my heart had been torn apart. I should leave as well, I knew. I should pack up the few belongings I'd need, and make my way out of here. I didn't know what Mary had told her, but I didn't disbelieve Rachel when she said I'd be in danger here tonight. I should hurry.

I should. But I couldn't.

She said she'd come back, and damn me for a fool, I believed her. More than that, I wanted it to be true. This place had never been more alive—*I'd* never been more alive—than when she was here. Lighting my darkness. A blazing sun shining her warmth on my endless night.

She might betray me, as I'd spent so much time convincing myself she would. If she did, I'd be damned. But I couldn't leave until I knew.

I went to the settee, lowered myself to it, bowed my head, and sat there, very still.

Who was I kidding? She wasn't going to betray me. I'd lost my heart to the woman, and when she came back I'd be here waiting. And I'd tell her, at last. My heart was in her hands.

Rachel sailed into the pub as if she hadn't a care in the world, though her heart was heavy. He'd be gone when she went back. He'd be gone, and she'd never see him again.

Still, she feigned surprise when she saw the men crowding the room, with Marney standing at the front of them all. "My," she whispered. "Business is better when I'm away, isn't it? And what's the celebration tonight that has half the village in attendance?"

"'Tis no celebration, Rachel." Marney stepped forward, clutching her hands as if she were his property. "But 'tis glad I am that you've returned. You'll be out of harm's way when we storm that damnable castle."

She frowned, and drew her hands from his. "An' why is it you're plannin' to attack an empty ruin?"

"Empty?"

"Aye," she said with a nod. "Donovan has gone. Only came for one last look at the place before leaving it for good. 'Tis a shame you didn't make him feel more welcome here, you know. He's a kind man."

"He's a beast!" someone yelled.

"Oh, I don't think that's true. He was kind enough to help me with my research before he went on his way." She walked behind the bar, reaching for her apron.

"I think you're lyin', Rachel," Marney said, eyeing her. "I think you're trying to protect him, an' you wouldn't be if you weren't under his spell."

"Spell?" she asked, wide-eyed. "Don't tell me you're fool enough to believe he's more than just an ordinary man?"

"You know he is."

She did. He was above and beyond ordinary and ten times the man of any in this room. But instead of telling them so, she only shrugged. "I know no such thing. But I do know this, Marney. I'll not allow you to harm him."

"Then he *is* still there!" Marney shouted, banging a fist on the table.

"I didn't say—"

"You didn't have to. You've been naught but cold to me since your return, Rachel. An' everyone knows you'd planned to marry me before you left. 'Tis that beast who's swayed yer mind."

"I never planned to marry you. The plans were all on your side," she told him. "And 'twas indeed a beast who made up my mind, Marney, but the beast was you. Not Donovan O'Roark."

"We're goin' up there, and when we leave there'll be nothing left but rubble. He'll not escape us...not alive, at least."

He turned and the other men rose. They piled out the door, Marney leading them. Rachel surged after them all, but they moved quickly, and though she caught hold of several of the men, tugging at them, pleading with them, they were too frenzied to listen to her. When they turned onto the curving castle road, Rachel ducked into the woods and raced for the shortcut Dante had shown her, so she could come out ahead of them.

But when she got to the frenzied men again, it was

to see the castle door opening to their pounding summons, and Donovan stepping out.

He eyed the crowd, shook his head slowly. He looked utterly calm, but she knew what he must be thinking. That she'd done this to him, just as her ancestor had done to his best friend. That she'd left him only to lead this crowd back here. That she'd betrayed him.

Then he lifted his head. "Where is Rachel?" he asked. "Have you harmed her?"

She blinked in surprise, unable to speak. He thought they'd harmed her? Then...

"Rachel's no longer your concern," Marney told him. "We all know you've bewitched her somehow, or she'd never defend you the way she has. Once you're gone, she'll be fine again."

"Defended me, did she? I'm not surprised," Donovan said, and she could have sworn he battled a gentle smile. "Once I'm gone, you say," Donovan went on. "So you intend to kill me, do you?"

"Aye," Marney growled.

"Just so long as you're honest about your reasons," Donovan went on. "You want me gone because of Rachel. Because it's me she loves and not you."

The men grumbled, and someone yelled, "Is that true, Marney?"

"So will you drive me out into the sunrise, Neal," Donovan went on, "or simply kill me here and now?"

"Here and now," Marney whispered.

"Are you sure you can?"

Marney's eyes narrowed and he lifted his rifle. Rachel screamed and lunged from the woods, slamming her body into Marney's, and groping for the gun. But she never found a hold. Marney staggered backward under the weight of her assault, and the shot cracked so loudly her eardrums split. Then she felt the burn...the heat. The rapid pulse of life from her body.

Blinking in shock, she would have fallen to the ground, had not Donovan lunged forward to gather her into his arms. "Damn you!" he shouted. "Damn you, look what you've done! Rachel? Rachel!"

She opened her eyes, studied his face. Then she turned to Marney. "Go," she told him. "Go away. If I see you again...."

Marney backed away. Already the other men were scattering, shocked from their fury, perhaps, to realize just what they'd been about to do. What had happened as a result of their foolishness.

Cradling her in his arms, Donovan bent over her, kissed her face. And Mary crowded through the retreating men, made her way forward while Marney stood in the road, blinking in shock. She leaned over Rachel, parting her blouse, and looking at her chest, where the pain throbbed and burned. Grimly, Mary lifted her gaze to Donovan's. "You can help her," she whispered. "Can't you?"

Through her fading vision, Rachel saw him nod. Then Mary turned away. "'Tis only a flesh wound," she called to Marney. "But I vow unless ye leave here now I'll inform the authorities an' have you arrested for attempted murder. An' if you ever bother these people again, I'll do it. Now go!"

Nodding, muttering that it wasn't his fault, Marney turned and ran away like the coward he was.

Mary faced the two of them once more. "I don't imagine I'll see you again, will I?"

Rachel said nothing, unsure what Mary meant.

"Goodbye, child. Be happy."

Then she was gone.

Rachel stared up into Donovan's eyes. "I was afraid you'd think I brought them…"

"I knew better."

"Did you?"

"You know I did. I kept telling you I couldn't trust, couldn't care…even when I already did. I doubted you, Rachel, from the start, and I'm more sorry than I can tell you. You didn't deserve that. But you never gave up on me, did you?"

"How could I? You're in my soul, Donovan O'Roark. You have been since I was but a wee girl."

"And you in mine," he told her. "You made me believe in you, Rachel. Made me…made me love when I'd vowed it was something I'd never do. I love you, Rachel Sullivan. Do you hear me? I love you."

"Of course you do," she whispered. "You always have."

He smiled very gently.

"I'm dying," she whispered.

"Yes."

"But you can prevent it, can't you, Donovan? You can make me…like you."

"'Tis not an easy way to live, child. Never again to see the sunlight. Always knowing there are those who would hunt you, kill you simply for being what you are."

"Wandering hand in hand beneath the moonlight, spending every moment in your arms," she said weakly. "'Tis the life I want, so long as I can live it by your side. That's the dream I've always had, Donovan. To be with you…as we're meant to be… together."

"Then together we shall be, Rachel. Always." He lowered his head and kissed her, and she knew she'd found her dream come true, at last.

*   *   *   *   *

Turn the page for an exciting excerpt
from Maggie Shayne's next project

''The Invisible Virgin''

coming in May 2003
as part of Silhouette Books'
thrilling anthology
BROKEN SILENCE.

Chapter 1

Mitch Conrad had escaped the party, with its "eligible" young women and their pushy mothers, at the first opportunity. He'd sneaked out the back and taken refuge behind the giant wall of green hedges that made up a genuine maze. Somewhere in the middle, one of the waiters had promised to stash a six-pack under a bench. Mitch found the right bench, peered underneath it and spotted the six-pack there, waiting.

Perfect. He twisted the cap off a bottle and took a long pull of beer. And then he heard a voice.

A woman's voice.

Frowning, Mitch leaned forward, craning his neck to see around the corner. There he saw a woman, leaning over, speaking to a rosebush. As she did, the strap of her garishly green dress slid down, baring her shoulder, and she pushed it back up again.

"No one wants you to be anything more than what

you are," she told a rose. "And that's enough. You're so lucky."

She heaved a heavy sigh as she straightened, then turned and started coming toward him. She was, he realized, the furthest thing from one of those society females inside the house. Her dress was ugly as sin, and too big, to boot. She kept tripping over the hemline but didn't seem to care. She wore round gold-rimmed glasses on her face, and her hair was fighting hard to escape the unimaginative bun it was pinned into, with pieces falling loose and hanging every which way.

She was, he thought, the anti-deb.

So he stayed where he was, intrigued, and wanting to know more.

She came a few more steps, then paused and reached out a hand to cup a flower blossom before she leaned in close and smelled it. She closed her eyes in ecstasy and he saw that she was pretty behind those glasses, standing there in her too-big dress, moonlight flowing over her.

"You're perfect just the way you are," she told the flower. He didn't know what kind of flower it was. Not a rose—something else. "People could learn a lot from plants."

"You can say that again," he muttered, not quite meaning to vocalize the thought.

She spun toward him, looking startled out of a year's growth, he thought, and tried to take a step backward at the same time. She caught her foot on the dress, tripped, and over she went, even as he shot off the bench to try to catch her in time.

He knelt beside her where she'd landed on her backside, slid a hand to cup her head and curled another around her shoulder, which was bare because the dress strap had fallen again. "Are you okay?"

She blinked at him, her eyes unfocused. "Yeah, um, do you see my glasses?"

He helped her to sit up, then looked around.

"Uh, unfortunately, yes." He picked up the glasses, held them up to her. Both lenses were shattered.

She took them from him, peered closely at them. "Oh, hell. I'm blind as a bat without them. Especially at night. Oh, and the orchid!"

He frowned, looking around them. "You landed on an orchid?"

"No. I came out here looking for one. Actually, that's the only reason I came to this party in the first place to see the orchid bloom tonight. It's supposed to be here somewhere." She peered around, squinting.

"If you describe it to me, maybe I can help."

"Gram said it was in a concrete pot with fairies on the outside."

"Oh." He glanced back at an urn he'd been using as a footstool. "Then this must be it here." Taking her hand in his—an act that sent a little tingle of awareness sizzling through him when her fingers laced with his and held on—he led her closer to the bench. "This one here?" he asked.

She leaned close to the plant. "Oh, yes. This is it. It hasn't opened yet, has it?"

"Not since I've been here." He sat down on the bench, guiding her to sit beside him. She did, leaning back, sighing.

"I, uh, have a contraband six-pack of beer under the bench here. Would you like one?"

"Oh, God, you have no idea."

"I'm taking that as a yes." Smiling, he reached

down, pulled out a beer, twisted off the top and handed it to her.

The woman took a long, slow pull on the beer, and then, to his surprise, leaned back on the bench and put her feet up on the edge of the flowerpot. They were bare, her feet. Bare, and cute as hell.

"So who are you?" she asked. "You working the party tonight?"

He blinked. So she thought he was staff. One of the employees. Well, that stood to reason. He couldn't think of another guest who would rather be in the garden drinking beer when he could be inside hitting on rich, eligible women. "Not by choice," he said, because it was the best noncommittal answer he could come up with. "You can call me Mitch."

"You can call me Rosie," she said.

"I like the way you think." He clinked the top of his bottle against hers. "So, Rosie, how come you're out here in the garden, barefoot, instead of in there dancing with some rich bachelor, hmm?"

"Don't tell me you broke your glasses, too," she said.

He frowned at her. "I see twenty-twenty. And I think you're adorable."

She held up her beer. "How many of these have you had?"

"Not that many."

"No? Well, thanks for that, Mitch. That's a sweet thing to say."

"Hell, I meant it, Rosie. I've always figured you can't really be sure what any of those primped and polished ladies actually look like unless you manage to take 'em down and scrub their faces clean, then wash all the goop outta their hair."

She laughed at that. "I tried to put some goop in my hair, and you can see the results." She drained the beer. He took the bottle from her and stuck a fresh one in its place. Then he reached behind her head and pulled a few pins from her hair. It fell around her shoulders, long and dark blond in the moonlight.

"I usually just wear it in a ponytail."

So why did you change it tonight?"

"Hell, Mitch, I couldn't show up here in a ponytail any more than I could arrive in my blue jeans. They'd never have let me in."

"They'd have called the police."

"And maybe the press," she put in. "As if I haven't already embarrassed my poor sisters enough tonight."

She sipped the beer, sighed and let her head fall back against the bench. "God, I haven't been this relaxed in a week. I figured this party was going to be one tense encounter after another."

"No tension here," he told her. "I came out here to get away from it."

"Me, too." She frowned, then, sitting up and looking skyward. "What happened to the moon?"

He looked up. "Dark clouds just slid over it."

"You think they'll pass? The orchid won't blossom without moonlight."

"You know, I don't think so. The clouds look to be pretty thick, and—"

The slow roll of thunder cut off his words, and then what had been a mild breeze grew stiffer. "I think we'd better seek cover," he said.

"Not back to the mansion. Can we slip around to the parking lot from here?"

Taking her hand, he drew her to her feet. "No, it's

all fenced in. Gates are all closed until after the party for security reasons. We can't leave without going back through the damn mansion."

"Then I'm here for the night," she said. "Rain or otherwise."

"There's something over that way. Come on."

The thunder boomed again; then the clouds burst all at once, and they were soaked to the skin in moments. Mitch was running, pulling her along beside him, and she was going full throttle even though she could barely see—and then he realized that she was laughing. Soaked by rain, running blind and barefoot over the wet paths, and laughing so hard it was making her gasp.

He stopped running, turned to face her, caught her face between his palms. "Have you lost it, Rosie?"

"I haven't had this much fun in years," she confessed. She blinked at him, water streaming over her cheeks and dripping from her hair.

And for some reason he couldn't have identified if he'd wanted to, he leaned down and kissed her. She didn't object. Didn't act all offended and shocked that he'd behaved like a normal, red-blooded male, the way any other woman in attendance at this event would have done.

Nope. She kissed him back. Sort of went all soft in his arms, then parted her lips and, to his heart's content, let him taste the beer she'd been drinking.

Damn, he liked this woman. Even though he knew it would only lead to disaster.

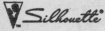

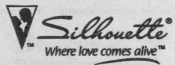

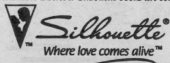

If you enjoyed what you just read,
then we've got an offer you can't resist!

Take 2 bestselling novels FREE!
Plus get a FREE surprise gift!

Clip this page and mail it to The Best of the Best™

IN U.S.A.
3010 Walden Ave.
P.O. Box 1867
Buffalo, N.Y. 14240-1867

IN CANADA
P.O. Box 609
Fort Erie, Ontario
L2A 5X3

YES! Please send me 2 free Best of the Best™ novels and my free surprise gift. After receiving them, if I don't wish to receive anymore, I can return the shipping statement marked cancel. If I don't cancel, I will receive 4 brand-new novels every month, before they're available in stores! In the U.S.A., bill me at the bargain price of $4.74 plus 25¢ shipping and handling per book and applicable sales tax, if any*. In Canada, bill me at the bargain price of $5.24 plus 25¢ shipping and handling per book and applicable taxes**. That's the complete price and a savings of over 20% off the cover prices—what a great deal! I understand that accepting the 2 free books and gift places me under no obligation ever to buy any books. I can always return a shipment and cancel at any time. Even if I never buy another The Best of the Best™ book, the 2 free books and gift are mine to keep forever.

185 MDN DNWF
385 MDN DNWG

Name		
	(PLEASE PRINT)	
Address		Apt.#
City	State/Prov.	Zip/Postal Code

* Terms and prices subject to change without notice. Sales tax applicable in N.Y.
** Canadian residents will be charged applicable provincial taxes and GST.
   All orders subject to approval. Offer limited to one per household and not valid to current The Best of the Best™ subscribers.
® are registered trademarks of Harlequin Enterprises Limited.

BOB02-R   ©1998 Harlequin Enterprises Limited

**These romances will entrance,
mesmerize and captivate...**

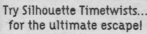